TROUBLE *in the* MANCOS VALLEY

Lowell F. Volk

Trouble in the Mancos Valley

Published by Wheatmark®
2030 East Speedway Boulevard, Suite 106
Tucson, Arizona 85719 USA
www.wheatmark.com

ISBN: 978-1-62787-809-8 (paperback)
ISBN: 978-1-62787-810-4 (ebook)
LCCN: 2020910260

Bulk ordering discounts are available through Wheatmark, Inc. For more information, email orders@wheatmark.com or call 1-888-934-0888.

CONTENTS

ACKNOWLEDGMENTS

I WOULD LIKE TO RECOGNIZE my wife, Mary Lou Volk, for all the help she has given me while I was writing this book. Not only has her dedication been a great help in editing, but her support has been the inspiration I needed to continue. She has been there for me as I have taken the Burton family through their trials as they strive to get ahead in the West.

I would also like to thank Tina Turner, who helped with the editing. She is a great friend, and her help is greatly appreciated.

Thank you both for your understanding and support.

Lowell F. Volk

1

NEW MEXICO TERRITORY

JAKE BURTON SAT AT THE Lazy L Ranch outside of El Paso, Texas, thinking about what had happened since he left home under less-than-good conditions with his father. Twenty-eight years old and six feet tall, Jake had worked on the family ranch since he was old enough to ride a horse, thinking someday he would take it over. His dark-brown hair and a face weathered from being in the sun day after day made his pale blue eyes stand out. When he was angry, the look in his eyes would make people's blood run cold and put fear into whoever had caused his temper to rise.

The one thing that had caused him to leave home was his father, who had not gotten over the death of his wife, Roseann. He blamed Jake for not being with her the day she died and wouldn't let him forget it. On the day she died, his mother had driven herself into town for supplies. On the way home, the horses became spooked by a mountain lion, causing them to run wild. When the wagon hit a rut, it overturned, and she was thrown to the ground, where she hit her head on a rock, crushing her skull. Just that morning, Jake's father had instructed him to go to town with his mother to help her. Instead, one of the hands rode in and told him they were finding dead calves. His mother told him to go find out what was killing the calves and that she would go by herself. It was the same day his father had gone to Durango on business.

It had been two and a half years since her death, and his father still blamed Jake. He had also not been able to quit blaming himself for what happened.

On the day he left, before his father's cattle ranch was out of sight, Jake stopped his horse and turned in the saddle. His hat shielded his eyes from the morning sun, but he still had to squint a little when it reflected harshly on the walls of the two-story whitewashed house. He didn't know when— or if—he would return to the Mancos Valley and wanted to sear a memory of his home into his mind. Seeing one of the men going about his work in the corral, roping a young horse to start breaking him, told Jake life would continue as normal with him gone. Watching his sister, Sally, wave from the porch, he knew there'd be tears in her eyes, and he felt the kick of guilt in his stomach for leaving her. He would miss her too, but after his mule of a father's constant reminder of his mother's death, Jake knew he had no other choice. He half-heartedly waved back to his sister and then, with a shake of his head, sighed as he turned away and kicked his horse on again. There was never a point in looking back. Sally's husband, Howard, would help his father run the ranch.

When Jake first got to Texas, he moved around a lot. When he started to run out of money, he decided to stay near El Paso, taking a job as a ranch hand at the Lazy L and writing a letter to his sister to tell her so.

It had been several months since Jake started working at the ranch. This night, as he sat in the bunkhouse, he started to think about returning to Colorado—its green valleys and mountains. He had not heard from his sister in some time and wondered how things were at home.

The next day, Jake rode into El Paso and went into the general store, where the post office was located, to send a letter to Sally. At the window, a young woman looked up and said, "May I help you?"

"I would like to post this letter."

Looking at the return address, she saw Jake's name and asked, "Are you Jake Burton?"

"Yes, I am."

"Just a minute . . . that name sounds familiar," she said. Going to the general delivery mail, she started looking through the stack of letters. It wasn't long before she said, "I have a letter for Jake Burton. I believe it has been here for about two weeks." She handed it to Jake.

When he looked at the envelope and saw Sally's name, he became excited, hoping to find out what had been going on at home. He put it in his pocket and left to find a place where he could be somewhat alone when he read it. Jake looked up the street and saw a café. It was dinner time, so he decided to go there and eat while he read.

Looking around, he found a table near the wall away from others. Jake ordered before he opened the letter, carefully taking it out of the envelope. His heart sank as he read what Sally had to say.

Dear Jake,

I hope this finds you before it is too late. I regret to inform you of what has been going on. After you left, a new man by the name of Gifford Clemens came to town and has been causing trouble for the local ranchers, trying to purchase all the ranches in the valley. Father was worried that our ranch was going to be next as some of our cattle have come up missing. When Father went to check on the herd in the north valley, he was shot. When one of our hands went to check the herd, he found Dad shot in the back. He was able to get him home before he died, but Pa never woke up before he passed. No one knows who shot him, but we believe that it was the new man who wants all the land in the valley.

I am afraid that is not all the bad news. When the sheriff was out investigating Pa's death, he was shot at the same place. I am afraid that Howard is now in danger and could be killed next. All these problems seem to have started since Gifford Clemens arrived in Mancos. He set up a law office in town and has bought several ranches in the area. Lately, he has been after me to sell the Double B. Several of the other ranchers sold out to Gifford when they couldn't pay their loans. Gifford had somehow ended up holding their loans from the bank. When they couldn't pay, he ran them out. Some were found dead, which left their ranches for the taking. Howard suspects that Gifford is behind the killings of our father and the other ranchers but can't prove it.

I hope this finds you soon and that you can come home as we need your help. Pa left half the ranch to you in his will.

Your sister, Sally

Jake was crunching the letter in his hand, staring at it, just as his food arrived. The waitress put his plate down. Seeing Jake's face and his clenched hand, she asked, "Is everything all right? You look like you just got some real bad news."

"I just found out my father was killed." Jake grasped the crumpled letter in his fist, holding back the desire to hit something.

"I'm sorry to hear that." The waitress left him alone, turning once to look back to make sure he was all right.

Putting the letter on the table, Jake felt a knot in his stomach as he thought about his father's death. When he left, they had not been on good terms, and now he would never be able to make amends.

While he ate, his mind was on what Sally had written and not on his meal. Finishing quickly, he picked up Sally's letter, put it in his pocket, and left, determined to go home.

He was gathering his things at the ranch when the foreman walked in. "I've been looking for you, Jake. Where have you been?"

"I rode into town this morning."

"What are you doing? It looks like you're getting ready to leave."

"I just got word that my father was killed and I'm needed at home."

"Sorry to see you go," the foreman said. "You've been one of the better hands we've had. When you get your things together, come up to the house, and I'll have your pay ready." He left in silence.

Jake finished gathering his gear and rode to the house, where the foreman gave him his pay. As he was riding away from the Lazy L, his thoughts were on if he would get home before anything happened to Howard and the ranch—or if it was already too late. The letter from Sally had been mailed over a month ago, and it had sat in town for two weeks while he had been out with the other hands rounding up cattle.

While traveling, he pondered if Howard was right about Mr. Clemens killing his father. How could they prove it? He feared for Howard and Sally's lives if he couldn't get there before something happened to them.

Jake put his horse in an easy canter that would allow him to go a long distance before he needed to stop and rest. He wanted to get home as soon as he could and knew it would take at least three weeks. Mentally kicking himself, he realized that if he had gotten the letter when it first came in, he would be close to home by now.

❦

It was after sunset of the third day. Jake was hot and tired, with dust plugging his nose. The grumbling in his stomach said he needed to eat. His horse was lathered, exhausted, and needed a rest and some grain. The sun had been unbearably hot throughout the day.

When Jake stopped on top of a small hill, he spotted the lights of a town. A sense of relief came over him, knowing he had reached Santa Fe. When he rode into town, his first stop was at the livery stable, where he called out for the owner. When nobody answered, he reckoned he would pay the stable fee later; right now, he needed to take care of his horse.

After his horse was cooled down and fed, Jake walked to a small café. Inside, the smells of fresh coffee and cooking meat filled his nose. After he placed his order, it seemed like it was taking forever for the food to arrive. When the waitress set the steak down in front of him, the only thing on his mind was to consume it. While he ate, he overheard two men talking about a poker game going on in the saloon. He finished and paid for his meal, looking at what money he had left. He had been lucky in poker before. *Maybe the game is a friendly one, and I can pick up some extra money while giving my horse a chance to rest.*

Jake walked across the street and entered the saloon. The inside looked like most other saloons he had been in. Located in the center of the room was a poker game in progress. A scarred wooden counter, stretched almost the length of the building, was used as the bar. In the middle of the wall behind the bar, he noticed a mirror and a painting showing a scantily clad lady. On each side of the mirror was a shelf stacked with whiskey bottles. Jake felt like he could have been in this bar before.

Four men were standing at the bar, drinking and talking. They all turned and looked at Jake as he walked over and ordered a beer. With his drink in hand, he turned his back to the bar and watched how the game was going.

He evaluated the five men sitting at the table. One of the fellows facing the bar was dressed in a black frock coat, silver vest, white shirt, black string tie, and black flat-brim hat. The man's face sported a black mustache below a large hooked nose between two dark eyes with thick black eyebrows above them. There was an old scar just below his left eye. Jake sized him up as being none too friendly and one he would have to watch. He had the look of a professional gambler.

The player next to him wore a bright red shirt under a black leather vest.

A dusty white hat sat on his head, looking like it had been there for some time. His light blue eyes watched the others as a new round of cards were dealt. He kept his hands on the table, tapping his index finger, indicating he was nervous. A small amount of money remained in front of him, showing that he was not doing well. Jake had seen men like him before, making careless bets, and knew he was one he wouldn't have to worry about.

The player to his left wore horn-rimmed glasses riding low on his nose. His gray hair fell in unkempt straggles across his shoulders. His leathery brown skin showed he had spent a lot of time in the sun. He wore a blue jacket with a hole in the sleeve of his left arm. His black pants were held up by a belt adorned with a wide silver buckle. He had a gun stuck in his waistband. Jake could see that he was tough, honest, and wouldn't back down.

Jake surmised that the man next to him must have been the local blacksmith who probably ran the livery stable. The man's arms showed enough strength to kill a person. He seemed to be playing conservatively with the money still in front of him. Jake figured he had worked hard for his money and wasn't about to throw it away. He was another one he wouldn't have to look out for.

The last man, who had his back to Jake, wore a brown jacket and hat. His black hair hung down to the collar of his shirt. When he turned his head, Jake saw that he had a dark beard and mustache. He, too, had a sum of money in front of him, indicating that he had been doing well. Jake wondered if he and the first man were working the table together. He would have to watch both.

The chair next to the last player was empty, so after watching a dozen hands, Jake walked over to the table and asked, "Is this a private game, or can anyone sit in?"

The man in the black coat sized him up and said, "Sit down, friend. This is a friendly game."

Jake noted that even the man's voice sounded black. He was sure that he was the one to watch.

Shortly after sitting down, Jake drew his Colt .44 from its holster and laid it on his leg like he always did when entering a game where he did not know the other players.

He started to relax after winning two hands; however, he kept his eye on the man in black. The blacksmith and the man with the blue eyes decided they had enough; they got up and left the game, going to the bar. Jake's luck turned some as he lost the next hand.

For the next two hours, the game continued to go back and forth. Jake was not winning a lot, nor was he losing a lot. After losing another hand, he began to wonder if the man who had offered him a seat—who was the dealer at this time—was taking cards from the bottom of the deck.

In the next hand, Jake got five good cards: two aces and two tens. He felt his luck was returning and raised the bet. The man in the black coat folded. The other two called, and Jake won a pot of two hundred dollars.

During the next hand, he received a good run of cards dealt by the man in the black coat. It didn't take long for the betting to get heavy as the pot grew to over a thousand dollars. Jake asked for two cards, while the man in black took one. Still not trusting him, Jake watched his hands and saw him start to draw his card from the bottom of the deck.

"Hold it, mister," Jake growled, still watching his hands. "Put the deck on the table before you draw and take the top card."

The dealer looked at Jake. "What are you saying?"

"I saw you try to take a card from the bottom of the deck."

"Are you calling me a cheat?" the dealer asked. Staring at Jake, he put the deck on the table in front of him while pushing back his chair.

"That's what we call men like you in the Colorado Territory," Jake replied, watching the man's eyes as he was pushing his chair back. "What do you call them here?"

Reaching inside his coat, the man pulled a .32 Colt from a cross draw holster. Watching his movements, Jake had moved his hand to his lap and was already grabbing his Colt. The dealer brought his gun out, and they both fired at the same time. The dealer's bullet whizzed past Jake's ear, but Jake's shot caught the man in the head. He fell back, slowly rolling out of his chair with blood pouring from the wound.

Those who had been sitting at the table had backed away as soon as the controversy started, knowing there was going to be gunplay. Not wanting any part of it, they watched as the scene played out.

Jake stood and moved around the table, putting his back to the wall and keeping his gun ready in case anyone had objections.

The man in the brown coat called out, "I didn't see him deal that card from the bottom."

Jake pointed his gun at him and ordered, "Come here and turn his cards over."

The man came over to the table and turned the dead man's hand over, showing it held three kings and a nine.

"Now turn over the top card on the deck," Jake commanded.

The man slowly reached for the deck and turned over the top card. It showed an eight, leaving the dealer with three kings.

"Now turn over the deck," Jake instructed.

He reached over and slowly turned the deck upside down, leaving the bottom card in place. It was a nine, which would have given the dealer a full house.

Jake ordered, "Now turn my hand over."

When he did, it showed three aces.

"I had him beat," Jake said. "Without my draw card."

The two men who had backed away from the table glanced at the cards before looking at Jake. One said, "You still can't prove that he was gonna take that card from the bottom."

"If he wasn't, why did he go for his gun?" Jake charged.

"Maybe he just didn't like being called a cheat," the man behind the bar called out.

With those at the bar starting to intervene, Jake knew he had to get out of there. His gun still drawn, he picked up his money and the money in the pot before putting it all into his vest pocket. "I won this fair. You two dropped out, and I had his hand beat before he tried to cheat."

Working his way to the door while keeping his gun ready, he backed out onto the boardwalk. He fired a shot into the ceiling, causing everyone to duck. Jake heard the men moving around inside and talking before he turned to head for the livery.

Someone called out, "We need to go after him. It ain't right that he took our money after killing Ben."

Reaching the livery, Jake looked around and saw that nobody had come out of the saloon. After saddling his horse, he led it out the back door, where he mounted and rode out of town. Knowing that the men in the saloon would be coming after him, he needed to get away from Santa Fe before they could get organized.

After riding at an easy gait for an hour, he stopped to let his horse recover. He needed to take it easy because his horse had only gotten a short rest while in town after the long ride that day. While in the stable, the horse had some time to eat the grain along with some hay Jake had put out for it.

After a half hour, Jake checked to see if anyone was following him before he mounted. During that time, he had not heard or seen anyone, so he decided to walk his horse with the hope that they could not follow him in the dark. Worried he might have lost the letter, he patted the side pocket of his coat. Feeling it, he was relieved that it had not fallen out.

Around midnight, Jake figured that he had put enough distance between him and Santa Fe that he could stop. Loosening the cinch on his saddle, he removed the headstall to let his horse graze. He lay down, and it wasn't long before he was asleep. He slept until daybreak. When light shined in his eyes, he woke with a start. Checking his back trail and not seeing any movement, he relaxed and ate a cold breakfast of jerky before going on. Even with the few hours of rest his horse had gotten, Jake knew that the animal wasn't up to its full strength and would not last if it had to go all day.

By midmorning, the red sun over Jake's head was causing sweat and dirt to run down his forehead, stinging his eyes and blurring his vision. He urged his horse through a narrow pass and into the lush valley that looked to stretch for miles. Realizing that the horse wouldn't be able to go much farther, he relaxed some when he saw a stand of trees that looked promising; there was shade that would allow them to get out of the heat.

The leather creaked as Jake turned in his saddle, looking at the open valley behind him where he had just crossed. He had a strange feeling crawling up his back when he saw a cloud of dust in the distance. He began to wonder if the men from the saloon had decided to follow him after all. He felt the urge to find shelter and protection.

His horse was stout but had become lathered from nose to tail, and its breathing was ragged. Stopping and dragging his leg over the saddle, Jake dropped to the ground to relieve the horse of his weight. After wiping the sweat from his eyes, he again looked at the stand of trees—only this time, he saw a swirl of smoke rising above them. Turning again to look behind him, he saw the dust was wafting above the mesquite into the clear blue sky and knew someone was causing it. He wanted to get back in the saddle but resisted, knowing his horse wouldn't make it.

While Jake led his horse, he watched the spiral smoke rising above the highest branches, not knowing what or who was in there. *Damn,* he thought. He could be heading into more trouble. Instead of entering, he made his way around the edge of the small stand of scrub oak and cotton-wood until he reached the north end. There, a rock wall seemed to materialize out of nowhere. Going behind the wall, Jake found that it would offer some protection and stopped. A dark indentation at the base of the wall provided shade that would shield him and his horse from the blazing sun shining overhead.

Near the opening of the indentation was a small patch of green, but his horse was too tired to graze; it just stood, hanging its head and breathing hard. Even after Jake loosened the cinch, the horse didn't move. Finally, twitching its nose in the air, the horse moved to a narrow pool that Jake hadn't noticed. The animal's thirst far outweighed its exhaustion.

Removing his lever-action .44 Henry, Jake left his horse at the pool's edge and made his way to an opening in the boulders that was carved out of the rocky wall. Finding it a perfect place to keep watch, he sat down. If it came to it, he felt that this was as good a place as any to make his stand.

2

THE PURSUIT

THE MEN WHO FOLLOWED JAKE stopped before they entered the valley. They stood looking at the lay of the valley before going on.

"How far ahead do you think he got?" asked Charlie, the man in the brown suit. "We saw where he stopped last night, and while we followed his tracks, we figured that his horse was about played out. I figure he can't be too far ahead of us."

"You reckon that could be him?" Gilbert wearing the red shirt and black vest remarked, pointing to the smoke. "He ain't been pushing his horse too hard."

Henry commented, "He can't be far enough ahead to where he would feel safe to stop and make camp unless he thinks no one followed him." "If it ain't him, he's probably out there somewhere, watching. He's got to be tired as hell. He had been riding all day when he came to the saloon, and he didn't get too rest much last night. I wonder if he even knows we're after him. Even still, that fire could be someone else."

"Maybe we ought to turn back," Art suggested.

"I ain't giving up that money he took. It belongs to all of us," Charlie growled. "I think he got me for more than three hundred dollars. And part of Ben's money should be mine if he was cheating us like the stranger showed us. Ben didn't have no kin."

"You ain't got no wife and kids neither," Henry said. "I do. Art might be right. I'm thinking that maybe we should go back—forget about the money. Hell, we know he was right. He showed us how Ben was dealing from the bottom, the old son of a bitch. Bet he's been doing that all along."

"All the more reason for us to get that money back," Art responded. "If Ben has been cheating us, that money should be ours and not with some stranger who come passing through."

"Wait . . . we got no idea who's in the trees. What if it's Indians?" Henry said. "I heard they've been raiding. That could be them in there. That's a lot of smoke for one man."

"I think it's him," Art replied. "If he knows he's being followed, he might just be setting up an ambush thinking that we'd ride in and try to surprise him."

"What if it ain't him?" Gilbert asked. "What if it's Indians?"

"If you don't want your share of the money, turn back," Charlie replied.

"Hell, I ain't no coward, Charlie. You know that. But we've been after him since early morning, and our horses are about played out. If it's Indians, we ain't gonna be able to outrun them on these horses," Art argued.

"Sitting here arguing ain't getting our money," Charlie said. "If it ain't him, he's getting farther away."

They moved forward, working their way into the trees, where they found a fire still burning with no one around. Tracks showed where two men had camped.

"They must've got wind of us; their tracks showed they left in a hurry before they could put out their fire," Gilbert said.

"He wasn't here because he was alone, but he might be near," Art said. "He could be watching and getting ready to ambush us. We need to spread out and keep searching for his tracks."

Leading their horses away from the camp, they searched through the trees without spotting Jake.

3

ON THE RUN

JAKE WAS UNSURE WHO WAS behind him. Was it a posse after him for killing the dealer, or was it just the men who had been in the poker game, now after his money? From where he sat, he thought he recognized a couple of the men who had been at the table. He watched them as they searched the trees. With the men out of sight, Jake decided to move. Leaving the protection of the rocks, he went toward the valley.

Keeping an eye on the trail behind him, Jake made his way across the valley as he walked and led his horse. He hoped to find a good trail through the hills into the mountains, where he could lose them as he slowly moved on. Concentrating on those behind him, he failed to see the second camp and almost stumbled smack into it. What saved him was his horse suddenly stopping; that brought Jake's focus back to what was ahead of him.

Jake spotted twenty Apache horses tied to a stringer between him and the camp. He took out his Colt as he moved closer to a dozen young Indians wearing war paint and sitting around two blazing fires. They were talking and inspecting items spread out on a blanket that were taken in a raid. Jake counted the men in front of him and wondered where the rest were as the string of horses numbered more than the Apaches in the camp.

While Jake was watching, two more Indians came into the camp. The distraction they created allowed Jake the time he needed to turn his horse and quietly lead him back the way he had come. The camp had been hidden mostly by tall sage and low mesquite, which also covered him as he slipped away. Being careful as he moved, leading his horse around the Indian camp, Jake cursed himself for his carelessness. He thought, *Being so tired almost got me into another bad situation.*

Before mounting, Jake led his horse to a spot where he felt safe. Just as he started to ride, he heard a ruckus that seemed to come from within the camp. His first thought was that he had been spotted. He needed to look for cover.

Stopping behind an outcropping of rocks, he waited and watched. It wasn't more than a few minutes before the Indians were mounted and rode through the scrub toward the tree line, where the men were searching for him.

Hidden behind the rocks, Jake found a spot of open ground, where he dismounted. He loosened the cinch on the buckskin to allow him to breathe easier. Taking his rifle, he got ready for the Indians if they were coming after him.

Jake had noticed that the Indians he saw in the camp were all young boys. To him, it looked like they were out to prove that they were warriors. Relief came as he saw them head for the men in pursuit of him. He was safe for now. After they were gone, he wondered if they had left some of their horses in the camp. He began to think that this could be an opportunity to get a fresh mount while the Indians were away.

He worked his way back to their camp, where he found four horses still there. Jake looked them over; he liked the casual bearing of a buckskin that had a brand on its hip, indicating that the Indians must have taken it in a raid. The buckskin looked strong, fast, and not too skittish. As he approached the buckskin, it raised its head and didn't shy away. While untying him, Jake heard gunfire erupt in the distance. Leading the buckskin, he returned to his horse, where he moved his saddle and tack to the buckskin. Taking the lead rope, he slowly left the protection of the rocks. He wouldn't be able to move fast with the weakened condition of his horse, which he would not leave behind since he had raised him from a colt. Jake hoped that the Indians wouldn't notice the horse missing for a while as they were busy with the other men. It would give him time to get away.

As he rode, the distant gunfire began to diminish. Jake found a ravine that was deep enough to hide him and his horses as he traveled. The ravine headed north and was wide enough for him to move without being seen.

Trotting the horses for about a mile, he stopped to give his horse a breather. Jake left the animals in the ravine and climbed to the edge, where he could look back to see if he was being followed. Not seeing any sign of pursuit, he waited and listened for gunfire. When he didn't hear any, he figured the men were either dead or captured. Then he thought he heard the scream of someone being tortured. That meant at least one of them had been captured.

His imagination ran wild with images of what the Apaches were doing to the men who had followed him. Even though he knew those gamblers would have gladly killed him had they caught him, he still felt a sense of guilt for not going back to help them.

After returning to the ravine, he rode the rest of the day and night without pushing his horses; he stopped often to rest them for an hour. When the pink glow of sunrise showed in the east, he looked for a place where he could rest. The land around him was dry and barren except for the sage that seemed to grow everywhere. Jake believed that the Indians would no doubt try to find him when they were finished with their captives and discovered the missing horse. However, he reckoned he had traveled far enough that it would be some time before they could find him if they did come looking. He thought that if they were torturing the men they captured, it allowed him time to escape. He had heard stories about Indians who had kept their captives alive for days just to watch them suffer. He was not sure if these young boys would do that or take their prisoners with them.

Not finding adequate cover but knowing he had some time, Jake dismounted and hobbled his horses. He kept them near where he sat on the ground and leaned back. It wasn't long before he dozed off.

With a jerk, he was awake and realized that he had fallen asleep and didn't know what had caused him to suddenly wake up. He also did not know how long he was asleep. Could they have gotten close to him? He stood and found that his legs had gone to sleep, making it hard for him to walk. He looked around but did not see any dust to indicate that someone was pursuing him, so he began to relax.

Jake had not eaten a meal since he was in the café in Santa Fe. He checked his saddlebags and found the remains of a small amount of jerky. While he chewed, he walked around, stomping his feet to get circulation in his legs. He poured water from his canteen and gave each horse a big slurp out of the ragged hat he wore. After an hour, he tightened the cinch, mounted the buckskin, and urged him on. It was now midmorning, and he would have to be careful while he made his way to the mountain range in the distance.

It was afternoon when he stopped. He'd ridden into a spot that was hidden from the trail and decided to make camp. A wide overhanging rock sheltered him from the sun, and water and grass were nearby to feed his horses. He hobbled the animals where they could get their fill without having to walk far.

Jake set a tin of water with a sprinkling of coffee grounds on a flat rock right in the center of a small fire he started. He didn't care if the coffee was bad, good, or so thick he could spoon it out. All he thought about was that he had to have some.

He spread his blanket and saddle next to the fire, where he lay back and watched the sky over his head as the sun moved toward the west. While he lay there, his thoughts went to his sister and her troubles, and he hoped he'd make it to her in time to help. After resting there awhile, he fell asleep.

It was late in the afternoon when Jake woke with a start. The horses had their heads up and their ears pointing south. He wondered who or what was out there. Had the Apaches found his trail? Had they started looking for him and the horse he took?

His campfire had died out early, so there wasn't any smoke that would give him away. He quietly saddled his horse and tied the buckskin's lead rope to his saddle horn. Spotting a small knoll that was high enough to hide him and his horses, Jake rode there. Taking his Henry, he maneuvered his animals to where they were hidden and waited. If they came after him, he would fight. He had made a promise to himself if it was Apaches, they wouldn't take him alive.

Jake continued to watch the skyline south of him as the cloud of dust being created continued to rise above the horizon just east of the ravine he had followed. As the cloud got closer, he could see that it was the Apaches. He watched as they rode between the sage and noticed that one of the Indians kept looking at the ground; he knew his tracks had been spotted.

As the Indians got closer, Jake saw two white men with them. The first man was bent over the saddle horn, and it looked like he was tied there to keep from falling. His head was uncovered. His face was all bloody from being beaten and cut. There was a lot of blood on his shirt sleeve and chest. He actually looked more dead than alive. The other man was in better shape. He was sitting up in the saddle and looking around. He, too, had his head uncovered, and Jake could see that he had been beaten as well. He had a scared expression that gave Jake a pang of guilt for not trying to help them.

Jake tensed when he saw one of the Apaches get off his pony and look closely at the ground. He stood and looked in the direction where Jake was hidden. After mounting, the Apache rode toward the overhang where Jake had stopped. Seeing him go, a second Indian turned and joined him. When he got alongside him, the first Indian pointed to the tracks, and they rode closer to the spot where Jake had stopped. They became cautious as they neared the overhang. Leaving their ponies, they crawled on the ground as they closed in. When they reached the campsite, they found it was empty. They searched the ground and found tracks where Jake had ridden away. They stopped and looked at each other, hesitating before deciding if they should follow or return to the others.

Jake grew tense as he watched the two Apaches return to their ponies. When he saw them turn toward where he was hidden, he knew if they found him that he would have no choice but to shoot his way out of it, and the rest would come to their aid. He continued to watch them, wondering what they would do next. They didn't move but instead sat on their ponies and looked at the knoll where he was hiding. A cold chill ran through Jake as he waited. Even though they were a hundred yards away, he wondered if the young bucks had seen him. Jake caught himself holding his breath so the Indians wouldn't hear him breathe.

They started to move, following his trail. Jake raised his rifle to his shoulder, preparing for the fight he knew was coming. Suddenly, a shout from one of the braves waiting to go on stopped the two Apaches in their tracks. Jake saw the brave who called out motion that they should return.

When they turned to ride back to those who were waiting, Jake let his breath out. He didn't relax until he saw them all start to ride west. Even so, he waited an hour after they were gone before he moved from behind the knoll. He was fearful that the two Indians who had searched for him would lag behind to watch their trail. When Jake started west, he didn't know how long he would have to follow the Apaches and hoped that they would leave the trail.

It was midafternoon when he reached the end of the canyon. When he came out of it, all he saw were miles of flat land. Not able to see any cover, he decided to hold back and rest until dusk.

Not wanting to risk a fire for coffee, he ate the rest of his jerky. While watering the horses, he was amazed that they could find anything to graze on in the dusty landscape. As soon as they finished drinking, they started pulling short stalks of peppergrass out of the ground.

Jake rested until the sun had dropped from the sky and the shadows grew long. Riding easy, he let his horses graze when they found a few spots of grass. Finally, he stopped for the night after he had not seen any signs of the Apaches. He figured they turned off somewhere, probably to head to their village, so he made camp.

Rummaging through the saddlebags, he found a can of beans he had forgotten about before he started a fire. Feeling good, he set about warming the beans and made a good pot of coffee.

While he sat and relaxed by the fire, he took out the letter from his sister to read it again. He wondered what kind of danger they were really in. When he left home, the ranch was doing well. They had money in the bank and a contract to supply cattle to the miners north of them. His sister had taken over running the ranch when their father was ill, so he knew she could handle it with the help of her husband, Howard, and their foreman, Logan. Sally had always been the apple of the old man's eye. She was also smart, so between her and Howard, they'd be capable of running the ranch without him.

She said in her letter that a few days after their pa had recovered, he went out to check the cattle and didn't return. When Logan sent one of the ranch hands out looking for cattle, he found him shot in the back in the north valley. Her letter also told him that their dad left half the ranch to him in his will. Jake wondered if she said that to get him to come home or if he had really done that. After all, they had never resolved the issue of his mothers' death.

Riding out early the next day, Jake noticed the change in the landscape. Since he had left Santa Fe, the land was desert with deep ravines, where water flowed during the rains. Low, rolling hills were mostly desert sand covered with sage and mesquite. Now he saw more green vegetation. It looked like there would be plenty of grass for his horses and maybe even some game.

That afternoon, after spotting an antelope, he left his horses and worked his way through the brush until the animal was in range. He aimed and dropped it with the first shot. With a fresh kill, Jake decided to stop early for the night to cook some of the meat and prepare the rest into jerky. He found branches that would work to make a rack to hang the meat to dry. After salting the meat, he hung the strips where the heat of the fire would slowly dry it overnight. For the meat to be cured, he would have to keep the fire going throughout the night to make sure the jerky was dried by daybreak.

The next morning, Jake thought about the ranch and the cattle they raised in the Mancos Valley. There was plenty of grass and water for the beef that they had always raised. His father had made agreements to take cattle to the mining camps, where the miners were willing to pay top dollar for them. The ranch that their father had claimed was made up of two thousand acres. With hard work over the years, they built up their herd to close to fifteen hundred head of cattle.

The Burtons had been one of the first families to move into the valley. Jake's father, Randolph, fought Jicarilla Apaches, Navajo, and Ute Indians, trying to keep his land while he built his home. When other settlers and homesteaders started to come into the valley, he had to fight some of them as well when they tried to settle on his land.

At noon, Jake stopped and cooked some of the fresh meat he had saved. With the knowledge that he was not followed, he relaxed and took his time to rest both himself and his horses. While scanning the land, he noticed a faint haze of dust rising toward the light-blue skyline about a mile away. While he watched, the dust kept getting closer. Not sure of what or who was causing it, he didn't want to chance being caught if it was Indians. Mulling over his options, he noticed that the land in front of him was flat and barren. If he tried to ride out now, he would most likely be spotted. Where he had stopped, there was a little protection from the tall scrub oak if he had to fight. He decided to stay put and see who or what was coming. He found a place that would conceal him.

As the dust got closer, he recognized that it was the second band of Apaches. They rode hard and did not follow his tracks. He realized that they had come up behind him without his noticing them, and that sent a chill up his spine.

Why had there been a young buck war party out in the middle of nowhere that now held two white men? And now another band was riding hard with a steely purpose. Something wasn't right. What's going on? he thought.

After they passed he broke camp.

4

THE HAMMANS

THE LAND WHERE JAKE DECIDED to stop had tall grass. A grove of pinion pine trees stretched north. He could see a few lodgepole pines dotting the landscape further on. He rode to the outer band of trees, where he set up camp.

With plenty of grass but no water near, Jake hobbled his horses to keep them from wandering. He made camp in the trees so that any smoke from his fire would disperse through the leaves as it ascended. He didn't want the Indians he spotted earlier to come upon him while he slept. He decided that once he finished eating, he would put out his fire and move. While cooking supper, Jake kept watching his horses in the hopes that they would alert him to any movement nearby.

Jake leaned back against a tree while he ate. Starting to fall asleep, he had to shake himself to stay awake. A gentle breeze blew as the night air became cooler. In the quiet, he could hear his horses munching nearby, which gave him comfort that he was alone. The rising moon lit the sky, allowing Jake to see across the open field. The few clouds floating overhead would cover the moon from time to time and turn the night into darkness as they moved across the sky.

He was still watching the clouds and thinking about home when he heard a sound off in the distance that suddenly made him alert. He cocked his head in the direction of what he thought was a gunshot. He waited and continued to listen, but all remained quiet. *Was it a gunshot, or was it just a tree branch breaking and falling?* Jake wondered. He had not gotten much rest over the past few days. He even wondered if he had dozed off and dreamt it. Not hearing it again, he relaxed and dozed off.

Jake woke with a start when he heard the horses snorting and moving about nervously. He shook his head, trying to clear it, and then sat up to look around and try to find out what had disturbed them. He cursed himself for falling asleep before he had moved on. He knew that this mistake could get him in trouble. Thinking the worst, he wondered if the Indians had turned back and found his camp.

Jake got up, picked up his rifle, and moved back into the shadows, where he could listen and wait. Cussing to himself, he saw that his fire was still burning bright, showing anyone where his camp was. Careless mistakes like that could get him killed.

He was watching his horses when he spotted movement near the edge of the camp. He couldn't tell if it was an animal or a man at first. Whatever was out there was moving consciously and stayed close to the ground. As he looked, the movement stopped. The next thing he saw was a man who stood up and glanced around before he made his way toward the horses, who became restless as the stranger got closer.

Staying in the shadows, Jake moved nearer the animals, trying to keep them calm. If he had to leave in a hurry, he wanted the horses close. His thoughts went back to earlier in the day when he had counted six Indians. If this was one of them, where were the rest?

As the individual inched closer, the cloud that had covered the moon moved, allowing the moonlight to flood the area. Jake saw it was a boy of about fifteen getting close to his horses. As the boy reached the buckskin, he bent over and started to remove the hobble. Jake silently moved from the shadows and grabbed him from behind before he could get the hobble off.

The young boy felt Jake's arms wrap around him. Thinking that he had been caught by an Indian, the boy started to kick and twist to get away as his fear set in. Unable to escape, he knew that he was dead. Shaking, he started to cry.

Hanging on to the boy, Jake tried not to get kicked. "Why are you trying to take my horse?" he asked.

While Jake held him, the boy turned his head and relaxed a little when he saw that a white man had hold of him. "I . . . I need to get help," he stammered.

Jake could see the boy was actually only twelve or thirteen. In the light, he saw his blond hair and blue eyes, which had turned red from tears. His face was covered in dirt with streaks where sweat had run down. "Stealing my horse is not going to get you help, but it could get you shot," Jake said. "What were you thinking, son?"

"I . . . I thought you were an Indian," said the boy. "That's why I tried to steal the horse."

"Well, you can see I ain't no Indian," Jake said, releasing his grip on the boy. "Now why do you need a horse?"

"Indians," the boy choked out. "My pa has an arrow in him, and my ma has been wounded."

"Where are they?"

"About two miles back there," the boy replied as he pointed west.

Jake remembered that he had thought he heard a gunshot but had dismissed it when he didn't hear it again. If both of his folks were wounded, they could be dead by now. "What are you and your folks doing out here alone?"

The boy still nervous about Jake, said, "We're on our way to Colorado."

Starting to gather his gear together Jake asked, "When were you attacked?"

"Just after we stopped to make camp near dusk, the Indians started shooting at us," the boy replied.

"How many Indians were there?"

"I . . . I don't know."

Jake wondered if it was the party he saw earlier that day that had come across the family traveling alone. They probably thought they would be easy prey, so they waited for them to stop before attacking.

"How did you get away?"

"When it got dark, Ma told me to go. She didn't think they'd be able to hold out, and she wanted me to get away," the boy answered. "You've got to help, or my ma and pa are going to die."

"They may be dead already," Jake commented.

Suddenly, he heard another gunshot and jerked his head up, realizing that it came from where the boy had indicated.

There might be a chance that they are still alive, Jake thought. He knew he couldn't just ride out and leave them and the boy alone. Jake finished gathering his gear together and saddled his horse. He put the boy on the buckskin, and they went to help his folks.

On the way, the boy told Jake that he thought his pa had shot two of the Indians but didn't know if they were dead. As they rode, they remained in the lower ground, trying to stay hidden as they approached the wagon. When they were a quarter-mile from it, Jake left the boy with the horses. Taking his lever-action Henry .44, he worked his way through the grass and sagebrush. In the moonlight, Jake could see the wagon and made out that the horses were still hitched to it.

They must not have had time to unhitch the horses or make camp when the Indians started attacking. He could see that the horses were nervous, and they kept looking toward the east. Jake was thankful, believing the animals had just indicated where the Indians were.

Jake could see movement behind the wagon. With a closer look, he made out that the woman was standing by herself. Worried that the horses could bolt and leave the folks unprotected, Jake slowly moved forward. Every few steps, he would stop and listen. The only cover available between him and the wagon was the tall grass and some sagebrush.

A drifting cloud blocked the moon and hid Jake as he moved. He stopped again and knelt in the grass when he heard someone moving near him. He realized that the Indians were closing in on the wagon, and he would have to do something soon. He strained his eyes until he caught the movement of the grass to his right. Not knowing if it was the wind or an Indian, he remained still. When the cloud passed, Jake saw an Indian in the brush about ten yards from him. The Indian was crawling on his stomach, inching his way toward the wagon. Jake was about to move when he heard a bird call from his right. The Indian in front of him stopped long enough to return the call. Jake aimed and shot. The bullet hit the Indian in the back and drove him forward into the dirt.

Moving to the right, Jake needed to locate the one who had made the first bird call. After he had gone a few feet, Jake was able to figure the general spot where the Indian was. Firing two quick shots in that direction, he heard the running feet of two Indians as they hurried away.

Hearing a noise behind him, Jake turned and spotted another Indian.

He fired his rifle and knocked the Indian backward, killing him. Jake levered his rifle and fired at the second Indian, who was trying to get away. The shot missed as the Indian rolled to his right, which caused Jake to lose sight of him. Before Jake could relocate him, the Indian moved again. Jake levered another round into his magazine. Now that the Indian was gone, Jake moved quickly to his left and dropped flat on the ground.

He didn't move until he heard a new bird call followed by someone running. He moved quickly as he tried to reach them. When the running stopped, he heard horses leaving in a hurry. Jake continued to listen to the beating of the hooves as they faded in the distance. After the sound died, he waited another fifteen minutes to make sure there were no other Indians around.

Returning to the boy, Jake said, "Call to your folks so they don't try to shoot us when we go in."

"Ma, Pa, it's me, Greg. I brought help, and we're coming in."

From the wagon, Jake heard a woman's trembling voice say, "Thank God."

Greg's mother was standing next to the wagon, shaking. She held an 1862 Spencer that had been in the war and was about worn out. When she saw her son, she dropped the rifle and ran to him, hugging him tightly when he got down from the horse.

The woman looked to be in her late twenties with blond hair. She stood about five-foot-four and wore a dark cotton dress with long sleeves. Her left arm had a blood stain from where she had been wounded. "Who's with you?" she asked.

"I don't know his name," Greg replied.

"Sorry, ma'am. My name is Jake . . . Jake Burton."

"You're the answer to our prayers, Mr. Burton. My name is Elizabeth Hamman, and this is my husband, Adam." She pointed toward the wagon, where a man was lying on the ground.

Jake saw that she had a rag wrapped around her left arm. "Are you hurt bad, ma'am?" he asked.

"No, but my husband isn't doing well," Elizabeth said. She went to kneel next to him and put his head in her lap.

"Have you got a lantern?" Jake asked, trying to see how badly her husband was wounded.

Greg went to the back of the wagon and returned with a lantern. The light from it showed an arrow protruding from the right side of Adam's chest.

"I don't know what to do," Elizabeth said, crying and shaking as she held her husband. "I don't know anything about a wound like this. I don't know how to remove the arrow."

Adam whispered to Elizabeth, "You can do it. You just have to be strong and do what he says."

Elizabeth looked at Adam with tears in her eyes, shaking her head and not saying a word.

"We cannot leave the arrow in him or he'll die. We'll have to be careful that the arrowhead doesn't come off the shaft when we remove it," Jake informed her.

"But . . . but how will you be able to remove the arrow and know if it's not coming out with the shaft?" Elizabeth asked, still holding Adam's head.

"I'll have to cut into him till I can feel the arrowhead and make sure it has room to come out as I pull on the shaft," Jake told her.

"Won't that kill him?" Greg asked, hanging on to the wheel of the wagon.

"It could," Jake said. "But if the arrowhead stays in him, it will certainly kill him. We're going to have to move him before I can work on him, but first we need to take care of your horses so they don't try to run off. Greg, you get some wood and get a fire going," he ordered as he went to unhitch the team.

The horses had calmed down since the shooting stopped, but there was still a chance they could bolt. Jake was able to unhitch them and tie them to the side of the wagon. After retrieving his horses, he tied them next to the team before going to help Adam.

Greg had a fire going, and Jake told Elizabeth to lay a blanket near it. Then she helped Jake move her husband onto the blanket. Adam, he let out a cry of pain as the arrow moved when he was picked up.

Once Adam was settled, the light from the fire gave Jake a clear view of the wound.

"Won't the Indians come back?" Elizabeth asked, looking out into the dark with fear in her eyes.

"I don't think so," Jake responded. "They don't know how many came to help you, so it would be risky coming back while it's dark. They may try again in the morning though."

Jake took out his knife and placed the blade in the fire. It was razor-sharp and would allow him to easily cut into Adam when he removed the arrow.

While the blade heated, Jake opened Adam's shirt to figure out how deep the arrow was lodged, hoping he could remove it without killing the man. It would depend on how much cutting it would take and how strong Adam was. Picking up his knife, Jake looked at Elizabeth. "You need to hold him so he doesn't move while I do this."

With a scared look on her face, Elizabeth took hold of Adam's left arm. "I . . . I don't know if I can do this."

"You have to 'cause if he moves while I'm working on him, it could kill him. Greg, hand me that lantern." Jake took the lantern and put it where the light shined on Adam's chest. "Now take your belt off and put it in your father's mouth. Then hold his other arm."

After Greg did so, Jake asked Adam, "Are you ready?" Adam nodded his head.

Jake ran his hand down the shaft of the arrow, gently moving it back and forth. He thought he felt the arrowhead move with the shaft. He was relieved that the arrow had not gone too deep and believed that it had hit a bone.

Adam started to writhe from the pain as Jake probed. "You've got to hold him still while I cut, or it could kill him," Jake growled again.

Jake took his time and started to cut next to the shaft. He figured that if the bone had stopped the arrow, he might be able to remove it without too much cutting When Adam felt the heat of the knife against his chest, he jerked. "Hold him still," Jake called out to Elizabeth.

Between the pain from the arrow and Jake's cutting, Adam passed out. Elizabeth started to relax her hold on his arm when he quit struggling. "Keep a hold of him. If he wakes up and moves, I could slip with the knife," Jake instructed her.

With Adam lying still, Jake cut a little deeper until he felt the blade of his knife hit what he believed was the arrowhead. When Jake felt that he had made a large enough opening, he started to pull firmly on the arrow, but it did not budge. Afraid that the arrowhead would not come with the shaft, he stopped.

Elizabeth asked, "What's wrong?"

"The arrowhead may be stuck in a bone," Jake replied.

Again, grabbing the shaft, Jake pulled. This time he felt the arrowhead move with the shaft as it started to come out. Relieved, he continued to pull until the entire arrow was out with the head still attached.

Afterward, Jake threw the arrow into the fire before taking a wet rag to clean the wound. With the arrow out, the blood started to flow freely. He covered it with a dry bandage and put pressure on it to stop the bleeding. While he held it in place, he said, "I need a needle and thread to sew up his wound before he wakes up."

Jake saw that Elizabeth had turned pale. She got up and walked unsteadily to the wagon to get her sewing kit. He continued to watch, afraid that she might pass out.

"Will he be all right?" Greg asked.

"I don't know," Jake said. "I didn't have to cut that deep. If he's a strong man and it doesn't get infected, he might make it."

Elizabeth returned with her sewing box. She opened it and handed Jake a needle that already had thread attached to it. Knowing what had to be done, she looked away when Jake started sewing Adam's wound. When he finished, he cleaned the wound, making sure the bleeding had stopped, before Elizabeth and Greg helped him put a clean bandage around Adam's chest.

Jake got up to look in the back of the wagon. "We need to make room for him here. Greg, I need you to hitch up the team. We're going to move out."

"Why are we moving?" Elizabeth asked.

"We don't want to be here if those Indians go get help and return in the morning."

Elizabeth helped Jake make room in the wagon while Greg hitched the team. Once Adam was inside, Jake asked, "Can you drive the team, Mrs. Hamman?"

"Yes," she said. "But won't moving the wagon make Adam's wound reopen?"

"Hopefully not," Jake said. "But we need to find a place that we can defend if those Indians return."

"Where are we going?" Elizabeth wanted to know.

"Just follow me. I'll find a place that's safer."

Jake was able to find his way by the light of a bright moon as the sky had become clear. They traveled between ravines, where the ground was flat but had numerous ruts created by previous rains. As the wagon bounced along, Jake could hear Adam moan and sometimes cry out. He knew that Elizabeth would be afraid her husband was not doing well.

"I need to stop and check on Adam," she called out to Jake.

"Keep driving," Jake called back. "When I find a place where we can stop, you'll be able to check on him."

Elizabeth became angry. Her face turned red, and she started to cry.

They had gone about four miles when Jake spotted a place that offered coverage and that he felt they could defend. He had Elizabeth place the wagon behind a pile of rocks that created a natural barrier and offered them more protection than just the wagon alone. The wagon would now protect their backs if an attack came.

When they stopped, Elizabeth climbed off the wagon and ran to the back to check on Adam. Greg took care of the team while Jake tended his horses.

Once the horses were put in a safe place, Jake sent Greg to look for wood. With a long night still ahead of them, he wanted coffee. He knew that if the Indians returned, they could follow the wagon tracks, so he would have to stay alert and stand guard throughout the night.

Greg returned with an armload of wood and got a fire going. Elizabeth left the wagon after Adam had gone back to sleep. Jake asked her to make some coffee. "Have you eaten?" he asked.

"We were just getting ready for supper when we were attacked," she responded.

Going to his saddlebags, he took out some antelope jerky and gave it to Elizabeth. "You may want to use some of it for a broth to give to Adam when he wakes up. You and your son need to eat some of this as well."

While Elizabeth made the broth for Adam, Jake decided to scout the area and walked away from the wagon. Ten yards out, he found a pile of large rocks that would offer protection to anyone sitting behind them while guarding the camp. The spot gave the advantage of being able to see movement coming from any direction. When he returned to the wagon, he told Greg, "I want you to come with me and bring a rifle with you."

Jake took Greg to the rock pile and showed him where to sit to keep watch. "If you see any movement, don't try to do anything. Just come back and get me."

Jake returned to camp and got his bedroll. He looked at Elizabeth and said, "Wake me in two hours." After he laid out his bedroll near the fire, he lay down and closed his eyes.

Elizabeth was still shaken from what had happened and knew she wouldn't be able to sleep. Worried about Adam, she went to check on him and found him resting, so she busied herself by setting up the camp. When she finished, she made sure the coffee pot was close enough to the fire to keep it warm. She poured herself a cup and sat down.

With nothing to do, she sat by the fire and watched Jake while he slept. Even in his sleep, she could see that his face was etched with exhaustion. Concern set in as she wondered what he was doing way out there alone. She was tired and started to imagine different things about the stranger. Was he on the run from something or someone? If he was an outlaw, she and her family might be in danger. She continued with evil thoughts of what he might do to them despite his help. What if he wanted their money? Would he try to take it? Maybe he would rape her. Thinking that, she started to shiver in fear. She got up and paced around the fire, knowing that neither Adam nor Greg would be able to stop him, whatever his intentions were.

The fear she felt and the exhaustion seeping into her body kept her from thinking clearly. It took a while before reasoning finally won out. It didn't make sense that he would have helped Adam if he was going to hurt them. Elizabeth reasoned that he could have killed her husband earlier if he wanted to. With that realization, she sat down and quit worrying about what Jake was going to do. Instead, she tried to figure out what they were going to do.

5

ATTACK

AFTER THE TWO HOURS PASSED, Elizabeth found Jake still sleeping soundly. She woke him by calling his name as she started to approach. Jake woke with a start, grabbed his rifle, and startled Elizabeth, causing her to jump back. "It's me . . . Elizabeth," she cried out.

It took a minute for Jake to recognize her and remember where he was. He relaxed his grip on his rifle and got up. With his head cleared, he saw Elizabeth standing in front of him, startled, holding a cup of coffee. Embarrassed, he said, "Sorry, ma'am. I guess I was asleep deeper than I intended. Is everything all right?"

"All is quiet," Elizabeth said, recovering from her shock. "You asked me to wake you in two hours."

"Yes, thanks. How is Adam doing?"

"He's resting."

Jake laid his rifle across his arm before reaching for the coffee. "Thanks, ma'am." With his rifle in one hand and coffee in the other, he left camp and went to relieve Greg.

As he approached, Greg sensed that someone was coming up behind him. In fear, he turned with his Spencer in his hand, pointing it at Jake. Relieved when he saw who it was, the boy lowered the rifle. Jake was surprised; he hadn't made any noise as he approached, but Greg had sensed him coming. Seeing the boy's reaction, Jake was glad to know that he was alert.

"I'm glad it's you, Mr. Burton," Greg said. "I thought that maybe it was an Indian."

"I'm glad you realized it was me. Have you seen anything?"

"No, it's been quiet."

"Thanks, you did a good job. You can go back to the wagon and get some sleep. I'll keep watch."

The spot where Greg had watched from provided a place to sit with good cover. Jake set his coffee on a nearby boulder and sat down. He rested his rifle across his lap as he sipped some of the dark liquid that warmed his insides, hoping it would keep him alert. Jake sat quietly for a while, not moving to let his ears adjust to the night sounds.

The first thing he heard was one of the horses stomp and snort. Next, Jake heard Greg and his mother getting settled down for the night as the camp got quiet. The sky was clear and allowed the moon to give off enough light to see in the distance. The night breeze gently blowing across the grass felt cool on Jake's face. He knew that the coolness would help to keep him awake. After becoming familiar with the sounds of the night, he felt confident he would recognize any change that would alert him of approaching danger.

After Jake sat for three hours without moving, the warmth of the night and stillness in the air made him drowsy. Getting up and walking around, he started to become alert again. By looking at the sky, he could see a red glow on the horizon telling him the sun would be coming up soon. Fighting the drowsiness, he picked up his cup and walked back to camp. The fire had died, but he found the coffee pot sitting nearby, still hot. Picking up the pot, he filled his cup. Before going back to watch, he looked around the camp and spotted Greg sleeping under the wagon. There was no sign of Elizabeth, so he figured that she must be in the wagon with Adam.

While the pot had sat near the fire all night, the coffee had gotten strong. Between the walk and the strong coffee, Jake was now fully awake. He sat and began to think about what he was going to do. Now that he had started to help this family, he couldn't just leave them. Still, he needed to get back to his sister, and traveling with these folks would slow him down. With the concern for his family and wondering if they were still alive weighing on him, Jake knew the wagon would delay him getting home. It would be faster if he was alone.

An hour later, when the sky turned lighter, Jake still hadn't figured out what he needed to do. He heard movement in the camp. The rattle of pots and pans told him that Elizabeth was up and had started cooking. The sun had just come over the horizon when she came to tell him breakfast would be ready soon.

"How is Adam doing?" Jake asked.

"He's still sleeping, but I think he has a fever. I'd like to let him rest for the day."

"Sorry, but we need to get moving as soon as we can this morning."

"I don't know if Adam will be able to travel," she complained.

"We can't stay here. Those Indians that attacked you may come back with more braves," Jake said. "We need to get as far from them as we can. After traveling some, we may find a better place that we can defend. Then we'll be able to let Adam rest."

"I guess you're right," Elizabeth agreed, hanging her head but knowing that it was best. "Come and eat. I'll get Greg to take care of the horses."

After Elizabeth left, Jake said to himself, "I guess I made up my mind to help these folks and not leave them alone."

He watched as the night shadows slowly crept across the valley and disappeared. The sky showed that it was going to be a clear day. Shaking his head, he knew it was also going to be hot. He was still looking at the sky when Greg came and told him that his food was ready.

As they walked back to camp, Greg said, "I took care of the horses as Ma asked. They've been fed and watered."

"Thanks," Jake said.

Elizabeth was very efficient, Jake thought as he walked into camp. She had made a fresh pot of coffee and handed the cup to him as he moved near the fire. She made a plate for him with cornbread, meat, and gravy.

Jake ate while Elizabeth took a plate of food to Adam. When she finished feeding him, she cleaned the campsite and loaded the wagon. Greg helped his mother while Jake hitched the team and saddled his horse. While finishing, he thought he saw dust on the southern horizon. He continued to watch it as it seemed to fade. Maybe he had imagined it, maybe the wind was blowing hard enough to cause dust to rise, or maybe it was because someone was moving around out there. He wanted to get going in case it wasn't the wind. "Greg, can you drive the wagon and handle the team?"

"Yeah, Pa had me work with the team some."

"Elizabeth, you ride in back with Adam and keep watching behind us," Jake said.

"What's wrong?"

"I thought I saw dust back there. I don't know what caused it, but we need to keep track of it."

Elizabeth asked, "Could it be Indians?"

"I can't be sure if it's someone following us or if it's just the wind blowing up dust."

Elizabeth climbed into the back of the wagon with Adam while Greg climbed onto the seat and took the reins in hand. When Jake saw that they were ready, he led the way. As they traveled, he kept watching for a place where they could defend themselves in case it was Indians. Throughout the morning, dust continued to appear on the horizon, and Jake grew uneasy, feeling like someone was closing in on them.

With Adam lying flat in the bed of the wagon, Elizabeth had to sit on some of their belongings to be near him and keep watch. Like Jake, she caught glimpses of the dust that appeared in the distance. When she felt Adam's head, she found it hot and became concerned that he was getting worse. She had wanted to stay where they had camped during the night to allow him time to recover but had been overridden by Jake. She was upset with him but knew that if the Indians were looking for them, they had to keep moving. Still, Adam was her first concern.

At noon, Jake wanted to stop and rest the horses. Not yet finding a place that would conceal the wagon, he kept looking. Luck was not with them as Jake did not find what he wanted, so they had to stop in the open. Being so exposed, he felt the tension continue to mount. He would only stop until the horses had rested some before they would continue to travel.

While they waited for the animals, Jake inquired again how Adam was doing. Elizabeth responded, "It feels like his fever has gotten higher. The jerking of the wagon is not letting him get the rest he needs. His wound started bleeding again, but I was able to get it stopped." Lowering her head, she added in a soft, fearful voice, "If his fever gets much higher, I'm afraid he will die."

Greg arrived at the back of the wagon in time to hear his mother say that and asked, "Is Pa gonna die?"

Elizabeth said, "I don't know. His fever has gotten higher."

"Why can't we stop for the rest of the day?" Greg demanded.

Jake said, "The dust in the distance looks to be getting closer. Whoever it is has been following us since we left this morning. We need to find a place to hide the wagon so we can hold up and find out who it is. If it's Indians, we need a place to defend."

Their noon meal consisted of the extra meat Elizabeth had cooked that morning along with the jerky Jake had provided. After giving the horses a short rest, they moved out as soon as they finished eating.

The dust from the distant riders continued to appear closer and closer as fear consumed Elizabeth. Jake had begun to worry about their chances of getting away. He kept searching the surrounding terrain for a place they could defend. After topping a ridge, he found what he had been looking for. A rock wall with an opening in the center large enough to allow the wagon to enter stood in front of him. They should be safe. Even with the opening, there was enough protection to hold off an attack.

Once behind the rocks, they unhitched the horses and tied them to the side of the wagon in hopes that if an attack came, they would be out of the line of fire. Jake instructed Greg and Elizabeth to get ready.

By the time they stopped, Adam was awake. Hearing Jake say it could be Indians following them, he did not want to be in the wagon and not helping. Still hurting from his wound, he tried to get out of the wagon. Elizabeth heard her husband moving around and climbed inside to try to keep him there.

When the dust settled, Jack was able to make out who had followed them. The Indians stopped at the top of the ridge, where they were outlined by the sky. Jake watched while they searched for the wagon. He wiped his brow, wet from the fear of knowing his worst thoughts were now a reality. Jake counted twenty Indians. He knew that the top of the wagon had to be visible to them when he saw one of them point in their direction.

Jake called to Greg and Elizabeth, "Get ready. They won't sit there long. They will want to find out how strong we are. If they are the same ones from last night, they know there aren't many of us here. Greg, you need to get a rifle."

"Mr. Burton, I . . . I ain't never killed anyone," Greg said with fear in his voice.

"You are going to be fighting for your life and your parents' lives. If you don't fight, they will kill you."

The sun was now high in the sky. Without any shade, the heat was merciless. Wiping the sweat from his eyes, Jake watched as the Indians started to advance.

After coming so far, they stopped and spread out, setting up to attack from two sides. Jake positioned Greg where he could watch the east and face the Indians, while Jake himself faced west. Seeing Greg by himself and looking scared, Elizabeth took the second Spencer and went to help her son.

As the Indians started to attack, Jake ordered, "Hold your fire until I shoot." With his .44 Henry, he could provide rapid fire while Elizabeth and Greg, with their single-shot Spencers, had to reload after each shot.

The Indians looked to all be young braves. Not knowing which ones had attacked the wagon, Jake wasn't sure if this was the same group from last night. Most were shirtless, and it looked like they had smeared some type of oil on their bodies, causing them to shine in the sun. Most of their faces were painted in red and yellow streaks. Some of them had covered half their faces in black and the other half in white. Their horses were also painted with different designs. None of the braves carried rifles. They all had bows and arrows.

Once they were in range, Jake opened fire. Levering a new round in, he fired a second shot. Hearing Jake shooting, Elizabeth also fired. Greg hesitated until he heard his mother shoot and fired while Elizabeth was reloading.

Hearing the gunfire, Adam couldn't stand by any longer. He grabbed his Bisley Colt model .44. Struggling, he crawled to the back of the wagon and spotted an Indian standing on a rock with a notched arrow aimed at Greg. He fired and hit the Indian in the chest, knocking him backward off the rock. A second Indian came crawling over the rock. Seeing him, Adam fired once again, and the Indian slid behind the rock. Thinking he had killed them both, Adam climbed out of the wagon in pain. As he reached the ground, the Indian who had slid out of sight had crawled back to the top of the rock. With an arrow notched in his bow, he hit Adam in the back just as he started to walk away from the wagon, knocking him to the ground. Adam turned over and, seeing the Indian who had shot him, fired—this time killing him.

Jake continued to fire at those who attacked from the west. The Indians were not ready for the rapid firing of the Henry and slowed their attack. By then, Jake had wounded or killed four of the braves. When they retreated, they took their injured and dead with them. When the Indians attacking from the east saw the others pull back, they also retreated. Jake turned to see how Elizabeth and Greg were doing. Seeing that they were all right, he continued to watch the Indians as they moved away.

During the momentary break in the attack, Elizabeth turned around and saw Adam lying by the back of the wagon. Running to him, she saw the arrow protruding from his back and turned him on his side for a better look. Adam opened his eyes and looked at her. He tried to smile, but the pain was too great.

Elizabeth started to cry and said, "Why did you get out of the wagon?"

When Jake heard her, he turned and saw Adam lying on the ground. He got up and went to help Elizabeth move him to where there was better protection, Elizabeth tried to address his injuries, but looking at Adam's pale face, Jake could tell he wasn't going to make it. Adam opened his eyes but appeared to look off in the distance with a blank stare. He tried to talk but couldn't get the words out.

Jake could feel what Elizabeth was going through. He had lost his mother and father, and now he was trying to get home before he lost the rest of his family. He was worried that he was not going to make it while trying to help this family.

Elizabeth was shaking and crying while she held Adam's head in her lap. The tears in her eyes were blinding her to what was going on around her. All her thoughts and concerns were for her husband.

Jake returned to his position in time to see that the Indians had started a second round. It looked like they were going to make an all-out attack and come at them from the west. He called Greg to his side and said, "Wait until I fire twice before you open fire. Save the second rifle in case they get too close."

"How is my pa doing?"

"Your mother is with him. Right now, we need to keep the Indians from overrunning us," Jake said. He needed Greg to concentrate on the battle.

Greg jumped, dropping his rifle, as he heard the Indians yell when they started their attack. It took him a minute before he recovered. Realizing he had dropped his rifle, he picked it up and got ready.

Jake shot at the first one who came into range, hitting him and knocking him to the ground. Seeing him get up again, he knew he had only wounded him. When the first shot was fired, the attack was launched. Levering a new round in his Henry, Jake fired a second time. Greg waited until then and fired. The Indians continued to attack, staying low and working their way closer to the rocks that separated them, hiding in the brush where they couldn't be seen.

Elizabeth had remained with Adam and was with him when he took his last breath. Crying uncontrollably and rocking back and forth, she sat holding him. Gazing toward the east with the tears in her eyes clouding her vision, she just made out an Indian coming over the rocks. In anger over the death of her husband, she grabbed Adam's Colt, blindly took aim, and fired. The Indian stopped, stood on his toes, and fell dead.

Hearing the gunshot behind him, Jake turned in time to see the Indian fall. When he saw that Elizabeth had Adam's revolver, he returned his attention to the attack as it came from the west. While he had looked away, Greg had fired, missed, and was reloading as an Indian came over the rocks, diving at Jake. He hit Jake, driving them both to the ground. Jake hit his head and was temporarily stunned. The Indian raised his hatchet to strike when he was hit with a bullet and fell on top of Jake.

Elizabeth had seen the Indian about to kill Jake and fired. In a panic, she went to fire a second round, only to find that the gun was empty. Jake managed to roll the Indian off and recover his rifle. Elizabeth knew that she needed to reload and looked in Adams' pockets, where she found more shells. Realizing Elizabeth had just saved his life, Jake knew he had to get back to help Greg. He would thank her later if he could.

Elizabeth, Greg, and Jake continued to fight until the attack started to wane. The toll on the Indians was high. They began to move back a second time, dragging their wounded and dead with them. After they withdrew, an eerie quiet came over the area. With the intense heat from the sun beating down, knowing that the Indians were still out there sent a chill up Jake's spine. Now they had to wait to see what their attackers would do next.

Jake turned and saw that Elizabeth had returned to Adam, holding him and crying. After what had just happened and what she had gone through with her husband dying in her arms, he realized just how strong she could be when needed. Adam had been lucky to have had her in marriage. Jake continued to watch and started to notice her in a different light, where she wasn't the frail, weak person he first thought she was. She reminded him of his mother, who had fought Indians with his father, saving their ranch. Shooting the Indian who was about to kill him had saved his life. He hoped that her strength would help her through the life she had ahead of her with her son.

The peace lasted for about half an hour before the Indians started another attack. Instead of coming in with a strong assault, they crept forward behind cover. Crawling close enough to the rocks, they started shooting arrows in the air, arching them into the area where Jake, Greg, and Elizabeth waited. Arrows were landing all around them. The only safe place was close to the rocks.

Jake saw that Elizabeth had stayed kneeling by Adam when the attack started and was in danger of being hit by an arrow if she stayed there. A couple had already landed near her. Jake rushed over and grabbed her, pulling her back just as an arrow landed where she had been kneeling. "What about Adam?" she screamed.

"Adam is dead," Jake said in a loud voice. "If you don't take cover, you will be too."

With anger in her eyes, Elizabeth leaned against the rocks, staring at Jake. When he turned away, she tried to go back to her husband. Jake grabbed her arm before she could get away.

Now Jake had a second problem: he saw the fear in Greg's eyes as he cowered next to the rocks. He was shaking and staring at his dead father's body lying nearby. Jake was afraid that Greg and Elizabeth had gone into shock and wouldn't be able to help if the Indians started a frontal attack.

While the braves continued to arch arrows into the camp, the three did not return any gunfire. The arrows continued to fly until the sun started to set.

All the while, Elizabeth had remained sitting with her back to the rocks, shaking and crying. She still held Adam's revolver close to her chest like it was the only thing left of her husband.

When the arrows quit coming, the day became quiet. Jake moved Adam's body and found that he had been hit with arrows twice after he had died. Removing them, he then covered the body to keep Elizabeth from seeing his wounds.

Greg asked, "What are they waiting for?"

"They ain't sure if we're still alive," Jake said.

While waiting, the Indians could not see any movement coming from inside the rocks, so they crept forward. The sun had started to set, and Jake had to look directly into it. He was lucky to spot one brave crawling toward them. "Here they come," He said and started shooting as they moved into the open.

Greg was still sitting with his head down and tears in his eyes when he heard Jake shoot. Setting aside his sorrow, anger took over because of his father's death. He grabbed his rifle, wiped the tears from his eyes, and stood up to help Jake.

Jake had to squint at the sun to see any movement. He was relieved to hear Greg shoot, knowing that the boy had again taken up the rifle. But when he did not hear Greg shoot again, he worried that they wouldn't be able to hold the Indians off. He turned to find out what was going on and saw that Greg had been hit and Elizabeth had started attending to her son's wound.

Jake spotted an Indian coming over the rocks near Elizabeth. Quickly turning, he shot and killed him before he could reach her. Elizabeth was startled when the Indian fell next to her. With Greg assuring her that he would be fine, Elizabeth realized Jake needed her help. She turned her attention to the Indians and started shooting.

Elizabeth and Jake kept shooting as fast as they could until the Indians started to withdraw. With the emotions that had built up inside of her, she kept shooting with tears in her eyes until Jake stopped her when there were no more Indians around.

All was quiet again as Elizabeth and Jake waited. After an hour with no activity from the Indians, Jake believed they had gone. Twilight was setting in as the sun got lower, and red and orange streaks showed up in the western sky.

With it still being light enough to see, Jake decided to look around. As he got up to leave, Elizabeth became afraid of being left alone. "Where are you going?" she asked.

"I'm going out to see if they left. I thought I heard horses earlier."

"What are we going to do if something happens to you?" she cried. "I can't do this by myself."

"I will be back," Jake assured her.

Behind the wagon, Jake climbed over the rocks to keep undercover as much as possible. His route kept him hidden from where the last of the Indians had been spotted. Taking his time, he found where the braves had left their horses and had gathered before attacking. Not finding any trace of them, he knew the three of them were safe for now. As the sun went down, with darkness setting in, he made his way back to camp.

"They're gone," he announced. "Greg, give me a hand to move these dead Indians out of here."

Once the bodies were removed, Jake said, "Get a shovel so we can bury your father."

Greg went to get the shovel while Jake checked the horses. He was relieved to find that they had not been hurt during the attack.

When the boy returned, Jake dug a grave while Greg helped his mother wrap his father in a blanket, and they said their goodbyes. With Greg's help, Jake lowered Adam's body into the grave and then covered it with dirt. He then took rocks and placed them on top.

"Why are you putting rocks on top?" Greg asked.

"They'll keep any animals from digging up your father."

Standing by the grave, Elizabeth held their family Bible. She began to cry as she opened it and started to read. Realizing she was having trouble reading, Jake took the Bible from her hands and read the passages she had selected. When he was done, he turned and walked back to the wagon, leaving Elizabeth and Greg alone. It was almost an hour before they left the gravesite. By then, Jake had started a fire and had coffee boiling.

Elizabeth went straight to the wagon, where Jake helped her take out some of the meat he had given them. While she was working on supper, Jake looked at Greg's arm. He saw that it was not a serious wound and would heal over time.

When Elizabeth finished cooking, she announced that supper was ready. They dished up their plates and sat quietly, each lost in their thoughts. Once they finished eating, Elizabeth asked, "What will happen to us now?"

"Do you have family back where you came from?" Jake asked.

Shaking her head, Elizabeth quietly replied, "No. We lost my family some time back."

"Who do you know in Colorado?"

"We don't know anyone. Adam had heard about some land there that he could farm. He wasn't sure what else he could do. Everything we own is in the wagon," Elizabeth said before breaking down in tears. After a while, she asked, "Where are you going?"

"I'm headed to my sister's place. She has some problems and needs my help."

"What can Greg and I do?" Elizabeth asked as she started to cry again.

"I guess you will just have to come with me. I can't leave you out here by yourselves."

Greg sat with his head down and tears in his eyes. He finally asked, "Do you think the Indians will come back?"

"I don't think they will try again."

While Elizabeth cleaned up camp, Jake fed and tended to the horses before settling them down for the night at the side of the fire. Elizabeth lay under the wagon near Greg. Jake was sure that if she were to go inside the wagon, it would only remind her of her husband.

Too tired to set up watch outside of camp, Jake counted on his horse to warn him if anyone came near. While lying there before going to sleep, he could hear sobs coming from both Elizabeth and Greg and knew he had made the right choice.

6

HOME

EVERYTHING REMAINED QUIET THROUGHOUT THE night. The next morning, Jake woke refreshed. Getting up, he looked around and found Elizabeth and Greg still asleep. They had had a hard time going to sleep after the loss of Adam, and Jake decided to check the area again to make sure that they were alone.

The first thing he did was check on the bodies of the Indians that they had carried out of camp. When he found that they were gone, he became concerned that he didn't hear any movement during the night. He scouted the area, discovering several spots of blood where either a dead or wounded Indian had fallen. From the number of such places, Jake figured that they had suffered heavy losses and would not be back because of their dead and wounded. He also thought that with the amount of pressure the Indians had put on him, Greg, and Elizabeth during the attacks, they had been lucky that Adam was the only one to die.

Elizabeth was just getting up when he returned. Her face was haggard, and her eyes were rimmed in red. Jake could tell that she had not slept much that night. While she made breakfast, Jake took care of the horses. Greg heard him and got up to help. As he came to water the horses, he asked, "What do you think will happen to us?"

"I don't know," Jake replied. "When we get to my sister's place, I'm sure that you and your mother will have time to figure out what you want to do."

Greg didn't respond. It was difficult for him to think about what he and his mother would do without Adam. He was afraid that they would be left on their own with no place to go.

After breakfast, Jake hitched the team to the wagon and tied his horses to the back as they prepared to leave. He helped Elizabeth onto the seat, where he climbed up next to her. Greg crawled into the back and nestled down where he could keep watching behind them as they traveled. The horses were eager to go and started to move when Jake took up the reins.

The land was flat, so the horses didn't have to strain while they pulled the wagon. An hour after they started, Elizabeth fell asleep. When she dropped off, she leaned against Jake and rested her head on his shoulder. Jake tried to keep as still as he could, knowing she needed the sleep. By noon, they had traveled ten miles. Elizabeth woke when they stopped. When she found that she had been leaning against Jake, she became embarrassed and said, "I am sorry."

"No need to be sorry. You needed the rest."

Elizabeth asked, "Have you seen anyone following us?"

"No. I don't think we have to worry about them anymore."

Jake was relieved as the further they traveled, he had not seen any sign of the Indians. When they started again, he hoped that their luck would hold throughout the day.

By late afternoon, Jake had become stiff and sore from bouncing around on the hard wagon seat. Wanting to get down and stretch, he began to look for a place to camp for the night. When he found an area with water and grass, he reined in the horses and stopped.

Jake had watched Elizabeth as she remained quiet most of the afternoon as they traveled. He had seen tears form in her eyes occasionally, and she would bury her head in her hands. He knew the loss of her husband would continue to weigh heavily on her.

When they stopped, Elizabeth climbed down from the wagon and stretched the tight muscles that had developed in her back. She walked around to try to get the blood to flow in her legs. She saw that Greg was doing the same. Walking over to her son, she wrapped her arms around him, both looking for and giving him comfort. She held him close for a moment while she silently wept. Noticing the dirty bandage on his arm, she went to get some water and a clean rag from the wagon. As she changed the bandage, she was glad that she didn't see any signs of infection. She knew his arm would heal.

Greg watched his mother as she walked to the wagon to put away the extra cloth she used to dress the wound. Not sure what to do, he followed and helped her take out what she needed to prepare supper.

Jake was taking care of the horses and hobbled them in the grass he found close to water. Then he returned to the wagon, glad to see that supper was cooking and they would be able to eat before long.

"Do you think the Indians have been following us?" Elizabeth asked when he returned.

"I didn't see any sign of them today. This morning when I looked around the area where we were attacked, I found several pools of blood. I think they had too many wounded and dead to try again."

Greg asked, "How long do you think it will take us to reach Colorado?"

"We came about twenty miles today. If we continue to travel like that, we should be there within two weeks."

The next week, they traveled without seeing any Indians, and Jake began to relax. But he was worried about what Elizabeth and Greg were going through, though he didn't want to interfere with their mourning. He continued to watch them as they coped with Adam's death. He saw the fear build up in them as they began to realize that they were now on their own.

Jake had also overheard them talking about how long he would continue to help them. They were lost without Adam and didn't know what they could do or where they would go.

He saw the fear in Elizabeth's eyes when she asked what it was like where his sister lived. After describing it, he again offered them the chance to stay with his sister at the ranch until they figured out what they wanted to do. However, without any knowledge of his sister, Elizabeth worried that she would not allow them to stay.

A week and a half after the Indian attack, Jake began to recognize the area they were in and knew that they were close to Mancos, Colorado. He told them that they would be at his sister's ranch within two days. Knowing he was close to home, he began to wonder what he would find.

A day later, they drove into the settlement of Mancos, where men were standing in front of the saloon, watching as they went by. Jake didn't recognize any of them but noticed that one of the men got up and crossed the street to the law office as soon as they passed.

Jake continued to watch the men as he drove through town. What he didn't know was that he had been recognized.

The man who crossed the street walked with the determination that he had something to report. When he reached the office, he hesitated before entering. It was a large one-room office with a desk sitting off to one side and two chairs in front of it. Behind the desk was a bookcase that contained several law books. Next to it was a safe. A large man sat behind the desk with black hair and a bushy mustache. His icy blue eyes were cold and piercing. He was a man of size and none of it fat. One look at him told even a stranger that he had known trouble and had learned to hate.

He looked up as Duke entered. "What do you want, Duke?" he growled in a voice that said he was not in a good mood.

"Jake Burton is back," Duke Sanders informed him.

Duke worked for Gifford Clemens as a hired gun and considered himself a gunfighter. He bragged that he had killed several men in face-to-face gunfights. However, there was some question if he had killed the men in a fair fight or shot them in the back. He was a thin man who stood five feet, ten inches and wore two pearl-handled Colt .44's on his hips. His black hat made him look over six feet tall. His eyes were green and set close together. His nose was crooked from being broken in past fights, and there was a scar over his left eye. He had a hard life that made him look older than his twenty-seven years. Being insecure, he always wore a white shirt with a black vest, stayed clean shaven, and kept his boots polished, trying to impress people that he was more important than he was.

"How do you know he's back?" Clemens asked.

Gifford Clemens had moved to Mancos and opened a law office after being run out of Denver for killing a man over land rights. He had plans to take over the cattle business in the Mancos Valley and sell to the miners to the north. The night after he arrived, he was in the saloon where Jake and Sid McFarland were playing poker. Overhearing an argument between the two about cattle had given him an idea. That night, he killed McFarland as he was riding back to his ranch. When the body was found, Gifford was able to put the suspicion on Jake based on the argument they had while playing cards.

After McFarland's death, Gifford purchased his ranch at an unreasonably low price, forcing his widow to go back east. McFarland's ranch was located near the Double B, and after taking possession of it, Clemens had set up headquarters in the house. He was not satisfied with just the McFarland ranch; he also wanted to get the Burton land. His efforts to run them off failed when he found out that Randolph Burton, not his son, was the owner, and Jake had left the area before he could be arrested. He had been unable to scare Randolph off, so he had brought in Duke Sanders and some of the men that rode with him.

"We just saw him come through town," Duke said. "Gil recognized him."

"Was he alone?"

"No, he was on a wagon and had a woman and a boy with him."

"I wonder if he got himself a wife and is thinking of taking over running the Double B Ranch," Clemens said.

"What kind of trouble do you think he will cause us?" Duke asked.

"I think we can control him. I heard that he was accused of killing Sid McFarland and left the territory the day after the body was found. If he got married and plans on moving back, maybe we can bring up the murder charge again. If we can't and he moves back on the ranch with his sister and brother-in-law, it is going to be harder to take control of it," Gifford informed him.

"What do you want to do?" Duke asked.

"I'll get the marshal to dig up the information on that murder charge."

"Do you think if it gets him arrested, it will help to get the ranch?"

"When I tried to buy it, Mrs. Ashley, Jake's sister, said that he was half owner and she couldn't sell it without his permission. If he is out of the way, she may sell. Tell Lew to follow them and make sure they go to the ranch," Gifford ordered.

Duke went back to look for Lew. He found him in front of the saloon and repeated Gifford's orders. "The boss wants you to follow Jake and find out where they go."

"They're going to his sister's ranch," Lew replied, not wanting to ride out as he figured that was where they would end up.

"The boss wants to make sure that's where they go," Duke said. "Get your horse and follow them."

Grumbling, Lew walked over to his horse and rode off.

Jake was relaxed as they drove through town, not worried about the men he saw. Once they were out of the settlement, Greg spotted Lew following them and said, "Mr. Burton, someone is behind us."

Jake looked back and saw the lone horseman.

"What do you think he wants?" Elizabeth asked.

Jake said, "He could be a rancher and just on his way home going in the same direction we are. I didn't recognize any of the men we saw in town. I don't think they know me either."

Two hours after they left Mancos, they topped a hill that overlooked the land in front of them. Cattle were scattered throughout the valley, grazing on the lush green grass. Jake stopped to let Elizabeth scan the land and the mountains that surround it. She could not believe what she saw. She couldn't get over how green the grass was and the river that snaked its way through the length of it. "This looks like good land," she said. "I can see why Adam wanted to come here."

At the furthest point of the valley, they could just make out the two-story ranch house with several outbuildings. A half hour later, they came to a gate. Elizabeth noticed that there were two Bs burnt into the crossbeam. "What is the name of your ranch?" she asked.

"It's called the Double B," Jake said.

As they were passing through the gate, the men at the ranch heard someone coming and came out of the barn to see who it was. Jake stopped in front of the house and recognized Logan, who had been his dad's foreman for years.

Logan was a no-nonsense man. He stood five feet, eleven inches, weighing 225 pounds. His brown eyes were clear, sharp, and always looking. His black hair hung over his ears under the dusty black cowboy hat that showed it had been on his head through a lot of work and sweat. His face was rugged but had kindness in it. His plaid shirt was covered with a brown leather vest that showed wear like his hat.

He walked over to see who had arrived in a wagon and was surprised to find that it was Jake. "Jake, it's good to see that you came back. We weren't sure if you were still alive. Mrs. Ashley said she hadn't heard from you for some time."

"Been moving around a lot," Jake said.

"Is that your missus?"

"Naw, this is Mrs. Hamman and her son, Greg."

"Howdy, ma'am."

"Is my sister around?" Jake asked.

"She's in the house."

While they were talking, the front door opened, and Sally came out. Younger than Jake at twenty-seven years old, she stood five feet, six inches tall with blond hair and blue eyes. She was wearing a green dress with white lace trim. Her face had a smooth complexion that lit up when she saw her brother. Running to the wagon, she said, "I was afraid you wouldn't come. Some of the men were saying that you might be dead."

"It took your letter a while to find me as I was out rounding up cattle for the ranch I was working on," Jake said. "I started back as soon as I got it."

"Who is that with you?" Sally asked.

After getting down from the wagon, Jake turned and helped Elizabeth down. When Elizabeth stood in front of his sister, he said, "This is Elizabeth Hamman and her son, Greg. This is my sister, Sally Ashley."

"Hello, Elizabeth," Sally said, holding out her hand and looking at her brother with questioning eyes. "Jake, did you get married?"

"No. Mrs. Hammam and her family were under Indian attack when I came across them, and she lost her husband."

"I am so sorry to hear that," Sally said.

Elizabeth looked down at the ground, holding back tears that suddenly filled her eyes. "We would have been dead if Jake hadn't come along and helped us."

Putting her arm across Elizabeth's shoulders, Sally led her toward the house. "Come inside, where we can sit while you tell me what happened."

Jake asked after her, "Is Howard around?'

"He's out checking the cattle with some of the men," his sister responded.

"We saw cattle as we came in, but we didn't see anyone," Greg commented.

"He headed north into the mountains," Sally said. "We have a herd up there that he wanted to check on. The cows you saw are ready to be driven to the miners."

When the women went into the house, Jake and Logan moved the wagon and unhitched the horses. Jake asked, "What has been going on?"

Logan stopped and looked toward the mountains before he answered. "Before your pa was killed, a man came to Mancos and set up a law office. That was just before you left. Since he arrived, he has been buying up ranches. Somehow, he has bought up the loans of those who can't pay their notes and forecloses on them, driving them out. The first one was the McFarland ranch after Sid was killed. He bought it for a pittance. After he moved there, the other ranchers around here started losing cattle, and it drove some of them out of the valley. Your brother-in-law believes that he's the one responsible for it. After the ranchers lose everything, he goes in and offers to help them by buying their land for half of what it's worth. Not knowing what to do, most of them sell out."

"Why hasn't the law done anything to stop him?"

"Marshal Owens was looking into it and suspected the lawyer was behind the cattle rustling. The problem was every time something happened to one of the ranchers, he was in his office. After the loss of their cattle, the ranchers were short of money and unable to pay their notes at the bank. When the notes came due, it looked like the lawyer would pay them off, foreclose on the ranch, and take over their spreads."

"What's this lawyer's name?"

"Gifford Clemens."

Jake asked, "Do you think he had anything to do with Pa's death?"

"Word around town is that he's got a man working for him who claims to be a gunfighter. His name is Duke Sanders, and I believe he does Gifford's dirty work for him. It seems that every time something happens to one of the ranchers, Duke is not around and Gifford is. The rest of the time you'll find him near the saloon or in Gifford's office."

"I don't understand why Marshal Owens doesn't do something about it," Jake said. "He's an honest man."

"Owens was found dead shortly after your pa was killed," Logan said. "He was out investigating your father's death when he was killed. He had a bullet in the back like your pa."

"Who's the marshal now?"

"William Shafer."

"How come he hasn't done anything?"

"He's one of Gifford's men. He hasn't arrested anyone since he became marshal. Seems all he does is serve papers on the ranchers for Gifford."

"Where did he come from?" Jake asked.

"He rode with Duke Sanders. Gifford got him appointed after Owens was killed," Logan stated. "Some of the townsfolks were against it, but it wasn't long before they changed their minds. Rumor is that Duke threatened them."

"You said this Duke Sanders spends most of his time at the saloon," Jake recalled.

"Yeah, most of the time you can find him hanging out there, just across the street from Gifford's office. That is, when he's not out doing Gifford's dirty work."

"Sounds like this Clemens guy is running the town," Jake said. "Has anyone gone to the Durango sheriff for help?"

"He won't come here," Logan answered. "He says it's out of his jurisdiction."

"Has anyone done anything about Pa's death?"

"Howard has done some checking and has some ideas on what happened, but he hasn't been able to prove that Duke was the one who killed him."

"I'll have to talk with Howard and see what he's thinking," Jake said. "For now, it's good to be home and find that everyone is all right."

"I know that Sally is sure glad you're back. She has indicated to us several times that she hoped you would return."

Leaving Logan at the barn, Jake went into the house. Looking around, he saw that nothing had changed; it looked the same as the day he rode out. Even his father's Spencer was still hanging on the wall where he had always kept it. In the kitchen, he found Sally and Elizabeth sitting at the table, talking. Greg was sitting with them, listening.

Sally said, "Come and sit. I will get you some coffee."

Elizabeth looked at Jake and said, "Your sister has invited us to stay here until I can figure out what to do. I said that I could help her with the cooking and taking care of the house. Greg can help feed the animals, chop wood, and anything else you would like him to do so we are not a burden on your family."

"I'm sure that you'll be a big help to Sally," Jake said.

Sally returned with Jake's coffee and sat down. "I'm glad you're back. Howard said that he could sure use your help running the ranch, and maybe you could help him figure out what happened to Pa."

"From what I saw coming in, it looks like the ranch is doing all right," Jake stated.

"Howard said we've been losing a few heads of cattle over time. He figured that our herd has been reduced by a hundred."

"Logan was telling me that there have been a lot of changes around here since I left. He said that Marshal Owen was killed shortly after Pa."

"There have been a lot of changes since Pa and the marshal were killed. Gifford Clemens came in right before it all started and has bought out most of the ranchers who got into trouble. He wants our valley and has been trying to buy it," Sally informed Jake. "He threatened me with buying our note from the bank if we don't pay it when it's due, and he'll have us run off."

"How much do you owe?" Jake asked.

"Five hundred dollars. When we sell the cattle, we'll have enough to pay off the debt, but it could leave us short on paying the hands."

"Does he know that I own half the ranch?" Jake asked.

"I told him that you would have to approve any sale, but if the note is not paid, he could foreclose without your approval."

"When do you expect Howard back?"

"He's supposed to return for supper," she replied.

"How come he didn't take Logan with him?"

"He wants Logan to stay near the ranch when he's gone. He believes that Gifford's men are the ones taking the cattle. He thinks that they might raid our place if they're both gone."

"That's good thinking. Where do you want me to put my bedroll?"

"You can stay in your old room. Elizabeth and Greg can stay in the spare room down here. Greg, I'm sorry that you'll have to sleep on the floor in the room with your mother. It's either that or the bunkhouse."

"What can we do with our things in the wagon?" Elizabeth asked.

"You can bring what you need into the house, and we'll make sure that your other things are protected. Come . . . I'll show you your room."

Sally took Elizabeth to the spare room while Jake put his things away. His room had not changed. Nothing had been moved. Even the water pitcher and basin he had left on the brown bureau were in the same place. There was a towel lying next to the basin, just like he remembered. Opening the drawer, he found the clothes he had left were still folded. Hanging on the wall was the picture of his mother and father holding him as a baby. The bed still had the colorful patchwork quilt that his mother had made. He remembered the many cold nights he had crawled under it to keep warm. As he looked around, calmness settled over him. Although he had been away for a while, it was like he had never left. He was glad to be home.

After putting his bedroll and saddlebags on the bed, Jake went outside to help Greg get their belongings from the wagon. With everything done, he figured he would ride out the next day and look over the ranch.

It was close to suppertime when Howard rode in with two men. Seeing the wagon, he questioned, "I wonder who that belongs to?"

"Logan will know," responded Bill Jenkins, who was riding next to him.

When they stopped at the corral, Logan met them as they left their saddles. Howard asked, "Whose wagon is that?"

"Jake's back. He brought a woman and a boy with him."

"He got married?"

"Naw. Seems Jake came across them and helped them, or they would all be dead. The woman lost her husband to Indians," Logan told him.

"Are they up at the house?"

"Yeah."

"Would you take care of my horse?" Howard handed the reins to Logan.

Jake was sitting in one of the leather chairs, watching the fire in the fireplace that held pictures of the family on the mantel. Off to the side, toward the front door, his pa's Spencer hung on the wall. A rack of pegs was located next to the door for hanging coats and hats. When Howard came in, Jake looked up and then went over to shake his hand.

"It's good to see you. Sally was worried that you wouldn't come back," Howard told him.

Sally came out of the kitchen with Elizabeth following her. Going over to her husband, she gave him a kiss and a hug. "This is Elizabeth Hamman, a friend of Jake's. She and her son, Greg, are going to stay with us for a while."

Howard held out his hand, shaking hers. "Nice to meet you." Looking at Jake, he added, "This is a surprise we did not expect. Did you meet in Texas?"

"I met her and her son coming here. She lost her husband a couple of weeks ago to Indians," Jake said.

"I'm sorry to hear that. You're welcome in our house, and you can stay as long as you need," Howard told her.

"It's very kind of you to let us stay," Elizabeth said. "We'll move on when we figure out what to do."

"May I ask why you were traveling by yourselves?" Howard asked.

"We lost everything we had, our home and our land, and Adam heard that there was good land out here that he could farm. We hadn't heard of any Indian troubles for some time, so we figured that we would be all right. If it wasn't for Jake, Greg and I would have been killed as well."

"Well, welcome to the Double B Ranch," Howard said.

Sally said, "Supper's ready. Would you call the men?"

Howard went out front and rang the dinner bell. It wasn't long before the men started coming into the kitchen and sitting down at the long table. Several of them greeted Jake and said they were glad to see him back.

Sally introduced Elizabeth and Greg. "You men are in for a treat. Jake informed me that Elizabeth here is one good cook, and she is going to be here helping out for a while."

During supper, several of the men wanted to know what Jake had been doing since he left. By the time they were finished eating, everyone was up to date on where he had been and what he'd been doing, including the killing of the man he caught cheating at cards.

When he had explained about Greg finding him and asking for help, tears sprang to Elizabeth's eyes. Jake didn't give a lot of details about what happened but did say that her husband had died from his wounds.

After supper, the men went back to the bunkhouse, while the women started cleaning up. Greg stayed in the kitchen with his mother. Howard and Jake went into the den and sat down.

"What can you tell me about Pa's death?" Jake asked.

"The morning he was killed, he had gotten up early to check on the herd we were getting ready to drive to Rico at the end of the week. I asked if he wanted me or one of the men to come with him, and he said that we needed to get things ready for the drive. Recently, there had been trouble for some of the ranchers—not all of them, just some. We got worried when it got late and he didn't come back."

"Who found him?"

"Later that afternoon, Logan and I went looking for him. When we got to the valley where we had gathered the herd, Logan spotted your pa's horse standing off to the side, somewhat hidden by rocks. We rode over and spotted Randolph lying on the ground."

"Was he dead?"

"He was still alive but badly wounded."

"Did he say anything?"

"He said he found the herd and was rounding up a few stragglers when he saw smoke coming from nearby. When he went to see what the fire was about, he was shot. Whoever was behind him shot him in the back. That was all he was able to tell us before he died. Logan and I loaded him on his horse and brought him to the ranch. I sent Logan and a couple of the men back to check on the herd. They returned and said the cattle were all there, and no one was around. The men must have gotten there before anyone could've returned and taken the cattle."

"Was there any sign of who did it?"

"We didn't look around at the time because we needed to get Randolph back to the ranch. Logan went back out, and I sent one of the men to town to get Owen. By the time he got here, it was too dark to look for any tracks. I have an idea of who was behind the shooting but no proof. Owen returned to town, and from what I heard, he questioned some of the men who worked for Gifford Clemens. The next day, Owen returned to the ranch and said he was going to look over the place where Randolph was shot. He mentioned that he thought he saw someone following him when he came here, so I sent Logan to ride out with him."

Jake asked, "Did he know who was following him?"

"He wasn't sure, but he thought it was Duke Sanders. He also mentioned that he had asked Gifford if any of his men had been out of town. Gifford was belligerent and said that he didn't keep track of every movement his men made."

Jake asked, "Did they find anything?"

"Logan said when he and Owen got to the herd, they separated. Logan went to check on the cattle, while Owen went to where we found your father. They were looking for anything that might tell them who had been there. Logan was watching the ground, looking for tracks, when he heard a gunshot coming from where the marshal had gone. Riding over, he found Owen lying on the ground, bleeding. He had been shot in the back. Logan was able to stop the bleeding and got him on his horse. He brought him to the ranch. After we got him in the house, we sent one of the men for Doc. Sally looked at the wound and did what she could. Owen said he thought the man who shot him was the same one who had followed him from town. He wasn't doing very well by the time the doctor got here. Doc did for him what he could, but Owen died that night."

Howard stopped to pour some whiskey. After handing a glass to Jake, he continued. "When we took Owen's body into town, word was that we were the ones who had killed him. Gifford had already appointed William Shafer as the new marshal."

"Didn't the townsfolk think it strange that a new marshal was appointed before they knew that Owen was dead?" Jake asked.

"Folks said Doc had already told them Owen had died."

"Why didn't the town council appoint a new marshal?" Jake asked.

"Gifford has them scared. Anyone who goes against him seems to end up getting run off or turning up dead," Howard said.

"Have you ever found any of our missing cattle?"

"We heard that some of them showed up at one of the mining camps with the Double B brand on them. By the time we got to the camp and questioned the miners, the cattle had been butchered. They said the men who drove them in had a bill of sale, so they didn't question them about the brand."

"Wasn't there any evidence to go after Gifford?" Jake asked.

"Without the cattle or their hides, we didn't have anything to prove it was Gifford. Even though we questioned the miners, none could testify against Gifford. Besides, he was in town while all this happened."

"Tomorrow I want to ride out to where Pa was killed."

"I don't think you'll find anything. It's been too long since your pa and Owen were killed, but if you want to go, I'll ride there with you."

7
THE NOTE

"DID YOU GET HOLD OF the marshal?" Gifford asked as Duke entered the office.

"He'll be here shortly," Duke said, taking a seat in one of the chairs.

Directly after Duke sat down, in walked Marshal Shafer, a man forty years old with a slight bulge around the middle, graying hair that hung below his hat, brown eyes, and a gray mustache sitting below a large, curved nose on a wrinkled face. "Duke said you wanted to see me?"

The marshal started to sit when Gifford said, "Keep standing. You won't be in here long."

Irritated at Gifford's attitude and being ordered around by Duke, Shafer asked gruffly, "What do you want?"

"I want you to find out why Jake Burton left the territory."

"Everyone knows that he was accused of killing Sid McFarland," Shafer said.

"Then you need to arrest him," Gifford replied.

"Marshal Owen said he didn't do it."

"You have the records that Owen kept. I want you to go through them and see what's in them," Gifford said. "If it doesn't say Jake didn't do it, you can arrest him and hang him. Now get busy."

Marshal Shafer left, muttering to himself, "He ought not talk to me like that. I'm the marshal."

After Shafer left Gifford, said to Duke, "I don't know why I made that idiot marshal."

"Cause you can control him. Why do you think those charges can be brought up again?"

"If Shafer finds any records stating that Jake Burton was charged for murder and not proven innocent, I'll have our fine marshal hang him," Gifford said sarcastically.

"What if Burton kills the marshal?" Duke asked.

"Then we'll charge Burton with his murder." Gifford began to think of ways to get rid of both the marshal and Burton. "If he doesn't kill him, maybe we can do something to help him along. We can frame Burton for the marshal's death and make sure that everyone knows it was Jake who killed him. Have one of the boys go out and watch Burton's ranch and let me know of his comings and goings."

Duke left to find Lew. Looking up and down the street, he couldn't spot the man, so he went to the saloon. Lew was at the bar when Duke entered. He looked up and nodded as Duke walked over to him. "Want a drink?" Lew asked.

"The boss wants you to go out and watch the Double B Ranch."

"What is he looking for?" Lew asked.

"He wants to know what Jake Burton is up to. If he leaves the ranch and starts nosing around, follow him and let me know what he's doing."

Lew left the saloon, got his horse, and rode out. Going to a spot where he had previously watched the ranch, he had no sooner gotten settled in than he saw Howard and Jake get their horses and ride out. Watching them as they headed north, he waited, thinking he knew that they were going to the pasture where Jake's pa was killed. However, Lew knew of a back trail that allowed him to arrive before the two men.

As Jake and Howard rode out to where Randolph was killed, Howard said, "After you left, Owen came out to the ranch asking questions about what happened in town. He said that there was a witness who identified you as the one who killed Sid McFarland."

"Do you know who the witness was?" Jake asked.

"I believe it was one of Gifford's men that said he saw you do it."

"When I left, I didn't know that McFarland was dead. I didn't know about it until I got a letter from Sally."

"McFarland's body was found the day you left. Owen considered that it could have been you. Whoever said you were the one who killed him described you and your horse," Howard told him. "His witness had to have been watching the ranch when you left as he even described the shirt you were wearing."

"Why would I kill McFarland? I had played cards with him, and that was the only time I saw him that night," Jake said. "Besides, most of the people in town know what horse I ride."

"Witnesses who were in the saloon told Owen that you and McFarland changed angry words while you were playing cards."

"McFarland lost and was upset when he left," Jake said. "The only words we had were about his lost cattle. He thought that the miners might be coming down and taking them."

"Owen came back a couple of days later looking for you. He said the witness against you was dead. He thought you might be in the area and that we had gotten word to you about who the witness was. Word spread around town saying you were the one who had killed him to keep him from talking."

"Who was the witness?" Jake asked.

"I don't know. Owen never said, and we didn't hear about anyone getting shot. We told Owen you had left two days before this witness was killed. He talked to the men, and they told him the same. Owen accepted our word and dropped the charge against you. But there was a reward put up for your capture."

"Who put it up?"

"Owen said the money came from Gifford Clemens," Howard replied. "A few days later, Clemens put together a posse to go after you. He even offered to increase the reward to capture you dead or alive. That got some of the men stirred up, and they went looking. Then after Owen was killed, Clemens got Shafer appointed marshal. With him owning the marshal now, he might push to bring the murder charge up again as no one has been arrested in McFarland's death."

"I'll keep that in mind," Jake said. "But I don't understand why Clemens would put up a reward for me. He was new in town and didn't know me."

"It is strange," Howard agreed. "But we hadn't thought much about it. Maybe we'll find a connection between Clemens and these killings."

When they reached the pasture where the murders took place, Howard showed Jake the spot where Randolph was discovered. Jake got down and started to look around before he asked, "Which way was he facing when he was found?"

"North."

"Was Owen facing the same direction when he was shot?" Jake asked.

"I don't know. Logan was the one who found him and never said. He did say that he was found at the same place your pa was. Like Randolph, he was face down too, shot in the back."

After Howard walked away, Jake kept looking around, when something caught his eye. Bending down to get a closer look, he saw there was a reflection from something partially sticking out of the ground. Picking it up, he found that it was a silver Concho that was well worn like it had been rubbed a lot. Putting it in his shirt pocket, he wasn't sure what it meant, but he would hang on to it.

While standing in the spot where the bodies were found, Jake turned around, looking over the valley. The place where his father and Owen were discovered was near the edge of the valley, where there was plenty of grass and water that would support a large cattle herd. The surrounding hills were steep, which made the valley into a box canyon that would hold cattle and keep them from wandering. The cows would be content and remain there if there were plenty of feed and water; this made it easy to round them up.

Since his father was shot in the back and found facing the north, Jake turned his interest to the south. He saw what he was looking for. Off in the distance, about three hundred yards away, was a pile of rocks. It looked tall enough for a man to stand behind and remain hidden.

Walking to the rocks, Jake kept looking for other places where a man might hide. Not seeing any, he walked behind the pile and stood thinking. The area where his father was found was visible from this spot along with most of the valley. Jake figured that this had to be where the shooter stood. He began to search the ground. Knowing there wasn't much of a chance of finding anything that would help him figure out who killed his pa, he kept looking anyway. If this was the spot where the gunman stood, whoever did it had to be a good shot and have a weapon accurate enough to hit a target at three hundred yards. Jake knew most rifles carried by cowboys were only accurate up to a hundred yards.

When his boot scuffed something in the dirt that was sticking out of the ground, he looked down and saw what seemed like a piece of wood. Jake prodded it with the toe of his boot, and it caught the reflection of the sun. He realized then that it was metal. Thinking it may be another Concho, he bent down and dug around the object until it was free. It was a bullet casing from a .52-caliber rifle.

Jake put it in his pocket, thinking that could be the round that killed his dad. Maybe if they found out who had a .52-caliber rifle, it might give them a clue as to who the murderer was. The caliber was an uncommon size carried by very few men in this part of the country. In fact, the only .52-caliber rifle Jake knew about was a Sharps Linen used during the war by sharpshooters.

Continuing to scout the area, he found that it was possible to get to this location without being seen from outside the valley. Following a path between more rocks, he came to the tree line. In among the trees, he found horse droppings. From the size of the pile of droppings, Jake could tell that a horse had stood there for some time or had been there more than once.

Meanwhile, Howard continued to search the area north of where the bodies had been found. He didn't find anything he could relate to the killings, but he did find fresh horse tracks. These indicated that whoever had been there had ridden away in a hurry. Maybe the rider had been scared off when he and Jake entered the valley.

Howard walked back to the horses and waited for Jake.

"When Pa was killed, what was the weather like?" Jake asked when he returned.

"It had rained for a few days," Howard said. "Why are you asking? Did you find anything?"

Jake reached into his pocket, pulled out the bullet casing and the Concho, and handed them to Howard. He looked at them and asked, "Where did you find these?"

"The Concho was where you said Pa was found. The casing I found stuck in the ground behind those rocks," he said, pointing behind him. "It looked like someone had stepped on it. The ground had to have been soft to push it in the dirt without damaging it."

"What do you think it means?" Howard asked.

"I ain't sure," Jake said, retrieving the items. "I figure that the casing had to come from a Sharps rifle. It isn't common. I know that the Sharps Linen .52-caliber was used during the war by sharpshooters, but I don't know of any cowboys around here carrying one. Finding it up behind those rocks makes me believe that's where the shooter stood. The Concho looks to be worn from being rubbed a lot. Do you think it was Owen's?"

"Can't say I ever saw him with it," Howard replied. "That doesn't mean it wasn't his."

"If we find out the Concho wasn't Owen's and belonged to whoever has a .52-caliber Sharps, we may have the man who killed Pa and the marshal." Jake put the items back in his pocket. "Did you find anything?"

"Some tracks indicating that someone was trying to move our cattle around. I found where they rode off in a hurry like we might have scared them off when we came in," Howard said. "I want to follow them to make sure they left. When we get back to the ranch, I'll send some of the boys up here to watch the herd."

Following the tracks out of the valley, Howard was sure whoever had been there was long gone. Giving up, they rode back to the ranch.

Lew had arrived in the valley before Howard and Jake. Finding some of the men from Gifford's ranch rounding up cattle, he warned them that the two men were coming. They hightailed it out before Jake and Howard arrived. Lew rode with them before he circled back to watch the two. He found them stopped at the edge of the valley, where they left their horses and walked around, looking at the ground. He saw Jake pick something up and put it in his pocket but could not make out what it was. He wondered if one of the men who were rounding up cattle had dropped something. He continued to watch Jake as he walked toward the rocks some distance from where they had stopped. Once Jake was behind the rocks, Lew couldn't see what he was doing.

Lew then watched Howard as he kept looking at the ground. He knew immediately that he had found the tracks left by the men but was relieved when he saw Howard go back to the horses and wait.

When Jake walked over, Lew saw him take whatever he found out of his pocket and show it to Howard. It was then that the sun reflected off one of the pieces. Lew noticed that Howard showed a lot of interest in whatever Jake had found.

After Howard handed the objects back, they mounted and began to follow the tracks left by Gifford's men. Lew continued to watch until they were out of sight. He was still there when the two men returned and watched as they rode south. He figured they were going back to the ranch.

Once they were out of sight, Lew scouted the area where Jake had picked up the item. Not seeing anything to give him a clue as to what it was, he mounted his horse and followed them to make sure they returned to the ranch. It didn't take him long until he had them in sight and could confirm where they were headed.

At sunset, Lew rode back to town, where he found Gifford's office was dark and the door locked. Duke saw him and crossed the street to where he was standing. "What did you find out?"

"Jake and Howard rode out to where Gil and the boys were rounding up some of the cattle," Lew said.

"Did they see them?"

"No. I got to them before they made it to the valley."

"What did they do there?"

"They were nosing around. I believe that Howard found the tracks Gil and the boys left while Jake was walking around and looking at the ground where his pa was killed. He found something," Lew said. "Then they followed the tracks before they returned to their ranch."

"Do you know what he found?" Duke asked.

"Naw," Lew said. "But when he showed Howard, I could tell it had to be something metal. I saw the sun reflect off it. They talked for a while before he handed it back to Jake."

When Duke heard that, he subconsciously reached into his pocket for his Concho out of habit. It wasn't there.

After shooting the marshal, he had found that he was missing his good luck charm. Whenever he got nervous, he would hold the Concho in the palm of his hand and rub it with his thumb. He didn't tell anyone that he had lost it. Duke also thought about the casing that he didn't find when he shot Owen. He thought it was still in the rifle, but when he got to where he hid the gun and checked the chamber, it was empty.

The only one who knew he had shot Owen and Randolph was Gifford. If they found the casing and could tie the rifle to him, he knew he'd be arrested for murder.

"Where's Gifford?" Lew asked.

"He rode out earlier this afternoon and hasn't come back. I'll tell him you're looking for him when he returns."

As Jake and Howard dismounted, Logan came out of the barn and took their horses. Howard told him about the tracks they found and his concern for the cattle. He also told him to send a couple of men out to keep watching the herd.

Logan asked, "Did you find anything to tell you what happened to Rudolph and the marshal?"

"Jake found a Concho and shell casing where they were shot."

"What does the Concho look like?" Logan asked. Jake took it out of his pocket and handed it to him. "I ain't seen one like this before. Looks to be worn some."

"Looks to me like wherever it came from, it was rubbed a lot," Jake said.

"What about the casing?" Logan asked.

"Not much to tell," Jake replied. "It's a .52 caliber. I believe it came from a Sharps Linen rifle. I wouldn't think there are many of them around here."

Logan said, "Let me show the Concho to the boys and see if any of them have seen it before." Jake handed him the Concho and headed to the house.

That night while they were eating supper, Logan commented, "I showed the Concho to some of the boys and asked if they had seen anyone who has one like this on their gear. None of them could remember seeing any like it. They couldn't recall seeing anyone with a Sharps rifle either."

"Well, the Concho may not mean anything," Howard said. "Maybe it was Owen's. When he was shot, Doc said that the bullet hole looked to be the same size as the one found in Randolph. If they were both shot with the same rifle, maybe our best lead is to find out who has the Sharps."

"What are you going to do with the Concho?" Sally asked.

"I think I'll just hang on to it for now," Jake answered. "And I think I'll check around town to see if anyone has been buying .52-caliber cartridges."

Sally asked, "Do you think Owen found the Concho, and that's why he was killed? When he was shot, he was looking over the place where Pa was killed. Maybe the marshal knew who it belonged to."

"That's something to think on," Jake commented. "If it didn't belong to Owen, then it could belong to the person who killed him and Pa."

Elizabeth, who had been sitting quietly and listening to the conversation, got up and announced, "Now that all of you have finished eating, I baked a fresh pie. Is anyone interested?"

All the men said yes at the same time.

Smiling at Sally, Elizabeth asked, "Would you mind helping me? I think these men want pie."

After being served, Logan remarked, "Ma'am, I think this is the best pie I ever ate."

"I told you she was a good cook," Sally informed them. Her comment, along with the men's remarks, was music to Elizabeth's ears.

Jake looked at her happy expression and asked, "Have you thought about what you want to do?"

"Sally told me that I could stay here and help with the cooking for the men as long as I wanted to. I think this is a good place for Greg and me to stay until I can figure out what we should do."

"Not to sound like I'm complaining, Ms. Sally, but her pie is mighty good," said Link, one of the ranch hands. "Course, your cook'n is mighty good as well."

Smiling at what Link had said, Howard turned to Logan and added, "Greg is old enough to help out with the chores and cattle if he's interested. Why don't you work with him tomorrow and see what he knows?"

"Sure, boss. But it might be easier if Greg moved into the bunkhouse with the other men."

Greg, who was listening to the conversation, eagerly said, "I'll get my things."

The men finished eating and returned to the bunkhouse. Greg gathered his belongings and walked out with Logan. "The men will pick on you being as you're a greenhorn," Logan told him. "How you react will determine how soon the men accept you as one of them."

"What do I need to do?"

"Just don't let them get you rattled cause they're only doing it in jest."

"I'll be on the lookout for them," Greg assured him.

Meanwhile, Howard and Jake went to the parlor and sat down. "Tomorrow we'll go back to the valley and gather the cattle. We'll put them with the ones I want to take to Animas Forks," Howard said. "If someone is trying to steal them, I want to get them closer to the ranch, where we can keep an eye on them."

"When do you plan to drive them to Animas Forks?" Jake asked.

"I figured to leave in two days."

"How many men will you take with you?"

"About half of them. We'll be gone for about three weeks, maybe four. If you want to ride along and see what goes on with selling our cattle to the miners, you can."

"Who'll look after the ranch while we're gone?" Jake asked with concern.

"Logan will stay here with the rest of the men. They can keep an eye on the remaining herd," Howard said. "With you being back, there may be people who have an interest in what you're doing. Going on the drive may lead them to think that you returned just to help us run the ranch."

"Sally wrote that you owed money to the bank. Do they know I own half the ranch?" Jake asked.

"As soon as we sell this herd, we'll have the money to pay off the bank," Howard responded.

"When does the note come due?" Jake asked.

"It's due at the end of the month. If we don't get the money we need from the sale of this herd, we won't be able to pay the bank. If they foreclose on the ranch, Gifford will take it over. He has already been trying to buy us out. Only you being gone has stopped him from forcing us to sign the deed.

Sally told him that you would have to agree to a sale. If the bank forecloses, we won't have a chance to stop him."

"Why do you think you might not be able to get the money?" Jake asked.

"We've been losing cattle over the past three months," Howard replied. "I've had Logan checking on the herd, and he said it seems that there are ten to twenty head missing each time he goes out. Selling to the miners, I need to keep enough cattle to grow the herd again."

"Has he found any carcasses?" Jake wondered.

"No. He said that he found signs the cattle had been driven off," Howard said. "I had Logan send men up to watch the herd when we first found cattle missing. When they're there, we haven't lost any animals. Logan brought the men back two days ago, and when we went up there today, it looks like we scared them off before they could drive more cattle out of the valley. I believe they have someone watching us all the time."

"Who else is losing cattle?"

"I haven't heard from the other ranchers lately," Howard said. "But those we are close to have lost some as well. It seems like Gifford is the only one around here who hasn't."

"While you're gathering the cattle tomorrow, I'll go talk to the bank," Jake said. "If it takes four weeks for us to get back, the note will be past due."

The women joined them in the parlor when they finished cleaning the kitchen. They sat down and started talking about the supplies the men would need on the cattle drive. The evening grew late as they finished putting together a list.

Looking at his wife, Howard said, "Jake is going into town tomorrow to talk to the bank manager. Maybe you can go with him and pick up what we need at the mercantile."

"I'll add what we need here at the ranch while you're gone," Sally agreed.

Standing and saying goodnight, everyone soon went to their respective beds.

Gifford Clemens returned early in the evening. Duke saw him ride in and take his horse to the stable. He waited until Clemens was back in his office before going to talk to him. As Duke entered the office, Gifford asked, "What did Lew find out?"

"Howard and Jake were out looking over the valley where Owen and Randolph were killed. He said it looked like Jake found something."

"Was it something that would connect you to the shooting?"

"Naw," Duke said, thinking again about the one casing he hadn't picked up. Even if it was the missing casing that Jake found, no one knew about his rifle. He kept it hidden and carried a Winchester on his horse. He had taken the Sharps from a man he killed four years ago, knowing that it had a long range. He knew that it was an uncommon rifle that could be easily identified. Even if they determined that both men had been shot with it, they would have a hard time finding out who owned it. Only Gifford knew he had it.

"Well, then, we don't have to worry about what they found," Gifford said. "Did Marshal Shafer find anything?"

"He didn't come up with anything other than Owen had dropped all the charges against Jake. The papers he found were signed by the district judge," Duke replied.

"Their banknote is due by the end of the month, and we have taken enough of their cattle that they may not be able to pay it off." Gifford sneered. "Even if they drive cattle to the miners and sell enough to satisfy the banknote, they won't be back before it comes due."

"Aren't you worried the bank will give them more time to come up with the money?"

"Mr. Dobbs won't extend the loan. I made sure he'll do what I want." Clemens said with a small grin of confidence on his face.

The next morning, Howard and his men rode out to round up the cattle, while Jake and Sally prepared to go to town. Before he left his room, Jake took enough of the money he had won in the poker game to pay off the loan. He put it in his pocket, figuring he'd pay off the note if he couldn't get additional time. He hadn't mentioned his poker winnings to Sally or Howard.

Arriving in town, Jake and Sally stopped in front of the mercantile. Jake helped his sister get down from the wagon. Looking around before going in, he noticed that several men were standing in front of the saloon, watching them. One of them was thin and wearing a black hat and vest. He stood out from the rest. He was also wearing two tied-down Colts with pearl handles and seemed to be taking a strong interest in Jake.

Sally noticed the men standing in front of the saloon as well. She recognized who they were and turned her back to them.

"Who is that?" Jake asked, indicating the thin man.

"That's one of Gifford Clemens's men. I've heard people call him Duke. All those men work for Gifford."

"While you're in the mercantile, I'll go to the bank," Jake said.

"You remember Mr. Dobbs, the bank owner? He's the one you want to talk to."

Jake walked across the street. Opening the door, he saw the teller standing in a small cage; behind him was the vault with its door open. The teller was a small man with horn-rimmed glasses. He was busy counting money and had a worried look on his face like something was not right. He stopped and wiped his brow before he started to recount. When he looked up and saw Jake, he asked, "What can I do for you?"

"Is Mr. Dobbs in?"

"Who's asking?"

"Jake Burton."

The teller put the money away before leaving the cage. He went to a door just left of the cage and knocked. It wasn't long before Jake heard someone say, "Come in." The teller disappeared through the door. When he returned, he informed Jake, "Mr. Dobbs will see you."

Jake walked over to the entrance and went in. He closed the door behind him as the teller went back to counting his money.

Mr. Dobbs, a heavyset man, was sitting behind a large desk. The top of his head was covered with thin hair. Horn-rimmed glasses sat halfway down the nose on his round face. He wore a black suit with a silver vest, a white shirt, and a black bowtie. On the desk in front of him were several papers and a large, open ledger book that had several entries in it. Looking around the room, Jake noted two chairs in front of the desk and a filing cabinet off to the side.

Looking up at Jake, Mr. Dobbs smiled and said, "So, Jake Burton, you are back. Have a seat. What can I do for you?"

Jake sat down and said, "I came to talk to you about the loan my sister and her husband have with you."

Mr. Dobbs got up and went to the filing cabinet. He opened the drawer, removed a folder, and returned to his desk. He opened the folder, took out a paper, and looked at it before he said, "The note is due by the end of the month. What is it that you want to know about it?"

"I was wondering if we could get some more time to pay it."

"Howard told me they were going to sell off some cattle soon and were planning on paying the note at that time," Mr. Dobbs responded. "Is there something wrong that you won't get the money?"

"They have lost quite a few cattle and don't know if they'll make enough to pay off the loan when it's due and pay their hired hands," Jake said.

Mr. Dobbs had a worried expression on his face and kept looking down at the paper. Sweat started to form on his forehead, which he took a hanky from his pocket to wipe. When he looked back at Jake, he said, "I can't extend the loan. If they can't pay it on time, the bank will have no choice but to sell the ranch to collect the money."

"Have we ever failed to pay the bank?" Jake inquired. "You've done business with my family for years before my father was killed."

"I'm afraid my hands are tied. I can't extend the loan," Mr. Dobbs said in a nervous voice. "I could offer you a new loan if you have something to use for security. I understand that you own half the ranch."

"Aren't you the owner of the bank?" Jake asked.

"Yes, I am," Mr. Dobbs said as more sweat formed on his forehead. "But it's the depositors' money that your family has borrowed, and I have a responsibility to them."

"How much do they owe you?"

"They borrowed four hundred and fifty dollars, but with interest, it will take five hundred to pay it off," Mr. Dobbs replied, still acting nervous.

Jake reached into his pocket and took out a wad of bills. Counting out five hundred dollars, he laid it on Mr. Dobbs's desk. "I want you to mark the note paid and return the title to the ranch to me."

Looking at the money, the bank owner began to shake. "Ah, I... I don't think I can do that," he said as the sweat ran down his forehead.

"Why can't you take the money and return the title to me?" Jake demanded. "I own half the ranch, so that makes me responsible for the debt.

You will take my money and return the title to me now. Now take it and mark the note paid."

As he looked into Jake's cold eyes, Mr. Dobbs knew that the man was not going to back down. The sweat continued to run down his face as he sat wondering what to do. His hands were shaking as he picked up a pen and marked the debt paid. He started to hand the note to Jake, who stopped him and said, "Date and sign it. You know that it's no good unless you sign it."

Mr. Dobbs laid the paper back down, took the pen, and signed and dated it. He handed the note to Jake.

"Now the title," Jake insisted. "Sign it back to Sally Ashley and Jake Burton." After Mr. Dobbs signed the title, Jake put it in his pocket along with the note and stood up.

The bank owner looked down at the money lying on the desk before he said, "You don't know what you have done."

"I just paid off our loan," Jake commented as he walked out of the office.

8

THE CATTLE DRIVE

WHEN JAKE WALKED INTO THE mercantile, he found Duke laughing and saw Sally upset. "What's going on?" he demanded, glancing at Duke and the two men with him.

"They won't let us get any supplies until we pay what we already owe and pay cash for what we need. It seems that Mr. Clemens has taken control of the mercantile," Sally replied.

Jake walked up to the counter and stood beside Sally with his back to Duke. Looking at Mr. Hanson, he said, "Fill the order."

"I . . . I can't until you pay what is owed," Mr. Hanson replied.

Duke started to laugh again and moved closer to Jake and Sally. He sat on a barrel at the end of the counter. "You ain't so big here, Burton. Maybe you were wherever you came from but not here." He sneered at Jake. "You got run out of town once, and I will see that you get run out again."

Mr. Hanson was frightened and started to shake as he looked between Duke and Jake. Mrs. Hanson had grabbed her husband's arm and tried to calm him down and keep herself from shaking.

Ignoring Duke, Jake asked Sally, "How much do you owe?"

"Thirty-five dollars."

Jake reached into his pocket, took out the money, and handed it to Mr. Hanson. "This should cover all of it."

Mr. Hanson took the money and tore up the bill.

"Now fill the order," Jake instructed.

"He can't do that," Duke yelled.

Jake turned his cold, gray eyes on Duke. "Are you going to stop him?"

"Mr. Clemens said no credit," Duke responded.

"Fill the order and then tell me what it costs," Jake said to Mr. Hanson. "If Mr. Clemens or Duke has any objections, they can take them up with me."

Hearing that, Duke took it as a challenge and stood up to face Jake. The icy-cold look in Jake's eyes told Duke that he wouldn't back down, nor was he afraid of him. Duke had heard some stories about Jake but wasn't sure how true they were. Standing in front of the other men who had come in with him, Duke didn't want to back down either. He started to drop his hand to the butt of his Colt.

Seeing the movement, Jake moved faster and had his Colt out and pointed at Duke before his opponent could clear leather. Seeing Jake's gun pointing at him, Duke froze. The two other men with him moved off to the side when they saw that Jake had outdrawn Duke.

"Fill the order," Jake said again to Mr. Hanson, keeping his eyes on Duke and the other two men.

Mr. and Mrs. Hanson started gathering the items. "I think it's time that you leave," Jake said as he backed Duke and the other two out of the store.

When they were outside, Duke said, "This ain't over, Burton. You will get yours."

Jake said, "Anytime."

Duke and the two others walked back to the saloon, while Jake stood by the door watching them. While the Hansons finished filling the order, Sally asked, "How much do we owe?"

"I . . . I am sorry," Mr. Hanson said, shaking. "I didn't want this to happen, but Mr. Clemens holds a note on the store, and if I don't do what he says, I'm afraid he'll take it from us."

"It looks like Mr. Clemens is taking over the town as well as the ranches," Jake observed.

"What do you mean?" Mrs. Hanson asked.

"Seems he has control over the bank too," Jake replied. "Has anyone been purchasing .52-caliber cartridges from you?"

"No," Mr. Hanson said. "I don't carry them. I would have to order them from Denver if someone wanted them. Why do you ask?"

"It's not important. I was just wondering about something."

Jake paid for the supplies and watched as Mr. Hanson loaded them on the wagon. Once he was finished, Sally climbed aboard, picked up the rifle from under the seat, and held it on her lap while Jake got up and took the reins.

He looked back at the saloon and saw Duke standing there, but he didn't see the other two men. Jake flicked the reins, and the horses started to move. "I didn't see where those two with Duke went. We'll have to keep an eye out for them in case they try to stop us."

As they rode back to the ranch, Sally asked, "Did you do any good at the bank?"

"Mr. Dobbs seemed awful nervous when I was talking to him. Seems that Mr. Clemens has a hold on the bank as well."

"What are we going to do?"

"Nothing," Jake said. Reaching into his pocket, he took out the note and title and handed them to Sally.

Sally opened the note first. Seeing that it was marked paid and signed by Mr. Dobbs, she opened the second and found the title. Surprised, she looked at Jake and asked, "How did you get him to sign these and give them to you?"

"I paid the note," Jake said.

"Where did you get that kind of money?"

"I got lucky at cards."

They rode the rest of the way in silence. Back at the ranch, Jake said, "You need to put those papers in the safe. I got a feeling that we have not heard the last from Duke or Clemens. You told me that he was trying to get the title to the ranch. If he was counting on getting the note from the bank, he may try something else."

Duke had watched Jake and Sally drive out of town before he went to see Clemens. He entered the office and said, "That Jake Burton and his sister were just in town and got supplies."

"I told Mr. Hanson not to give them any supplies on their account," Gifford said. "How come you didn't stop them?"

Duke said, "He paid what was owed and got the supplies Mrs. Ashley wanted."

"Well, I'll still get the note coming due at the bank," Gifford stated. "He may have paid that small amount in the mercantile, but I'm sure he couldn't pay off the note."

Duke said, "When they came to town, Jake went to the bank before the mercantile. He didn't seem upset when he came in."

"What did he do at the bank?"

"He didn't say," Duke answered.

"Go to the bank and find out."

Minutes later, the teller saw Duke coming and went to warn Mr. Dobbs. Duke entered the bank and went straight to the owner's office. He walked in without knocking and found Mr. Dobbs waiting for him.

"What did Burton want?" Duke demanded.

"He wanted more time to pay off their loan," Mr. Dobbs said.

"Did you give it to him?"

"No."

"What did he say when you told him no?" Duke asked.

"He was upset and walked out."

"Is that all that happened? You know that Mr. Clemens is counting on getting that note," Duke told him.

"Yes," Mr. Dobbs replied.

Duke walked out. As soon as he was gone, Mr. Dobbs called the teller in and said, "Lock up. We're going to close early today."

The teller asked, "How come?"

"I don't feel well and need to go home," Mr. Dobbs replied.

The teller pulled the shade down and locked the front door. They both left by the back door.

Shortly after, Duke returned to Clemens's office. "Well, what happened?"

"He wanted extra time to pay off their note," Duke said.

"Did Dobbs give it to him?"

"He said that he didn't."

"We'll have to wait and see what they do next when they can't pay the note as it comes due," Gifford said. "The land they have is the only section keeping me from controlling the northern valley. We've gotten the other ranchers to sign over their land or leave."

"You want us to stop them from driving their cattle to the mine?" Duke asked.

"We've cut their herd enough that they can't pay off the note and their men when they sell the cattle," Gifford said. "Even if they get enough money, they won't be back before the note comes due. I'll still get the ranch."

♋☯♋

The next day, Howard and the men herded the cattle into the corral. "How many head have you got?" Sally asked as she walked out to look at the cattle.

Howard said, "We have two hundred and fifty head that I can afford to sell. If we don't have any problems taking them to the miners, we'll get enough money to pay off the note. I just don't know if we'll have the money to pay the men and get through till we can sell more."

"You don't have to worry about the note," Sally told him.

"What do you mean?"

"Jake paid it off yesterday when we were in town. I have the title in the safe with the note marked paid and signed by Mr. Dobbs."

"That means that the ranch will be all right, and when we sell these cows, the men will get paid. We won't have to worry about selling more cattle right away, and we can build up the herd."

As they went into the house, Howard asked, "Did you get the supplies we needed?"

"Yes. I almost forgot . . . that was another problem Jake took care of."

"What do you mean Jake took care of it?"

"Mr. Hanson wasn't going to let us get any supplies when Duke and a couple of Mr. Clemens's men followed me into the mercantile. He told me that we had to pay off the account and pay cash for any new supplies we got," Sally explained.

"What did Jake do?"

"He paid off the account and then ran Duke and his two men out of the store."

"How come the Hansons wouldn't let us get supplies on our account?" Howard asked.

"He said that Mr. Clemens is holding their note from the bank, and he threatened to run them out of business if they didn't do what he said."

"Gifford is going too far. I think it's time to get the ranchers together and run him off," her husband stated.

Elizabeth came in and said, "Supper is ready. Will you call the men?"

Howard went out to the porch and rang the dinner bell. The men heard it and started to clean up before heading to the house.

While they were eating, Howard said, "We'll start to move the herd tomorrow morning. If everything goes well, we should be back in three weeks, four at the most. Logan, I want you to select five men to stay with you and keep an eye on the place. The way we have been losing cattle, we need to keep watch on the herd as well. We'll need the stock we have to rebuild the herd."

Logan asked, "Are you expecting trouble?"

"Sally has been telling me some of the things that are going on in town. All of them seem to be at the hand of Gifford Clemens. Jake drove some of his men out of the mercantile when Sally was getting supplies, so they know we're getting ready to move cattle. With Clemens trying to get our ranch and knowing that most of the men will be gone, he might try to take the rest of our cattle or hurt Sally."

"What about the herd you're taking? Do you think he might try to take it?" one of the men asked.

"He might," Howard said.

Jake said, "You'll have to watch out for Duke. I think he's Clemens's hired killer."

"Word got around that he's a gunfighter," Logan said. "Some say he claims to be fast."

"I don't think he's that fast," Jake said.

"Why do you say that?"

"He backed down real fast when we were at the mercantile. I think he would rather shoot you in the back than face you."

"Do you think he owns that Sharps rifle?" Logan asked.

"I asked Mr. Hanson if he had sold any .52-caliber cartridges, and he said no. I was hoping that he had so he could tell us who might own that Sharps."

"Are you going to stay here?" Logan asked Jake.

"No, I'm going with the herd."

"Mr. Ashley, can I come along?" Greg asked.

Elizabeth started to protest, but Sally placed her hand on her new friend's arm. "He's old enough to go on a trail drive. Jake was fifteen when he first went."

"What do you think, Logan?" Jake asked. "You've been working with him. Do you think he can handle it?"

"I think he can," Logan said.

"All right," Howard agreed. "Be ready to go at sunrise."

Elizabeth and Sally were up early the next morning and made breakfast for the men. When the chuck wagon was loaded, the men started out. Logan opened the gate to the corral as they drove the cattle out and started to push them toward Durango. The trail to Animas Forks led them to the Animas River before they would turn north.

With plenty of water and grass along the way, the cattle settled down after they were driven for a while. The first day passed without any problems.

The cook had supper ready by the time the cattle were bedded down. Howard left half the men with the herd; the rest rode back to camp to eat. While they were eating, Howard said, "Greg, I want you to ride herd until midnight with three other men. You might as well get use to the life of a cowboy."

Jake volunteered. "I'll ride with him."

When they were done eating, Jake and Greg got their horses and rode out to the herd. Jake instructed Greg about what he needed to do. "While you're riding around the herd, you could sing to help keep them calm. Don't make any loud noises, or you could spook them and cause them to stampede. I'll be near if you have any problems."

While they watched the cattle, the night riders rode in opposite directions, meeting each other as they circled. Sometimes when they met, they would stop and talk before they moved on. Greg was a fast learner, and he became relaxed as he rode around the herd.

Jake watched the boy and was surprised at how well he was doing on his first cattle drive. *Greg is going to make a good cowboy,* he thought.

Four cowboys showed up at midnight to relieve them. Tired and weary, Jake and the boys went back to camp to get some sleep. In the morning, some of them would have to relieve these men so that they could eat before the herd was moved out.

Greg was dead tired and almost fell asleep in the saddle. Not used to being on horseback all day and half the night, he was exhausted. Even when he finally got to lie on the hard ground, it felt better than sitting in the saddle. It didn't take long before he was sound asleep.

It was still dark when the cook started to roust everyone. Greg opened his eyes and felt like he had just gone to sleep, when he heard the cook holler, "Get up! Breakfast is ready and getting cold. Get moving. I ain't gonna heat it up for ya."

Jake watched Greg get out of his bedroll and saw that he looked a little stiff. "I guess spending a day in the saddle got to ya," he said, laughing.

Howard rode in just as the rest of the men were ready to eat. "Hurry up and eat," he said. "We need to relieve the men with the herd. I want to get moving at first light."

It was still dark when the last man finished eating. As soon as the sun started to come over the mountain, they moved the herd.

Over the next two days, the work became routine. Each man knew what he had to do and didn't wait to be told. Greg even learned what was expected of him and pitched in. The men were impressed that he was doing his share, and they were accepting him as one of the regular hands.

Once they were north of Durango, the terrain became steeper. Moving the herd became more difficult. The cattle began to stray, which made the horses work harder to keep them together. At the higher altitude, the horses tired more quickly and needed to be changed often. As time wore on, even the cattle slowed down as they continued to climb.

9

ANIMAS FORKS

EACH DAY, GREG LEARNED MORE about how to work with the cattle. After eight days of being on the trail, he understood why cowboys had to be tough. Howard finally moved him from the back to the side of the herd. Riding behind the herd since they left the ranch, Greg had eaten a lot of dust. Jake always rode with him at night when they covered the first shift. Spending time with Jake, Greg learned a lot and started to grow close to him. Their relationship took away some of the hurt from losing his father. While he rode the night herd, he learned to get along with only four or five hours of sleep. He would look forward to being relieved and would fall asleep as soon as he was in his bedroll.

Two weeks after leaving the ranch, they arrived at the Animas Forks valley. The scattered cabins throughout the valley mostly housed miners. Greg was riding with Jake when he saw the buildings and asked, "Is this Animas Forks?"

"That's what they call it," Jake said.

"It sure don't look like much," Greg replied. "Who buys the cattle?"

"There's a store in town that will purchase the cattle and sell the meat to the miners."

"How do you know that they'll buy the herd?"

"Our family has been bringing them beef since we moved into the valley," Jake said. "They know that Howard will bring cattle in every few months. He knows how many cattle to bring to last them till the next time he comes."

Entering town, Jake rode to the front of the herd to join Howard.

Isaiah Brown, the store owner, saw the herd and came out to greet them. "Howdy, Howard. Glad to see you made it."

"Howdy, Isaiah. You remember my bother-in-law, Jake Burton."

"Glad to see you again. I got the word you had gone to Texas," Isaiah said.

"I was there for a time," Jake told him.

"I was sorry to hear about your pa. Is that what brought you back?" Isaiah asked.

"I got word that they were having problems at the ranch," Jake said. "I decided to come back and find out what was going on."

Howard asked, "Are you ready for this herd?"

"Several men showed up two months ago with some cattle. They said they worked for the Clemens ranch," Isaiah explained. "They offered to sell cattle for half of what I've been paying you."

"We suspected that Clemens bunch have been stealing cattle," Howard told him. "With stolen cattle, they could afford to sell at half price."

"They looked like they were all wearing fresh brands," Isaiah said. "When we butchered some of the steers, we saw the brand had been altered. Some of them had been branded over the Double B."

"What did the fellows look like who drove them?"

Isaiah said one of the men was wearing a black coat, silver vest, and two pearl-handled Colts. He went on to describe the other men who rode with him. When he finished, he asked, "Do you know who they are?"

"Yeah, they sound like Clemens's men all right. The one with the two Colts is Duke Sanders. The others sound like the men who follow him. Do you still have any of the hides?"

"No, I got rid of them a while back. They told me they had bought the cattle from the ranchers near Mancos and that some had come from your ranch. The one you think was Duke said that Gifford Clemens bought a ranch and hoped to supply cattle to the miners," Isaiah explained.

"Did they have any proof that they had bought the cattle?" Howard asked.

"They showed me a bill of sale that they said was signed by you."

"Have ya got that bill of sale?"

"It's in the store," Isaiah said. "When we go in, I'll show it to you."

"I'm interested in knowing who signed it for me." Turning to Jake, Howard said, "We've been losing cattle, and so have some of the other ranchers. The boys thought they might have wandered off or gotten killed by wolves or mountain lions. Now we know for sure that they're being rustled by Clemens's men."

"I don't know who Gifford Clemens is," said Isaiah.

"We believe he's been causing problems for some of the ranchers. He has bought their ranches and indicated that he wants our ranch as well," Howard told him. "If you see my cattle here without me or Jake bringing them, you can be assured they are stolen."

"How many head have you got with you?"

"Two hundred and fifty," Howard said. "I figured they would last you through the winter."

"Come on in the store, and I'll get you a draft from the bank and show you that bill of sale," Isaiah said.

Jake left Howard to work out the details with Isaiah and went to help the men take care of the herd. When the cattle were in pens, they headed to the saloon. They kicked up dust while they crossed the street. Greg heard music from inside the saloon. He had never been inside one and didn't know what to expect.

When they entered, Greg was surprised at what he saw. Sitting off to the side of the room was a man playing the piano, who stopped to see who had come in before he turned back to his instrument. Before he started to play, he reached for the glass of beer sitting on the piano and took a drink. At the bar, five men stood drinking beer. They looked like they were miners. They had dirt on their faces, and their clothes were covered in it. When the cowboys headed for the bar, the men standing there made room for them, knowing that these guys were thirsty and there was fresh beef in town.

Two men and a girl sat at a table, drinking and laughing. The girl sat between the two men and had her arm around one of them. She was leaning against him and looked like she had been doing a lot of drinking herself. She wore a dark red dress with black lacy trim. It was cut low in the front and showed a lot of cleavage. Her skirt was cut up the side almost to her hip and hung open, where it showed off the net stockings that covered her legs. She sat there with her legs exposed from the ankle to mid-thigh, and seeing her got Greg's hormones going. She had on black high heels that looked like they would be hard to walk in.

When she noticed the look on Greg's face, she shifted her position to make herself even more enticing. She smiled as she watched the young man's expression. Because of the reaction she was causing in Greg, she continued to tease him subtly.

He stood and stared at her, unable to look away. Jake saw what Greg was looking at and started laughing. Pete, one of Howard's men, asked, "What are you laughing at?"

Jake pointed to Greg, and Pete started laughing, poking the man next to him. Soon, all the men had turned to watch Greg. "I bet he ain't never had a drink either," Pete said. "Step up here, boy. Let me buy you your first drink."

Tearing his eyes from the girl, Greg moved to the bar between Pete and Jake. Pete ordered a drink for Greg and himself. Jake had already received a whiskey. When their drinks were poured, Pete lifted his glass to Greg and said, "Drink up, boy, and become a man."

The girl continued to take an interest in Greg and kept an eye on him when she saw what the men were doing to him. She poked the man next to her and leaned over, whispering in his ear while she pointed at Greg. Hearing Pete say he would buy the boy his first drink, she wanted to see what would happen next.

Greg watched as Pete took his drink and downed it in one gulp. He looked at Jake, who did the same. When he saw that it didn't seem to bother them, he took his drink and downed it. When it hit the back of his throat, it felt like liquid fire as the whiskey ran down and hit his stomach. He gasped and started to cough. His face turned red, and his eyes started to water. The gal sitting at the table laughed. She had seen boys take their first drink before, and the results had always been the same.

Seeing Greg's reaction, the barkeeper handed him a beer. Greg took a couple of gulps of the beer and finally stopped coughing. By then, everyone was laughing.

Jake asked, "Do you want another drink?"

Greg answered in a hoarse voice, "I think I'll wait."

The girl got up and went to the bar. Pete saw her coming and moved aside to give her room to stand next to Greg. Greg was still trying to recover from the whiskey when she put her arm around him. She rubbed up against him and whispered in his ear.

Surprised to hear a female voice, Greg turned to find the girl next to him. He blushed with embarrassment. "Hi, honey. Let's have a drink together," she said as she leaned over and kissed him on the cheek.

Jake watched her and said, "Let me buy you both a drink."

Speechless, Greg was enchanted with the girl standing next to him. With her arm around his shoulder, he could only nod while Jake ordered the drinks.

The two men at the table watched as the bartender brought the drinks to them. The man who had been buying her drinks got up and called out, "Hey, kid, she's with us."

Pete turned to him said, "Just sit down. She's only having a little fun with him."

"Are you his ma or something?" the man asked.

"Them ain't kind words, mister," Pete replied.

"What are you going to do about it?"

Greg turned to see what was happening. The girl said, "Don't pay any attention to them, honey. I'm here with you now."

With Greg's attention back on the girl, she raised her glass, indicating that he should raise his as well. They both drank their drinks as a fight broke out behind them.

The miner came at Pete, swinging his fist. Pete ducked, swinging at the same time. His left fist punched the miner in the stomach. While the miner was bent over, Pete swung a right, catching him on the side of the head and sending him to the floor. The miner lay there, not moving. His friend got up to help. He picked him up and dragged him back to the table, where they both sat down.

With the fight over, the barkeeper brought Greg another drink. "Here, kid, it's on the house."

"What about her?" Greg asked.

"Sure. Why not?" the bartender said, pouring the girl a drink.

When Greg downed the whiskey, he again started to cough, and his eyes watered. The men, along with the girl, began to laugh again.

She wrapped her arms around Greg and said, "Don't worry, honey. You'll learn."

Howard entered the saloon and found the men still laughing. Greg seemed to be the cause of it. His face was red, and his eyes were wet. The girl who stood next to him had her arms around him, and Howard quickly figured out what the men had done. He walked over and asked, "Did the boys buy you a drink?"

Greg could only nod his head.

"First time?"

Greg could only nod his head. Now Howard started to laugh. "We have all been there, son."

Jake said, "He learns fast. The women even seem to take a liking to him."

"I knew you men were up to no good when I came in," Howard said. "Now I need a drink."

Jake asked, "What did you find out from Isaiah?"

Howard took the bill of sale out of his pocket and showed it to Jake. "We didn't sell any cattle to Clemens, and that ain't my signature. I'd like to find out who did sign it."

"It doesn't look like it was a cowboy who signed it," Jake said. "There ain't that many who know how to write. Most sign with a mark."

"Isaiah described the man who gave him the bill of sale. It sounded like Duke. I think we need to talk to the marshal about losing our cattle to rustlers."

"We need to catch them in the act," Jake said. "The new marshal ain't going to do anything as long as he works for Gifford. They could say that they bought the cattle from someone else and thought it was legal. Without proof of them taking the cattle, there's nothing we can do. If we had some of those hides, it would help."

Greg was now a little drunk. He had his arm around the girl, and it was hard to tell if it was for support or not. Feeling responsible for Greg, Jake had to pry him away from her to allow them to leave. When Jake got Greg's arm off the girl, she smiled and said, "You come back and see me some time, honey."

They left the saloon, and Jake had to help Greg get on his horse. Once in the saddle, he had to hang on to the saddle horn while they rode back to camp.

It was late in the afternoon, and the cook had supper ready when they arrived. Some of the men were ready to get some sleep after they had spent the afternoon in the saloon. Those who had stayed with the cattle and horses had already eaten and were anxious to go to the saloon. By the time they returned to camp, the rest were already sleeping.

Greg was drunk and had some trouble eating. He kept talking about the girl. The cook heard him talk and asked Jake, "What did you do to that boy?"

"We didn't do anything," he said. "We bought him his first drink, and the girl at the saloon came over to him and put her arms around him. Seems he ain't never been that close to a female before, except his mother."

The cook started to laugh as he walked back to the wagon. "I wish I had been there to see it."

In the morning, they were up early like every morning since the drive started. They ate breakfast before sunup and were on the trail by daylight. Between the movement of the horse and his head hurting, Greg had trouble keeping his breakfast down. Pete saw that the boy had a sick look on his face and went to give him advice. "If you hadn't eaten the cook's greasy pork, you wouldn't feel sick."

Greg thought about all the grease that he ate, and it started to make him throw up. Pete moved away, laughing.

Three days later, while going through Durango, Howard stopped at the bank. He cashed the bank draft Isaiah gave him and paid off the men. He put the rest of the money in his saddlebag, and they headed for home.

Late the next day, they arrived at the ranch, and Logan met them as they rode up. "Did you have any problems?"

"No," Howard said. "How were things here?"

"I sent Zeb out to watch the herd two days after you left, and he saw someone nosing around the ranch. When he went to find out who it was, they rode off. Since then, I've had the boys keep watch, and we ain't seen anyone."

Lew had been watching the Double B Ranch, waiting for their return.

When he saw that the number of men was more than the day before, he rode to town to let Gifford know they were back.

Lew ran into Duke and said, "I couldn't get close to the ranch. They have men watching the trails. But I believe by the number of men around the ranch that they are back."

Duke began to wonder what triggered them to keep that close a watch on the trails. He also wondered why they hadn't come to town to pay off their note. Concerned about what Lew just told him, he said, "We need to see Gifford."

They found Gifford at his desk. He didn't look like he was in a good mood.

"Well, what did you find?" he asked.

Lew said, "It looks like they're back at the ranch."

"I've been wondering why none of the boys have seen them in town since they got back," Duke added.

"Did you see any of them coming to town?" Gifford asked.

"I didn't see if anyone was coming here. But while I was watching them, I saw that they have men watching the trails and the cattle," Lew said.

"Maybe they found out that we sold some of their cattle in Animas Forks," Duke said.

"If they figured out it was us, why haven't they come after us?" Gifford asked.

"Maybe they can't prove it, and Marshal Shafer won't do anything about it anyway," Duke figured. "What I don't understand is why they haven't tried to pay off the note and Dobbs hasn't had the marshal go foreclose on them."

"Are you sure that Dobbs didn't give them more time to pay it off?" Gifford asked angrily.

"He said he didn't," Duke replied.

After standing in front of Gifford for a while without anyone talking, Duke and Lew started to get nervous. Duke reached into his pocket and started rubbing his new Concho. Finally, he asked, "You want us to go after them?"

"Not now. I need to think first."

They left Gifford while he was trying to figure out why the family had not done anything about their banknote. What was Dobbs doing that he hadn't come to him with the note like he had been instructed? Maybe they got into town and paid the note off without his men seeing them. Suddenly, he remembered that the money owed to the mercantile had been paid the day that Jake and his sister were in town. Could they have paid the note off too? Knowing that the note was now past due, Clemens decided to visit Dobbs.

Leaving his office, he went to the bank. The clerk saw Gifford crossing the street, heading their way, and went to warn his boss. "Mr. Dobbs, Mr. Clemens is walking toward the bank."

With the note paid off, Dobbs wasn't sure what Gifford would do. Legally, there was nothing that he could do, but what he wanted to do in the first place was not legal either.

The door flew open, and Gifford walked straight into Dobbs's office. Sweat was already forming on the bank owner's forehead and dripping into his eyes. His hands grew sweaty, and he couldn't keep his leg still. "What can I do for you, Mr. Clemens?" he asked in a shaky voice.

"You know what I've come after. I want that past-due note on the Burton ranch."

Mr. Dobbs said, "I . . . I can't give it to you."

"Why not? It's past due, and I have the money here to pay for it," Gifford said, reaching into his coat pocket and taking out a roll of bills.

"I . . . I don't have it," Mr. Dobbs said, knowing that Gifford was going to be mad. He wasn't sure what was going to happen to him. He squirmed in his chair as he waited to see what Gifford would do next.

"What do you mean you don't have it?" Gifford shouted.

"It's . . . been paid off."

"What do you mean it's paid off? No one has been here from the ranch, and you know that I was going to buy it when it came due. You told Duke you didn't give them an extension, and it came due while they were gone. Now I want it."

"I didn't give them an extension," Mr. Dobbs said. "I . . . I don't have the note. It's been paid."

"Who paid it?"

"Jake did when he came into town."

"You weren't supposed to let them," Gifford said. "I told you to stall them until it was past due."

"There was nothing I could do," Mr. Dobbs protested. "He wanted to see the note, and I had to show it to him. He had the money, and I had to take it and sign the note as paid."

Gifford's face turned red with anger when he heard that the note was no longer available. He slammed his fist on Mr. Dobbs's desk and stormed out of the bank.

Mr. Dobbs breathed a sigh of relief when Gifford was gone. The clerk came in to make sure that he was all right.

Across the street, Gifford returned to his office and sat at his desk. The anger on his face continued to show as it turned redder and redder. Gifford sat there trying to figure out what he could do next. With no loan at the bank and the cattle sold, they would have the money they needed to run the ranch. His plan to bankrupt them had been destroyed by Jake Burton's return. He would have to get rid of him. There had to be something in the files at the marshal's office still connecting Jake to the murder that caused him to leave.

Howard and Jake went into the house after they put up their horses. Sally met them when they came to the door. Elizabeth stood with her. When she saw Jake, she smiled and asked, "How did my son do?"

Jake smiled back. "The men said that he has become a cowboy. He learned a lot on this drive."

Howard smiled when he heard what Jake had said, thinking about Greg's experience in the saloon. Greg would have to be the one to tell his mother about that. Neither he nor Jake would tell.

"What did he learn?" Elizabeth asked.

"You're gonna have to ask Greg," Jake responded. "After this, he may want to remain a cowboy."

Elizabeth began to become concerned about what her son had done on the trail that Jake and Howard would not tell her. She would have to get Greg alone and find out what happened. If Greg wouldn't tell her, she would get Jake alone and talk to him.

"How's Isaiah doing?" Sally asked.

"He said he's doing fine. He bought some cattle from the Clemens ranch, and some of them showed our brand. He had a bill of sale from someone who stole them," Howard explained.

"What?"

Howard took the bill of sale out of his pocket and showed it to her. "Isaiah gave this to me. He described the man who gave it to him. It sounded like Duke."

"What are you going to do?" Elizabeth asked.

"We can't prove that it was him," Jake said. "We're going to have to try to catch him taking cattle."

"Do you think he'll continue doing that?" Elizabeth wondered.

"I don't know what he'll do," Howard said. "With the note paid off, Clemens lost his chance to take the ranch by foreclosing on us. From what Jake found out when he went to the bank, Gifford must have something on Mr. Dobbs that he didn't want Jake to pay the note. We know that Gifford wants to control the valley, and as long as we own this ranch, he won't be able to."

"We're going to have to be careful," Jake said. "He might try to kill us like Pa and the marshal. If we could prove that, we could get rid of Clemens. I believe finding out who owns that rifle would give us the proof we need."

"Maybe we need to keep an eye on Duke and the rest of Gifford's men too. You said you think they're watching us," Sally said. "Why shouldn't we be watching them?"

"We have men looking after the herd and making sure no one is watching our ranch," Howard told her. "Logan said that they haven't seen anyone around for a few days. Maybe we need to have a man at the Clemens ranch to watch and learn where they're getting their cattle. I'll talk to Logan about sending someone over there."

10

HOWARD

The next morning, Howard and Sally drove into town to get supplies. With the money they had from selling the herd, they knew they wouldn't have a problem as they could pay for what they needed.

Gil, one of the Clemens men, was standing in front of the saloon when they stopped by the mercantile. Seeing that Jake wasn't with them, Gil watched as the couple went into the store.

Howard spotted Gil but paid no attention to him as there was always one of Gifford's men outside the saloon. He tied the horses to the hitching post and helped Sally off the wagon. He took her by her elbow as they went inside. Mrs. Hanson was busy stocking the shelves. "Hi Sally," she said. "What can I do for you and Howard?"

"We need some supplies," Sally told her.

"We have the money to pay for them," Howard added. "Jake told me that you couldn't give us credit anymore."

"I am so sorry," Mrs. Hanson said. "Mr. Clemens is holding the banknote for the store. Until we pay it off, he controls what we can and cannot do."

"Well, we have the cash to pay for the things we need," Sally repeated, handing Mrs. Hanson the list.

Howard stood at the front of the store and looked out the window, where he saw Gil crossing the street. He remembered what had happened between Duke and Jake, so he wasn't sure what Gil was up to. He continued to watch Gil until he entered the store.

Mr. Hanson and his son, Bobby, came in from the back of the store when Gil entered. They saw the Ashley's and Clemens's man at the same time. "What do you want, Gil?" Hanson asked.

"I thought Mr. Clemens told you not to sell to them."

"He told me not to give them any more credit," Mr. Hanson corrected.

"I think that means you aren't to sell to them," Gil said.

Howard heard the exchange and decided that he had had enough of Gil. "I think you should leave."

"You don't tell me what to do," Gil said, turning to face Howard.

When Howard started moving toward him, Gil pulled his gun and fired, hitting him in the chest. Howard fell backward into a barrel of flour before he fell to the floor.

Sally screamed and ran to her husband, who was still alive but bleeding badly. "He needs the doctor," she cried out, putting her hand over the bullet hole to stop the bleeding.

"Bobby, go fetch the doctor," Mr. Hanson stated.

Bobby ran out the back door and down the street to the doctor's office.

"If he dies, you are going to hang for murder," Mrs. Hanson told Gil.

"He drew on me."

Sally looked up at Gil with bloodshot eyes, shaking in anger. "He's not wearing a gun."

Gil turned back to Howard to see inside his jacket and noticed that he was unarmed. If Howard died, he was in trouble and would hang. When he saw the marshal cross the street on the way to the mercantile, he turned pale, knowing he was going to be arrested. He started to panic, looking for a way out before the marshal got there, but froze.

Marshal Shafer opened the door and saw Howard lying on the floor, bleeding. He found Gil standing with his Colt still in his hand and asked, "What happened?"

"He shot Howard," Sally said. "Arrest him."

Gil turned his Colt on the marshal. "You ain't gonna arrest me. He came after me and started to draw his gun. I shot in self-defense."

"Howard doesn't have a gun," Sally countered.

When Marshal Shafer turned to look at Sally, Gil saw his chance. Running to the door, he shoved Mr. Hanson out of the way, knocking him over as he escaped. He ran to his horse and rode out of town, heading west.

Once out of sight, he circled back to bypass the town to the east and rode toward the mountains.

Early that morning, Gifford had gone to the marshal's office to look at the files on the McFarland case but was unable to find any documents that accused Jake of the murder. Returning to his office, he knew he needed to come up with a new plan. The problem was that he didn't think Marshal Shafer would be strong enough to come up with a way to get rid of Jake. He would have to count on Duke to do it. Maybe he could frame Jake again as he did with McFarland's death. He could set him up to kill the marshal and have his men in place as witnesses. But he would have to figure out a plan to get the marshal alone with Jake and wait for the right opportunity.

Gifford was sitting at his desk, trying to come up with a new plan, when he heard the shot. He assumed that his men were out at the ranch as he had left orders for them to round up the cattle, so he waited before he got up to see what happened. When he looked out the window, he was surprised to see Gil running to his horse and was puzzled as to why he was in town. Gifford began to realize from the way Gil was acting that he must have been involved in the shooting.

When he looked at the mercantile, he saw several people gathering. If Gil was involved, he knew he needed to find out what happened. When he left his office, he saw the doctor hurrying to the store. His first thought was that Gil had shot Mr. Hanson and ran.

By the time Gifford had reached the mercantile, he was cussing Gil under his breath as he moved people aside to get to the door. Inside, he saw someone lying on the floor. The doctor was kneeling over the injured person and blocked his vision. Not able to make out who it was, Gifford looked around and saw the marshal talking to Mrs. Hanson. He motioned for him to come over and asked, "What happened? Is that Hanson?"

"Gil shot Howard Ashley," the marshal said.

"Why?"

"Mrs. Hanson said that he tried to stop the Ashley's from getting supplies. He said that it was your orders not to sell to them."

"I didn't send him in here. Gil was supposed to be at the ranch. I had left orders for the men to stay there."

"Well, he wasn't at the ranch," the marshal said. "Mrs. Hanson said her husband told Gil that you had instructed them to not give the Ashley's any credit. Gil didn't believe that and said what you meant was not to sell them any supplies."

"She's right. I didn't say they couldn't get supplies. I told Hanson not to give them credit," Gifford explained. "It must have been self-defense. I heard that Howard has been upset and must have pulled his gun on him."

"Howard couldn't. He wasn't wearing a gun."

The marshal started to get nervous talking with Gifford. He knew that with the Hansons and Sally as witnesses, he would have to go after Gil. He wondered what Gifford would do now that one of his men was involved in the shooting of an unarmed man with reliable witnesses. How was he going to go after Gil if Gifford wanted to let him get away?

"If he dies, Gil will be charged with murder," the marshal told him.

"How do you know he didn't have a gun and it wasn't self-defense?" Gifford asked.

"You can see for yourself that he isn't wearing a gun. The Hansons saw what happened. If Howard dies, the people will want Gil to hang for murder. He needs to turn himself in. Do you know where he went?"

Gifford pulled the marshal away from the others and took him toward the back of the mercantile, where he could talk to him alone. "He rode out of town toward the west." Lowering his voice to make sure no one else would hear, he then said to the marshal, "Don't try too hard to catch him. I'll get him out of the territory."

Marshal Shafer indicated that he understood but said, "If I don't find him, Jake Burton will go after him."

"We'll find him first and get him out of here," Gifford replied.

Pointing to some of the men who had come in to see what had happened, the marshal said to them, "I need four or five of you men to ride with me. Get your horses and meet me in front of the jail."

While the marshal organized a posse, Gifford decided to leave the store. He knew Jake Burton would go after Gil as soon as he heard about Howard being shot and who did it. If he got to Gil before Duke or the law did, Jake would try to get information out of him. If Gil talked, Gifford knew that Burton would be coming after him, especially if Gil said that he had ordered him to shoot Howard.

Gifford had to go to his ranch and get his men looking for Gil. He got his horse and rode hard out of town. Duke was at the corral with some of the men when he rode into the yard. With Gifford not stopping until he got to them, Duke hurried over to see if something was wrong.

"What happened?" Duke asked.

"Have you seen Gil?" Gifford asked.

"He rode into town earlier," said Lew, who had come up and was standing by Duke. "We ain't seen him since."

"You need Gil for something?" Duke asked.

"I need you to find him," Gifford said. "Gil shot Howard Ashley at the mercantile. I need you to get to him before the marshal or Jake Burton does."

"The marshal ain't going to do anything to him if he finds him," Duke stated. "He'll just let him go."

"He doesn't have a choice this time. He has a posse riding with him made up of men who were at the mercantile and heard what happened. The Hansons saw Gil shoot Howard, who was unarmed."

"Where do you think he went?" Duke asked.

"He headed west when he went out of town," Gifford said. "I thought he might have turned north and come here."

"Like Lew said, we ain't seen him. Lew, do you know where he might go?"

"He sometimes goes up in the mountains southeast of town. I ain't been up there with him, but I might be able to find where he goes. Most of us have heard him talk about an area up there where it seems he found some old Indian ruins."

"Duke, you and Lew find him before the marshal does," Gifford ordered. "Take the supplies you need. When you find him, make sure he does not come back."

Duke got the supplies together while Lew got their horses saddled. As they rode out, Lew said, "Gil is gonna be hard to find if he didn't leave a trail. From what he said, there are a lot of places a man could hide in the mountains. We might not find him."

"If we can't, maybe Jake and the marshal won't be able to find him either," Duke replied.

Still in a foul mood, Gifford was cursing Gil under his breath for his impetuous behavior. With a face like he'd sucked on a lemon, he walked over to his house after Duke and Lew had left, stomped up onto the porch, and slammed the door behind him. That gun-happy fool Gil had left Gifford with problems he did not need, and now he didn't want to go back to town; most people were probably already thinking Gil was acting on his orders. He would claim Gil had done this on his own. That was the darn truth, but he doubted anyone would believe him.

As the posse headed west, they found that Gil's trail was easy to follow at first. About half a mile out of town, the trail had gotten harder to follow, but the marshal saw where Gil's tracks had turned north, and he hoped that no one else had seen it. He wanted to lead the posse away from where Gil had ridden; he wanted to move on.

One of the men near the back of the group spotted Gil's tracks turning north. He pointed it out to the marshal, and they again started to follow the trail.

The marshal thought that Gil might be heading to Clemens's ranch. A mile further, his tracks turned east. One of the men following the tracks said, "I think he might try to throw us off and go to Clemens's ranch."

The marshal said, "Take another man with you and go check it out. We'll continue to follow his trail in case he isn't going to the ranch. If he shows up there, watch him. Don't try to arrest him until we get there. One of you come back and tell me. We'll catch up to you later."

The two men rode off, while the rest of the posse continued to follow Gil's trail as it headed east. They continued to search for tracks until late afternoon, when they found that he had gone into Mesa Verde, but then they lost the trail before finally giving up. The marshal was relieved and ordered everyone back to town. It was dark by the time they returned.

Riding hard, Gil didn't take the time to hide his tracks. He knew that if Gifford had sent the marshal to find him, he wouldn't make much of an effort to locate him. Checking his backtrail, he did not see anyone. Relieved that no one was following, he slowed, wanting to hide his trail if he was followed later.

East of town, the ground became hard, and Gil knew his trail would become difficult to follow. Wanting to make sure that he couldn't be found, he turned north before turning east again. Going slow, he stayed on the rocky soil leading to Mesa Verde. Entering it, Gil continued to go deeper and deeper in, knowing a place where he could hole up and be hard to find.

While Howard still lay on the floor of the mercantile, the doctor was able to get the bleeding to stop. "Some of you men pick Howard up and carry him to my office so I can remove the bullet."

As the men carried Howard out, Mr. Hanson said, "Bobby, ride out to the Ashley's ranch and tell Mr. Burton what happened." Sally heard that, so she stayed with her husband.

After the store had cleared, Mrs. Hanson began filling the order that Sally had given her. Mr. Hanson asked, "What are you doing?"

"She is going to still need these things when she gets ready to go home," his wife said.

"What about Mr. Clemens?"

"I think it's time we stand up to him," she said.

"He could just as well shoot us," Mr. Hanson complained.

"When they shoot unarmed men, they have gone too far," Mrs. Hanson said. "We need to keep a gun handy for when he or one of his men comes here so we can protect ourselves and our customers."

"But what about the money we owe him?" Mr. Hanson asked. "He could put us out of business."

"I have had enough with Clemens and his trying to run our lives. We have the money to pay him. Now he has gone too far, allowing his man to shoot an unarmed customer of ours. We need to force him to take the payment and get that note back so he'll leave us alone."

"How can we force him to take the money?"

"After what happened here today, it's time for the people of this town to stand with us and against Clemens to stop him. Here . . . you fill this order. I'm going to the doctor's office to be with Sally."

When the men had reached the doctor's office with Howard, they put him on the operating table and left. The doctor's wife stood by to help him operate. "Sally, you need to wait in the other room while we take the bullet out," Doc said.

"I want to be with him," she protested.

Margaret, the doctor's wife, took Sally's arm and escorted her to the outer room. "We will take care of him, and as soon as we get the bullet out, you can see him."

Sally was sitting in the outer room with her head in her hands when Mrs. Hanson opened the door. "How is he doing?" she asked.

"Margaret is helping the doctor. They just started working on him," Sally said, looking up at her. "They won't let me be with him and told me I needed to wait out here."

"Let me sit with you," Mrs. Hanson said. "I am so sorry about what happened."

"It's not your fault," Sally told her. "Gifford has gone too far. I'm afraid Jake is going to go after him, and Gifford has a lot of men. If Howard dies, this will be the start of a range war."

"You're right; Gifford has gone too far," Mrs. Hanson agreed. "Several of the townspeople know what happened today, and they agree that Gifford has crossed the line. Mr. Hanson is filling your order and will have it ready for you when you go home."

"I have the money," Sally said.

"Don't worry about that right now. Worry about how Howard is doing. You can pay us later."

"Thank you," Sally said, taking hold of Mrs. Hanson's hand. "You are a very dear friend."

The ladies sat together holding hands while they waited, giving Sally the strength, and comfort she needed.

Bobby raced to the Double B Ranch and was riding in when Logan came out of the barn. Logan saw him coming fast and knew something had to be wrong. When he saw the look on Bobby's face, he rushed over to see why he was in a hurry. "What's wrong, son?"

"Is Mr. Burton around? It's Mr. Ashley."

"He's in the house," Logan said. "Come on. I'll take you to him. What happened?"

"Mr. Ashley has been shot."

Hearing that, Logan hurried Bobby into the house and found Jake at the kitchen table, talking to Elizabeth. When they entered, Jake asked Logan, "Who do you have here?"

"This is Mr. and Mrs. Hanson's son, Bobby. He came looking for you. Howard's been shot."

"What happened?" Jake asked as he jumped up from his chair.

"Pa sent me to tell you that Mr. Ashley was shot in our store by one of Mr. Clemens's men."

"Is he still alive?" Elizabeth asked.

"The doctor was with him when I left," Bobby said.

"Who shot him?" Jake asked.

"I think his name is Gil or something like that."

"Where is Mr. Ashley now?" Logan asked.

"He was in the store when I left."

"Did Mrs. Ashley get hurt?" Jake asked.

"No, she's fine," Bobby said. "Only Mr. Ashley was hurt."

"Sit down," Elizabeth said. "Would you like to rest and have some lemonade before going home?"

"Thanks," Bobby said, sitting down.

"Logan, get the horses. We're going to town to find out what happened," Jake said. "Then I'm going after the man who shot him, and I'm going after Clemens."

By the time Logan got the horses ready, Jake had gotten the full story from Bobby. As he left the house, Elizabeth said, "I'll get the room ready for Howard when you bring him home."

As they rode into town, Jake saw the ranch wagon in front of the doctor's office. When they stopped and went in, they found Sally sitting in the waiting room with Mrs. Hanson. "How is Howard doing?" Jake asked.

"The doctor hasn't come out since they took him in," Mrs. Hanson replied.

"How long have they been in there?"

"About two or three hours," Sally said.

"I am sure that the Doc is doing all he can to save him," Jake told her.

The door opened, and the doctor came out. Sally stood up and asked, "How is he? Can I see him?"

"He is very weak and has lost a lot of blood. If he doesn't get an infection or pneumonia, he could recover. The bullet hit his lung, and he's having a hard time breathing. I need to keep him here overnight. For now, you can go in and see him, but he needs to stay here."

After Sally saw Howard, she came out of the room and said, "I want to take him home. With Elizabeth's help, one of us can be with him all the time and take care of him."

"I don't recommend you taking him home," the doctor warned. "He could die before you get him there."

Crying, Sally said, "I want him at home. We can be with him all the time."

"I cannot be responsible for him if you take him."

With tears in her eyes, Sally nodded in understanding.

Mrs. Hanson was standing with Sally when they were getting ready to take Howard to the wagon. "My husband put your supplies in your wagon."

"How much do we owe you?" Jake asked.

"You can pay for them the next time you're in town."

"Thanks," he said. "But won't you get in trouble with Clemens?"

"Don't worry about that," Mrs. Hanson said. "It's about time we took our store back."

With the doctor's help, Logan and Jake got Howard into the back of the wagon. They helped Sally onboard next to him, and Jake said, "Logan, you drive them back to the ranch."

"What are you going to do?" Sally asked.

"I see the marshal and the posse are coming back. I want to talk to them. It doesn't look like they found Gil."

After Logan tied his horse to the back of the wagon, he climbed onto the seat, and they headed out of town. Jake walked to the jail and waited for the posse to stop in front. "What happened?" he asked.

"We lost Gil's trail east of here going into the mountains," Marshal Shafer said.

"Are you sure he didn't go to Clemens's ranch?"

"I sent two men there to see if he doubled back again," the marshal explained. "I don't see how he could have doubled back from where we lost his trail."

"Maybe he'll go back later," Jake said.

"He might. How's Howard?"

"He's still alive, but the doctor isn't sure about his chances. Logan and Sally are taking him back to the ranch."

"I'm sorry to hear he's not doing well," Shafer said.

"When do you expect the two men you sent to Clemens's ranch?" Jake asked.

"That's them riding in now." They stopped in front of the jail, and the marshal asked, "What did you find out?"

"He didn't show up at the ranch."

"Maybe you should have someone watch it in case he goes there later," Jake suggested.

"I don't have anyone to sit out there," the marshal replied.

"I think you need to find him," Jake said.

"What are you going to do?" the marshal asked.

"If you can't find him, I will. I know Gifford is behind this, and I'm going after him as soon as I find Gil."

"You ain't the law," the marshal stated.

"You ain't doing your job sitting here. Where did you lose his trail?"

"About ten miles northeast of here. It looked like he headed into Mesa Verde. If he went in there, he'll be hard to find. I ain't got the men to go looking for him."

"Well, he can still be found," Jake said. "He can't stay there long without supplies, and he'll have to come out to get them."

"If you find him, you bring him here," Marshal Shafer said. "I mean alive. He will stand trial for what he did, and if Howard dies, he will hang."

The sun was down when Jake rode back to the Double B. He knew that with the marshal working for Gifford, he wouldn't hang one of his men. If the marshal caught Gil, he might have to take him to Durango. Jake decided that in the morning, he would get supplies and go looking for Gil himself.

⊱⟡⊰

The ranch hands saw Logan pull into the yard and came out to see how Howard was doing. Word had spread fast at the ranch that he had been shot. Elizabeth came out as they stopped in front of the house. Logan got a couple of the men to help carry Howard into the house. Some of the others helped Elizabeth unload the supplies and put up the horses and wagon.

Once Howard was in bed, Sally gave him some of the medicine the doctor had given her for his pain. Soon, he went to sleep. It wasn't a restful sleep as he was still having a hard time breathing. Sally could see he was in a lot of pain and stayed with Howard while Elizabeth went to make supper for the men.

When Jake rode in, he found the yard empty. After he put up his horse, he went to the house and found the men in the kitchen. He pulled up his chair, and Elizabeth dished a plate for him. "How's Howard?" he asked.

"He's in bed, resting," Elizabeth said. "Sally is with him."

"What did you find out from the marshal?" Logan asked.

"They lost Gil's trail east of town going into Mesa Verde. I'm going to head up there in the morning and see if I can pick up his trail."

"I'll send Lance with you," Logan said. "He has been up there hunting and knows some of the areas. He said that the last time he went, he found some old dwellings built in the cliffs. Maybe Gil is hiding in one of those."

Jake turned to Lance and said, "We'll get started right after breakfast."

"Do you know how long we'll be gone?" Lance asked.

"I don't know. If we can't find any sign of Gil, we should be back in a day or two."

"Is the marshal going out again?" Lance asked.

"He said he didn't have the men to look for him. Logan, you might want to send someone over to watch the Clemens's place. Gil doesn't have any supplies; he may try to go there and get some."

"Do you think Gifford ordered Gil to kill Howard?" Logan asked.

"I ain't sure," Jake said. "I know that Gifford ordered the Hansons not to give us credit. When we get Gil, maybe we'll find out if he was acting on Clemens's orders."

II

THE HUNT FOR GIL

AFTER JAKE LEFT, THE MARSHAL waited before getting his horse. He needed to tell Gifford that Jake was going after Gil and would be coming after him as well. As he rode, he knew that Jake would tie Gifford to the shooting, which would mean trouble for all of them. He had heard about the incident that happened between Jake and Duke in the mercantile.

Shafer knocked, and Gifford opened the door. "Did you find Gil?"

"We lost his trail going into Mesa Verde," Shafer said. "Jake Burton was in town when we returned.

"What did you tell him?"

"I told him where we lost his trail."

"What did Burton say he was going to do?"

"He said that he was going after Gil and that he'd be coming for you as well."

"Do you think he'll find him?"

"He ain't gonna find him in there with all the underbrush and canyons. If you don't know where he went, you ain't gonna find him. Even if he comes across his trail, Gil will see and hear him long before Jake finds him," the marshal commented.

"Go back to town," Gifford ordered. "Tomorrow, ride out and continue looking for Gil. Stay away from town so the people will think you're making an effort to find him. When you come back, if someone asks, tell them you believe that he has ridden out of your jurisdiction."

Now Clemens had another problem. If what the marshal said was true about Jake coming after him, he needed to get rid of Jake Burton once and for all.

⚘

To keep a lid on things, Gifford decided to stay at his ranch the next day instead of going back to town. If Gil did show up, he wanted to make sure that he would leave the territory.

In the morning, he watched Duke and Lew ride out. He had ordered them to find Gil before Jake did. If they came across Burton while looking for Gil, this would be a good opportunity to get rid of him—he instructed them to kill him and Gil. Killing Jake would solve two problems. First, it could be blamed on Gil, and, second, it would eliminate one of the owners of the Double B Ranch.

⚘

Before daylight, Duke and Lew threw their gear together, along with supplies, and tied it on their horses. They were in a hurry to leave, knowing that Jake Burton would be out looking for Gil. They wanted to get to Mesa Verde at first light and find Gil before Jake got there.

They reached Mesa Verde while it was still dark and stopped. They hoped that Gil would be on the lookout for anyone coming after him, so they built a fire bright enough for him to easily see, hoping he would come to them.

While they waited, Lew said, "I ain't heard much about this area. Not too many people have been here. To me, it seems like if someone wants not to be found, this would be the place to come. The brush is so thick, it's hard to get through, and one could easily get lost in here."

"Gil has been here several times before," Duke said. "Whoever lived here before has been gone a long time. Right now, we need to find him before Burton does, or the boss could be in trouble that would lead to us as well."

"What about the marshal? Do you think he'll come back?"

"The marshal ain't gonna be a problem," Duke assured him. "The one we gotta watch out for is Jake Burton. He could be trouble."

"Gil shouldn't have shot Howard Ashley," Lew commented.

"Gil wasn't too smart about some things, and you're right: he shouldn't have shot Howard. If he dies, there will be a range war when they come after Clemens—unless we get rid of Burton first."

That morning, Howard was not any better. Sally had stayed up with him all night. He continued to have a hard time breathing and would cough now and again.

Elizabeth got up early to make breakfast for the men and knew that Sally had stayed with Howard. Going to their room, she saw Sally dead on her feet. "You need to get some rest. As soon as I clean up, I'll come and sit with Howard, and you can get some sleep."

"Have Jake and Lance gone yet?" Sally asked.

"They're getting ready now," Elizabeth told her. Sally nodded, and Elizabeth went back to the kitchen.

Jake and Lance went out to the corral to saddle their horses. Jake decided to take a packhorse with them, not knowing how long they would be gone. Going back to the house, Jake found Elizabeth in the kitchen as she finished putting food together for them. She handed Jake the supplies and smiled.

Jake smiled back. "How's Howard doing this morning?"

"Sally said he didn't rest well last night," she replied. "I'm going to let her get some rest as soon as I get the kitchen cleaned up."

"Thanks for putting together these supplies for us," Jake said.

Elizabeth went over and put her hand on his arm. "You and Lance be careful. I know that Sally and I would not want anything to happen to you two. Do you know how long you'll be gone?"

"Shafer said he lost Gil's trail going into Mesa Verde, and according to Lance, it could be some time before we find him," Jake said, aware of the feeling of comfort he felt from the warmth of Elizabeth's hand on his arm.

"You be careful," she repeated. "Howard and Sally will need your help more than ever now."

Jake took the food bundle and walked out to tie it onto the packhorse. Elizabeth followed him out the door and stood on the porch, where she watched as they rode away. Sadness was in her heart as she watched Jake leave. She said a silent prayer for their safe return.

Reaching the base of Mesa Verde at noon, Jake and Lance stopped to look for signs of Gil's passage. They had been able to follow the tracks made by the posse and could see where they stopped. The tracks showed that the posse had milled around without going into Mesa Verde. It wasn't until later in the afternoon that they found fresh tracks from two horses ahead of them. Knowing Gil had ridden alone, Jake wondered if the horses belonged to two people out looking for Gil. Had Gifford sent men to find him, or had he given Gil supplies and a packhorse? As they followed the tracks, they determined that it had to be two riders.

When it started to get dark, Jake and Lance decided to make camp. They could pick up the trail first thing in the morning.

While they were setting up, Lance asked, "Do you have any idea who could be following Gil?"

"No. It could be Gifford's men. I don't think the marshal would do it."

"You think they know where Gil is?"

"They might," Jake replied. "If it is Gifford's men, we need to make sure they don't see us before we see them."

"Those tracks were made just today," Lance commented.

"Let's follow them in the morning, and maybe we can catch up to them and find out who they are."

An hour after they started the next morning, they came across the camp where Duke and Lew had stopped. Jake looked around and found that two men had been there, confirming it wasn't Gil they were following. While Jake looked over the camp, Lance found where the tracks were headed, going deeper into Mesa Verde.

Going back to Jake, Lance asked, "What did you find?"

"The two camped here last night. Seeing that it's not Gil and knowing the marshal wouldn't make an effort to capture him, I think Gifford sent some of his men to find him. If they stay as careless as they have been, we should be able to follow them, and maybe they'll lead us to Gil."

They continued to follow the tracks. At noon, they stopped to rest the horses. While eating, Lance got a chill on the back of his neck, a feeling he had before when he was being watched.

Seeing Lance looking around nervously, Jake asked, "What's wrong?"

"I ain't sure. I got this feeling we're being watched."

"We're gonna have to be careful until we know for sure if we've been spotted. The tracks here are still fresh," Jake observed.

While they were talking, the horses started acting up. Looking across the camp, the two saw movement in the brush. Jake caught a glimpse of something as it moved but couldn't make out what or who it was.

Turning to Lance, he said, "Hold the horses. I'm going to see what's out there."

Jake took his rifle and went into the brush. Checking the ground, he found prints of a large cat that had passed where he had spotted the movement. Relieved that the animal appeared to have moved on, he returned to Lance.

"Looks like you were right," Jake said. "We were being watched by a mountain lion."

They mounted their horses and continued to follow the tracks. By late afternoon, they still had not spotted who it was. "Whoever we're following seem to be looking for Gil as well," Lance said.

"If they don't know where he is, maybe they ain't Gifford's men," Jake replied. "We ain't seen any tracks other than those we've been following. Maybe Gil started in but came out during the night, hoping that anyone following him would spend a lot of time looking for him while he got away."

"Didn't you say that the marshal lost Gil's trail at the entrance into here?" Lance asked.

"That's what he said. You know the marshal might have been lying to throw us off."

"Maybe we need to go back to where the posse turned around and see if we can find Gil's trail," Lance suggested.

"We could, but if the two in front of us are Gifford's men, they must think Gil is in here," Jake reasoned. "Let's see if we can find out who they are first."

They continued to follow the trail until it got dark. When they stopped, they set up camp without building a fire. Settling down, they ate some jerky. While sitting there, Lance spotted a glow in the sky just south of where they camped. "Ain't that a campfire?" he pointed out. "You think that could be Gil?"

"It's probably the men we've been following," Jake said.

"How far away do you think they are?"

"It doesn't look to be far. This could be our chance to see who's there without them knowing we're following them. We'll leave the horses here and go on foot."

After hobbling the horses and checking their guns, they set out. About a quarter of a mile from their camp, they heard voices. Jake cautioned Lance to stop. The clouds were covering the moon, making it dark and hard to see. Still, they had to be careful not to make any noise as they slowly proceeded. When they got closer, they could overhear what the men were saying.

"I ain't sure Gil is in here," Lew said.

"We saw his tracks heading this way this morning," Duke replied. "I'm sure that he's still here. Maybe he's close enough to see our fire."

"You don't think if he sees our fire, he'll go further up the mountain thinking we're the law or Burton?"

"Gil will want to know who's coming after him," Duke said. "I would bet that he finds a spot to watch the trail and see who comes up it. If he sees it's us, he should come to us."

"What about Burton?" Lew asked.

"You heard what Gifford said."

"Yeah, I heard," Lew replied. "You think he's looking for Gil?"

"He ain't gonna let Gil go after shooting Howard," Duke stated. "He'll come after Gifford as well. You heard Gifford say we should get rid of both of them if we can. Build up that fire."

"If Jake is looking for Gil, won't he see it?" Lew asked.

"That could save us time looking for him."

Suddenly, Lew heard a noise in the dark. "What was that?"

"Sounded like a twig breaking." Duke motioned for Lew to back away from the fire and move into the brush.

Once they were hidden, they waited. "Maybe it's Gil," Lew whispered.

"If it is, he may not come into the camp if it's empty," Duke said. "We can only hope it is him and he watches for us tomorrow."

Lance had accidentally stepped on a branch and felt it break with a loud snap. He stopped and didn't move. After the clouds slid away from the moon, it allowed Lance to see that he had wandered into an area where the ground was covered with several branches lying about.

When Jake heard the branch break, he stopped as well. *Did they hear it in camp?* Jake wondered. They had just put more wood on the fire. Maybe they thought it was a burning branch. Motioning to Lance, Jake had him move back, not taking any chances.

Once they were a safe distance away, Jake said, "That was close. If they heard the twig break, they might come looking for who or what caused it."

"With it being so dark, I didn't see it," Lance apologized.

"Maybe we should have waited for more light. Anyway, we did find out who we've been following. Gifford must have sent Duke and Lew out to find Gil. We're going to have to be careful now. From what I heard them saying, it sounds like they're looking for me as well."

"Do you think they might look for our camp?" Lance asked.

"They might. We need to keep guard."

Lance said, "I'll go first."

"Wake me at one. I'll relieve you."

Duke and Lew continued to wait in the dark until their fire started to burn down. Finally, Duke said, "We might as well go back into camp. If it was someone out there, they're gone by now."

"What if it was Gil?" Lew asked heading back toward their spot.

"If it was, he'll find us tomorrow."

Hoping Gil had seen their fire, they let it die down.

The next morning, Duke was up first. As the sun was coming up, he left camp and scouted the area where they had heard the noise the night before. There, he found two sets of footprints. He was careful not to disturb them as he followed them. Once he found that they had come from the west, he knew they were being followed. He only tracked them a short distance before going back to camp.

Lew was just waking up when Duke arrived. "Where have you been?"

"I went out to check the area around our camp and found two sets of footprints nearby."

"You think it was Burton?" Lew asked.

"I don't think it was the marshal. He would have come into camp when he found it was us," Duke said. "We know Gil was alone, so it has to be Burton."

"What do you want to do?"

"Maybe we can draw them into a trap. If they're watching, we won't let on that we know we're being followed."

The morning started out looking like it was going to be a clear day. Jake and Lance ate before mounting their horses to continue to follow Duke and Lew. Reaching their camp, they found it empty. While they stood there, the wind suddenly changed, coming from the north. It increased, and the sky filled with dark clouds

"When we got up, it looked like the sky was clear. Now it looks like rain," Lance observed.

"If it rains, it will wipe out any tracks we're following," Jake said. "Let's get going."

Duke and Lew had gone about a mile when the weather started to change. Lew said, "We need to find shelter. From the looks of those clouds, it's going to come down hard."

They stopped for shelter under an overhang with room for them and their horses. When the clouds opened, it rained so hard that they couldn't see more than two feet.

"We were lucky to find this shelter before the downpour hit," Lew said.

"Maybe those following us were not as lucky and are caught in it," Duke said.

Jake and Lance weren't so lucky and were caught out in the open when it started to rain. It came down so heavily that it went straight through their slickers and as Jake yet again blew away water that dripped from his nose, he muttered that they may as well not have bothered with them. The downpour continued for over an hour until it finally slowed to a drizzle, and Jake looked up to see a few welcome breaks had begun to appear in the solid gray sky.

They found some dry wood that had been protected by a rock overhang—the irony of them only now finding a place to shelter was not lost on Jake—and drank coffee by the fire while their hats and clothes dried. While grateful the rain finally stopped, both men remained quiet with miserable expressions on their unshaven faces. They were cold and wet and had lost the trail. All they could do was hope to pick up some new tracks while the ground was still soft.

Duke and Lew remained dry while it rained. When it finally stopped, they again started looking for Gil. Duke didn't want to leave any tracks but knew it couldn't be avoided because of the mud. He wanted to get far enough ahead of Jake to set up an ambush.

Taking it slowly, they went about a mile before Duke spotted a place where they could hide and wait. He made sure their tracks were visible as they rode past it before they circled back.

The sun came out while they sat and waited. It was hot and muggy as the ground dried. By the middle of the afternoon, they had not seen any sign of Jake and Lance. Sweat was running down Lew's back, causing it to itch and making him move around, trying to scratch it. Getting impatient and irritable, he said, "It's too dam hot to just be sitting here. I think we need to keep looking for Gil. I think they got caught in the downpour and turned back."

"Naw. If Burton is following us, he ain't gonna give up," Duke said. "They'll be coming."

Two hours after getting a fire going, Jake and Lance had dried their clothes and were ready to move. They continued to ride further into Mesa Verde at an easy pace. The sun continued to beat down on them, which helped to remove the chill in their bones and warm them.

"How far do you think they got before it started raining?" Lance asked.

"If they know that we're following them, they might have gotten an early start," Jake said. "We just need to keep going and look for any sign of them."

It was late in the afternoon when Jake spotted their tracks. He got off his horse to take a closer look, when two shots rang out, and Lance was knocked from his horse.

Jake ducked undercover and drew his Colt as he moved. Looking back, he saw Lance lying on the ground, not moving. Not sure where the shots had come from, he waited. He was looking for a way to check on Lance as another shot rang out, hitting the rock near his head. This time, he located where it came from and returned fire.

Not having enough coverage, Jake fired a second shot and moved. He no sooner got behind cover than two more shots were fired. Jake looked at his rifle strapped on his horse; he wished he could get to it, but his horse was too much in the open to risk trying. Looking at his Colt, he realized the distance between him and the ambushers were too far for his handgun to be effective.

Still thinking, he realized if he could keep the horses between him and the ambushers, he could get his rifle. He was looking at his horse when he saw movement coming from Lance. If the others had seen him move, Lance wouldn't have a chance. Jake needed to get him under cover.

Reloading the empty cylinders of his Colt, he dashed for Lance. Jake's sudden movement must have taken the ambushers by surprise as they didn't open fire until he was almost to him. He fired as he reached Lance, causing the ambushers to remain behind cover. Grabbing Lance's arm, he dragged him to safety, firing as he moved.

Once under cover, Jake saw where a bullet had grazed Lance's head. He also saw where he hit his head when he landed on the ground. "You're lucky. The bullet only grazed you, and it looks like you hit your head when you fell. How do you feel?"

"A little dazed," Lance said. "But I can still shoot."

"You stay here, and maybe I can work my way behind them."

Carefully looking around the area, Jake found the best way to get behind the ambushers. Running from cover to cover, he drew fire from Duke and Lew. Lance began to shoot; due to his head wound, his aim was off, but it was still close enough to make the ambushers take cover. Jake was able to make his way to the side where Duke and Lew were.

From Jake's new position, he caught sight of Duke. He aimed and fired just as Duke moved, hitting the spot where he had been. Jake was almost hit as Duke returned fire at him, so he quickly moved to better cover. From there, Jake saw Duke motion to Lew before moving to their horses, quickly mounting, and riding off.

When Jake heard the horses running off, he went to where they had been to make sure Lew and Duke had gone. Not finding them, he went to help Lance. He retrieved a piece of material from his saddlebag to wrap around Lance's head to stop the bleeding. Lance winced as he put his hat on and asked, "Did you hit any of them?"

"I got a shot at Duke but missed. Are you able to ride?"

"I'll be all right," Lance said. "I have a headache, but I can still ride."

"Now that they know we're following them, we need to be careful," Jake warned when they mounted their horses and rode on. "They might try to ambush us again or when we set up camp tonight."

"You remember hearing them say they had found Gil's tracks?" Lance asked. "We know that they won't be able to follow them since the rain."

"We know the direction they're headed," Jake said. "If we go the same way and stay off to the side of the trail, we should be able to avoid them."

Before they could go much further, Lance needed a chance to rest. Jake found shelter, where he set up camp and cooked. Lance went right to sleep after eating. While Lance was asleep, Jake walked away from camp, hoping to spot a campfire that could belong to Duke and Lew. The heavy growth restricted Jake's vision, making it impossible to see very far.

Duke and Lew rode hard, going deeper into Mesa Verde. While riding, Duke noticed that Lew was bleeding. He stopped and asked, "When did you get hit?"

"When Jake was running, he got lucky, and one of his shots got me in the arm."

They dismounted and led their horses into the trees nearby. Duke got busy taking care of Lew's arm. "You were lucky it's only a flesh wound and didn't hit the bone."

"How are we going to find Gil now that the rain wiped out the tracks we found?" Lew asked.

"Maybe he'll find us," Duke said. "We need to keep going."

A while later, the sun was starting to set when Duke and Lew stopped to set up camp. Lew asked, "Are you going to build a fire again?"

"I will. I don't think Jake and whoever's with him will be coming tonight. The man you hit didn't look too good. He had to be dragged to cover, so he's hurt more than you are. Jake is going to have to take care of him before they can follow us. If he's in bad shape, he might have to take him back to town or the ranch."

Duke gathered wood and got a fire going. After getting coffee started, he made supper. While eating, they heard a noise. Moving away from the fire, they hid and waited again. It wasn't long before they heard, "Hello in the camp."

"That's Gil," Lew said.

"Show yourself," Duke hollered. He kept his Colt out, waiting for Gil to come forward. When he saw Gil was alone, he put his Colt away and walked back into camp.

Gil walked into the light of the fire, leading his horse. He looked tired and worn out. "Ya got any extra grub? I ain't eaten for two days."

"Looks like you ain't slept for two days either," Lew said.

"Get your cup and plate," Duke told him. "Help yourself to the food; there's plenty."

Duke cared for Gil's horse while he ate. "Are you two the only ones looking for me, or is the marshal still out there looking?"

"Gifford took care of the marshal," Duke assured him. "We ain't the only ones looking for you though."

12

GIL

By late afternoon, dark clouds filled the sky, threatening rain. The temperature continued to drop as the sun went down. After finding shelter, Jake and Lance made camp. During the night, Lance developed a fever. When he woke in the morning, his vision was blurry. He started to get up, became dizzy, and fell back.

Jake had built a fire and was starting to cook breakfast when he heard Lance move. "There's coffee ready," he said.

Lance carefully made his way to the fire. When he tried to fill his cup, he missed it and spilled the hot brew on his hand. Jake took Lance's cup and filled it. "Are you all right?"

"I'll be fine as soon as I have some coffee," Lance replied, trying to clear his vision.

While they ate, Jake kept an eye on him. He could see that Lance's face was flush, and he kept rubbing his eyes. Jake was wondering if the area where he was grazed by the bullet had become infected, causing his fever. He also noticed that Lance seemed to be having a hard time focusing on his plate. By the time they finished breakfast, Lance's head was starting to clear. "Are you going to be all right?" Jake asked again.

"I'm just a little dizzy, and I'm seeing double."

Jake took his time before breaking camp and saddling their horses to give it a chance for Lance's vision to clear. By the time they were ready to return to their search for Gil, a drizzle of rain had started.

"If it rains hard, we'll need to find another shelter," Jake said. "With you being hurt, you need to keep dry and out of the rain. If we come across Duke before then, are you going to be able to see well enough to shoot?"

"I'll try. My head still hurts, but it isn't as bad as when I first woke up, and my vision is starting to clear."

With that, the two men mounted their horses and rode out.

❧

Duke was the first one up with a fire going. "Looks like we're in for more rain," he said as Gil and Lew got up.

"That should slow Jake down," Lew replied.

Duke made a pot of coffee and prepared breakfast. While they ate, Gil asked, "Who sent you?"

"Gifford wants you out of the territory," Duke said. "He's afraid that if Jake Burton finds you first, you'll tell him you acted on his orders to shoot Ashley. Besides, Burton will take you back to town and see that you hang for murder."

"Why does Gifford care if they hang me?" Gil asked. "He didn't tell me to shoot Ashley. Anyway, it was self-defense. I thought he was going to shoot me."

"Gifford told us Ashley wasn't armed, and if you tell Burton that you were following his orders not to let the Hansons sell supplies to them, Burton will go after him," Duke said. "Gifford knows you were told he wasn't armed."

"Where does he want me to go?" Gil asked.

"He wants ya out of the territory where Burton can't find ya," Lew said.

"What makes you think Burton can find me?"

"We found you, and he has been following us. Now it's up to you to get out of here," Duke said. "If you do get caught by Burton, make sure you don't tell him that Gifford told you to shoot Ashley."

"Are you going to do anything about Burton?" Gil asked.

"We're gonna kill him and the fella riding with him," Lew said.

While they talked, the clouds opened, and rain started coming down. Gil said, "Get your horses; there's an old dwelling near here that will give us shelter."

They rode a mile further into Mesa Verde, where they found the old dwelling that was built out of rocks under the overhang of a cliff. After hobbling their horses, they took their gear into one of the rooms. Gil had been there before and had left wood for the next time he returned.

They started a fire, and before long, the room was warm and dry. The light from the fire showed that someone had lived there a long time ago. The ceiling was covered with soot from several fires of long ago. There were indentations in the wall that looked to have been used as shelves. An entryway at the back of the room led into another room that went deeper into the cliff. Walls defined the different rooms that were built by carefully stacking rocks to form a tight seal.

"How did you find this place?" Duke asked.

"I was hunting near here and came across it by accident," Gil said. "When I want to get away, I come here so I can be alone."

"Are there more places like this near here?"

"I ain't found any others. The canyons are hard to get into, and I don't know for sure."

"Well, when the rain lets up, you need to hightail it out so you can get as far away as you can," Duke said, knowing if Jake found Gil, he could kill them both.

Jake and Lance continued to ride in the direction that Duke and Lew traveled. When the weather looked like it was about to turn bad, Jake started to search for shelter so they could get out of the rain before it came. While they rode, the sky continued to grow darker, and the rain started to fall before they found shelter. The heavy clouds caused the day to grow as dark as night. With the rain came lightning that would light up the area for a moment, and then it would go dark again.

They wandered off the trail and entered into a canyon. Lightning struck a tree near them and caused it to splinter, spooking the horses. If lightning was striking that close, they knew they had to find shelter soon. With the next bolt of lightning, Jake saw an opening in the wall.

"Did you see that?" he asked.

"See what?" Lance asked.

"Looked like a cave."

They rode to the wall, where Lance could see what Jake had spotted. Lightning flashed again, and they could see that the opening was large enough to allow room for the horses. "That ain't no ordinary cave," Lance said.

Exploring along the wall, they found several openings that would get them and the horses out of the weather.

"I ain't never seen anything like this," Jake said.

Several layers looked like rooms that had been built by someone. They rode up to one and dismounted, leading their horses into one of the rooms. Lance waited in the room with the horses, while Jake went to search for dry wood to build a fire. When Jake first looked around the room, he found an opening in the back that led to a second room.

Carefully checking some of the surrounding rooms, with help from the ongoing lighting, Jake found dry wood in a corner of one of them. He gathered as much as he could and carried it back to where Lance waited with the horses. He asked Lance to unsaddle the horses and store their gear while he went to the room next door and started a fire. With the fire lit, he went outside to gather more wood.

The wood outside was wet, but it would dry quickly when laid out near the fire. After he had gathered an armload, he returned to the shelter. By then, Lance had unsaddled the horses and was waiting near the fire. The cold rain had caused his fever to increase. As his clothes dried, his body began to get warm, which made him feel better.

"Who do you think made these rooms?" Lance asked.

The light from the fire allowed Jake to see the amount of work that someone had put into their construction. Each stone looked like it had been carefully selected and placed where it would remain for centuries to come. Small stones and clay had been placed in between the larger stones to keep wind and weather out. Niches had been built into the walls for storage.

"I heard stories about a tribe of Indians that lived here long ago. The storytellers didn't know who they were or where they went. Most of the dwellings they talked about were in open areas. I never heard anything said about a place built in the cliffs."

The room where they built the fire had others adjoining it, like the one the horses were in. Jake took a burning branch from the fire and used it as a torch, carrying it into the next room. This room was about the same size as the first one. Along the wall were two low-lying shelves that looked like they were used as beds. As he stepped into the room, he saw a broken piece of pottery. When he searched further, he found a larger piece and picked it up. One side of the pottery was red. It resembled the red clay that was common in this area. On the other side of the piece was a unique black design. He went back to show Lance what he found, but Lance had fallen asleep. Jake placed the piece of pottery on a nearby shelf and decided he would show it to him when he woke up.

While Lance slept, Jake decided to check on the horses, who were standing on one side of the room, resting. With nothing there that needed his immediate attention, Jack went to the entrance of the shelter and stood to watch the rain. He looked up at the sky, and all he saw were dark clouds. He shook his head, knowing that the storm was not going to let up anytime soon. As hard as it was raining, he knew that Duke and Lew had to find shelter as well.

He went back by Lance and sat near the fire. With his back to the doorway, there was suddenly a blinding white light that lit up the interior of the room. Jake was momentarily blinded by the light, which was followed by a deafening boom that echoed throughout the room. Lance jumped to his feet, disoriented.

"What was that?" he asked, shaking his head to clear it.

Jake could hear the horses had started to move nervously. He went to the doorway and, looking out, found that the lightning had struck a tree no more than fifty yards away. Turning toward Lance, he said, "Lighting hit right outside here."

"It sounded like it was in the room," Lance commented.

"How are you feeling?"

"I feel better, but my head still hurts. My eyesight is better though."

"I need to go check on the horses again to make sure they're all right," Jake said.

He found that the horses were nervous but fine. Standing with them, he rubbed them until they started to calm down. When they were settled, he went back by Lance, walked over to the shelf, and picked up the pottery he found earlier.

"What do you have?" Lance asked.

"Looks like a piece of pottery," Jake said, handing it to Lance.

"Where did you find it?" he asked as he turned the piece over, looking at both sides.

"In the other room. Have you ever seen a design like that?"

"Can't say I have," Lance replied. "Maybe it has something to do with the Indians who lived in the area."

"I guess we'll never know for sure."

After handing the pottery back to Jake, Lance asked, "What does the weather look like?"

"Doesn't look like it's going to let up anytime soon," Jake said. "Seeing that we're out of the rain and have a fire, it'll give you a chance to recover."

"I'll get some supper together. After we eat, we can look around in some of these rooms and see what we can find," Lance said.

After they ate, they wandered around the adjoining rooms. Only finding a few more pottery pieces, they returned to the fire. The rain was still coming down, and it was night when they settled down.

Duke sat by the fire, thinking as he watched the rain. If Gil hadn't shot Howard, he could have put together a plan that would have gotten rid of the Ashley's as well as Jake. But Gil messed that up.

He felt the bulge of money in his pocket that Gifford had given him and thought about what he had hinted at about getting rid of Gil. He didn't say to kill him, but Duke thought he might still be able to get rid of Gil and Burton. He could blame it on Jake and keep the money for himself. He looked over to where Lew and Gil were talking and kept thinking of ways to get rid of Gil. Then Duke leaned back against the wall and closed his eyes. It wasn't long before he fell asleep.

"You need to get out of the area," Lew said to Gil. "Where are you going to go?"

"Maybe Santa Fe. Been there before, and I know a couple of fellows if they're still there."

They sat quietly for a bit before Gil asked, "You think Burton is still out there looking for me?"

"If they didn't find shelter, I don't think they'll stick around," Lew said. "This weather ain't helping the wounded fella with him. I figure when this rain lets up, we can ride out of here, and you could head for Santa Fe."

It wasn't until late at night that the rain finally stopped.

Jake woke as the sun was coming up. The rain had stopped sometime during the night, and the sky was blue with scattered clouds. He went to check on the horses and led them outside to a pool that had collected rainwater. Near the pond was a patch with grass, so he left the horses hobbled so they could feed.

Lance woke up when he heard Jake moving around. Getting up after Jake had gone out, he put a pot of coffee on and started to prepare breakfast.

When Jake returned, Lance asked, "Where do you think we should start looking for Gil?"

"I don't think they went very far. With all that rain yesterday, any tracks they left yesterday are gone. If Gil is with him, he knows this area, and there might be more places like this one that they held up in when the rain started."

"I been doing some thinking about what Gil did, shooting Howard. Do you think he could have killed your pa?"

"I don't know," Jake said. "I believe Pa's murder was planned. Shooting Howard just happened. Gil doesn't look like a fella who would own a Sharps. When we find him, maybe we can get him to talk and tell us who shot my pa."

They loaded their gear onto the packhorse and resumed their search. The rain had made the ground soft and slick. The horses had a difficult time climbing the hills without slipping. Going slowly, the two men didn't make much progress as they searched for tracks.

Near midmorning, Lance spotted tracks from a single horse. "You think it could be Gil?"

"I don't think Duke and his partner split up unless they did it to look for us," Jake said.

"If we backtrack, we might find the others," Lance said. "We could tell what they are up to."

"If we backtrack and these were made by Gil, he'll get away. Maybe Gil didn't run into Duke. I got the feeling that we need to follow these tracks since they're the only ones we found. They look to be heading north. Whoever is ahead of us is looking to get out of the Mesa Verde. It could be Gil," Jake said. "By now, he has to be hungry as he wasn't able to get supplies before he came in here. He might be trying to get out to get supplies."

"Maybe you're right and it is Gil," Lance agreed, so they rode on.

A few hours earlier, Duke had woken up, looked around, and saw that Gil was asleep. Seeing that Lew was awake, he moved next to him and said, "You know that Gifford gave me money for Gil to get away so that Burton wouldn't be able to find him."

"Yeah," Lew said.

"If we kill Gil, we could tell Gifford that Burton was the one who did it," Duke said. "Then we can split the money. What do you think?"

"Gifford would believe that, but won't he expect the money back?"

"We can tell him that we had given the money to Gil and he left. That way he would think that Burton took the money when he killed him," Duke explained.

"Why don't we kill him now?" Lew asked.

"As long as we have Gil with us, we know that Burton will come looking for us. If we wait till Burton finds us, we can kill them both." Duke took the money out of his pocket and put it in his saddlebag.

Gil had been lying there with his eyes shut when he heard Duke and Lew start talking. Curious what they had to say, he listened to Duke planning to kill him and Burton. Now it was his turn to wait for them to go to sleep.

Gil lied quietly, putting together a plan to get away. After he was positive that Duke and Lew were asleep, he got up and searched Duke's saddlebags. Finding the money, he put it in his pocket. He also needed the supplies, so he gathered them before he saddled his horse.

The rain had not yet stopped, but it had let up some. Gil felt it would help him get away by covering his tracks. The clouds hid the moon and made it hard to see where he was going, which caused him to go slower than he wanted. He hoped that he would get far enough away before Duke woke up that he would not have to worry about them.

The slippery ground made it dangerous for his horse. If the animal fell and got hurt, Gil would be in trouble. While getting his horse ready to leave, he almost woke the others and had to get out of there. He couldn't take Duke and Lew's horses as they would have slowed him down, and Jake could find him. Gil's plan was that while he was traveling alone, Burton would continue following the other two, thinking that they had not found him.

An hour after Gil had left, Lew woke up and found him gone. He woke Duke. "Gil and his horse are gone. What do you think made him do that? You think he heard us talking?"

"He must have heard us," Duke replied.

"What do you want to do now?"

Duke got up to check his saddlebags. "The money's gone. He must have taken it. We need to find him before Burton does. If Jake finds him, Gil could cause us all trouble."

"He also took our supplies," Lew added.

"We can't do anything now; we need to wait till morning to follow him," Duke said. "The rain has let up, and with the ground so wet and slippery, he'll have to take it easy. If he did hear us, he'll be heading out of here."

When morning broke, they mounted and started to track Gil. The going was still slow and dangerous for the horses. When Lew's horse slipped and fell, throwing him from the saddle, they had to stop. Once he recovered, he checked his horse; finding it wasn't hurt, they continued. It was late morning before they found the tracks left by Jake and Lance, who appeared to be following Gil.

"Looks like Burton is ahead of us," Duke said.

"Do you think he caught Gil?"

"Nah, it looks like they're following him. I don't think Gil knows they're behind him."

Gil rode half the night and kept going until midday. Wanting to be safe, he had to put as much distance as he could between him and Duke. The wet ground made it hard for his horse to walk without slipping. When he finally accepted the need to rest his horse, he moved off the trail and into some trees to let it graze. Ever watchful, he tried to eat some dried meat, but his stomach was churning; he now had Duke wanting to kill him as well as Burton.

He thought he saw movement on the trail and wondered, *Could that be Duke and Lew?* He was several hours ahead of them, and they would also have to go slow as he did on the slick ground. *Maybe it's Burton.* He began to feel uneasy and needed to find a spot where he could hole up to find out who was behind him.

Gil got his horse and looked for a spot that would hide the animal and allow him to ambush whoever was behind him. A quarter of a mile down the trail, he found what he was looking for. He tied his horse and took his Winchester with him behind a rock, where he sat and waited.

Twenty minutes later, Gil saw Jake and Lance come into view. He aimed his rifle and fired. Gil cussed as the shot missed Burton, who had moved; he must have seen something. Gil saw Jake shove Lance from his horse before he dove from his own, grabbing his rifle as he left the saddle. He continued to watch, trying to aim as Burton hit the ground rolling and was soon back on his feet, running for the nearest cover while Lance fired a shot in his direction. He guessed they must have seen a flash of the sun reflecting off the barrel of his rifle.

Peering around the rock, Gil raised the rifle again and fired a shot at the other guy as he headed for cover. The bullet hit a rock, causing him to drop to the ground and crawl out of sight as the echo of the ricochet faded away.

Jake called out, "Gil, you ain't going to get away. We got you pinned down. Let us take you in."

"I ain't gonna hang," Gil replied as he took a wild shot in Jake's direction.

The shot came close but missed. Jake knew that he would have to move if he was going to take Gil alive. He glanced over at Lance to make sure he was all right before he began to work his way behind Gil.

Lance couldn't see Jake and wondered where he was. When he rose to take a shot at Gil, a bullet hit the rock, causing splinters to spray in his face.

It caused him to duck, and he tripped just as a second bullet hit where he had been.

Jake worked his way behind Gil and called out, "Gil, give up."

Hearing Jake behind him, Gil panicked. Turning, he fired in Jake's direction.

Lance had moved, and when he saw Gil turn to fire at Jake, he shot and hit Gil in the shoulder, causing him to drop his rifle. He ran over to Gil as he lay on the ground.

Jake saw Gil get hit and rushed to him. He grabbed Gil's rifle and held his Colt on him while Lance helped him up.

"Why didn't you kill me?" Gil asked.

"If Howard dies, I'm going to see you hang," Jake said. "Lance, get his horse. We're going to take him to the marshal."

Lance returned with the horse while Jake tied Gil's hands behind his back. After hoisting him into the saddle, he led Gil's horse over to where they could retrieve their own horses. Soon, they mounted and headed to town.

Duke and Lew continued to follow the tracks, when they thought they heard shooting. Not sure how far away it was, they continued. When they arrived at the spot where Gil had been captured, they stopped. Getting down, they looked at the ground, trying to figure out what had happened. They could only find blood in one spot, and Duke said, "Looks like someone was wounded."

"Do you think it was Gil? Reckon he's dead?" Lew asked.

"There isn't that much blood. Whoever was hit is probably just wounded. There are three sets of boot prints coming to this spot and only one set of hoof prints. There had to be two other horses around here someplace." They continued to look until they found were Jake and Lance had mounted.

It was already late in the afternoon. Not knowing the area, Duke was sure they wouldn't reach the edge of Mesa Verde before dark. He decided to make camp for the night.

"Why are we camping here?" Lew asked.

"We can't move fast with the ground this soft. Your horse already fell once, and if it falls again, it could get hurt or killed. We'll spend the night here and head out at first light."

By the time it started to get dark, Jake and Lance had not gotten out of Mesa Verde. "We need to make camp," Jake stated. "I want Gil alive when we get to town. I don't want to risk a horse falling in the dark."

"We're gonna need to keep guard," Lance said.

"You're right, especially with Duke behind us. They might keep riding in the dark."

"Do you think they'll try to free him?" Lance asked.

"Don't know. It's strange that they let Gil leave on his own."

Finding a place to camp, they stopped. Jake hauled Gil off his horse and tied him to a nearby tree. Lance started supper while Jake looked at Gil's wound. After he removed his shirt, Jake found that the bullet wound in his shoulder had festered some. He would have to get the doctor in town to remove the bullet. He wrapped the wound as best he could and put Gil's shirt around him. It was then when he felt a lump in the pocket. Jake reached in and took out a large sum of money. He looked at Gil and said, "You got a lot of money on you for a cowhand. Is this what Gifford paid you to kill Howard?"

Gil sat there with a blank look on his face, not saying a word.

"Maybe you're the one who killed my pa. How much did Gifford give you for that?"

"I ain't telling you nothing," Gil said.

"If Gifford didn't tell you to kill Howard, why did you shoot him?"

"I told you I ain't gonna tell . . . ow!" Gil cried out as Lance grabbed his wounded shoulder.

"Now answer him," Lance said.

The anger in Gil's eyes was piercing as he looked at Lance, who reached for his shoulder again. "I didn't kill your pa," Gil cried out.

"Who did?" Jake asked.

"I don't know," Gil lied. "All I heard was that your pa and the marshal were killed by the same person."

"Where did you hear that?" Jake asked.

"Around town."

"Did anyone at Gifford's ranch talk about killing them?" Lance asked.

"No one said anything about it at the ranch."

"Where is Gifford getting all his cattle?" Lance asked.

"I don't know."

Lance went to reach for Gil's wound again. "From ranches in the area," Gil said suddenly.

"Is he stealing them?" Jake asked.

"He takes a few at a time."

Jake set his jaw. "Did Gifford pay you to shoot Howard?"

"No."

"Why did you shoot him?" Lance asked.

"I thought he was going for a gun."

"He wasn't wearing a gun," Jake said. "If you didn't intend to kill him, why did you follow him into the mercantile?"

"Gifford gave orders not to let him get supplies from there," Gil said.

"Gifford told you to stop him?" Lance asked.

"I just went in to stop him. When I was there, I wasn't going to let him do to me what you did to Duke," Gil said, looking at Jake.

"Well, if he dies, you are going to hang," Lance said. "I know that the boys and I will be there to see it."

"Where did you get this money if you weren't paid to kill Howard?" Jake asked.

Gil refused to talk again until Lance grabbed his shoulder. "Ow! I took it from Duke."

"When did you see him?" Lance asked.

"Last night I was with him and Lew."

"How come you weren't with them when we caught you?" Jake pressed him.

"I heard them talking, and they said they were going to kill me, so I took the money and left during the night."

"You all work for Gifford, so why would they want to kill you?" Lance asked.

"They wanted to keep the money for themselves and blame Jake for killing me."

Supper was ready, so they ate. Afterward, Lance took the first watch, and Jake relieved him at midnight. As the sky became lighter with the coming dawn, all was quiet and still. It looked like the storm had passed as the sky was clear of clouds and turning blue.

After breakfast, they broke camp, and the three men headed for Mancos. While they were riding, Lance kept checking their back trail. At one time, he thought he saw riders, but they were too far back to be sure.

13

GIL'S ARREST

WHILE THEY RODE INTO TOWN, Jake saw Gifford looking out his window, watching them. When they stopped in front of the marshal's office, he and Lance got down and tied the four horses. Jake then got Gil off his horse.

They opened the door to the jail and found Marshal Shafer sitting at his desk. The marshal looked up, angry at the disturbance. When he saw Gil being shoved into his office, he asked, "What the . . . ?"

"Here he is, Marshal," Jake said. "He's still alive and knows how to talk."

"Who shot him?" Shafer asked.

"I did," Lance said. "He's lucky he's not dead. He tried to ambush us. You need to get the doctor to take the bullet out of his shoulder."

The marshal got up and shook his head before he got the keys to open a cell. Jake waited until the cell door was open and Gil was inside before untying his hands. Gil went to the bunk, sat down, and stared at Jake with fear in his eyes. The marshal closed the door and locked it.

Jake asked, "Have you heard anything about Howard?"

"Last word was he was still alive. The doctor was out to see him and said that he didn't look good and there was nothing else he could do for him." Jake and Lance turned to leave, when the marshal asked, "Where are you going?"

"Home," Jake said. "I'm going to check on Howard. If he dies, I'm coming back to get Gifford. When I come back, I expect to see Gil in jail. I don't what to hear that he escaped or that Gifford left town. If I go after him again, he won't be alive when I bring him back. If he's gone, I'll hold you accountable for it."

"You can't threaten me," the marshal said.

"I ain't threatening you. Just making you a promise."

Lance and Jake went out the door, got their horses, and rode out of town. Marshal Shafer watched them ride away before going to get the doctor to look at Gil's shoulder. On the way, he spotted Duke and Lew as they rode in from the east. Not paying any more attention to them, he continued to the doctor's office.

Gifford had been sitting at his desk when he looked out the window and saw Jake and Lance bring Gil to the marshal's office. He became worried and wondered how Jake got him and where Duke was. How long had they had him, and what did he tell them? What happened to Duke and Lew?

When Jake and Lance rode out and the marshal left, Gifford figured this would be his chance to see Gil alone. He opened the door before he spotted Duke and Lew. When he saw them, he decided to wait as they stopped in front of his office. He returned to his desk, where he sat down and waited for them to come in.

When they entered, he asked, "Well, what happened that Jake got Gil and you didn't?"

"We had Gil until the other night," Duke explained.

"Then what happened? I thought I told you to get rid of him if you could."

"He left during the night while Duke and I slept," Lew said. "We were going to take care of Gil and Burton together."

"Why did he leave, and how did Jake end up with him?" Gifford demanded.

"He kept acting nervous with us and said he wanted to get out of the area as quickly as possible. With the money you gave him, he left during the night," Lew said.

"Burton came across his trail after he rode out," Duke added. "Gil tried to ambush them but got caught."

"You two wait here. I'm going over to the jail to talk to him," Gifford said, getting up.

The marshal had returned to the office with the doctor before Gifford arrived. Shafer had just sat down at his desk when Gifford walked in and said, "I see you got Gil."

"Burton brought him in."

"How bad is he hurt?" Gifford asked, seeing the doctor tending to him.

"He was shot in the shoulder," the marshal said. "Doc can tell us when he gets done."

When the doctor finished, he called for the marshal to let him out of the cell. When Doc saw Gifford, he said, "He will live to hang if Ashley dies."

"You already got him hung," Gifford stated. "Don't you think he should have a trial first?"

"He won't get away with killing Mr. Ashley. Everyone knows Gil shot an unarmed man." The doctor looked at the marshal and added, "If his wound becomes infected, call me."

After Doc left, Gifford said, "Marshal, I want to talk to Gil."

"Go ahead."

"Alone," Gifford stated.

The marshal got up and left the office. When he was gone, Gifford walked over to the cell. Gil saw him and said, "You gotta get me out of here."

"Why didn't you stay with Duke and Lew?"

"I heard them say they were going to kill me."

"I sent them to find you and tell you to leave the territory," Gifford lied, knowing he had instructed Duke to kill both Gil and Burton if he got the chance. "I gave them money to give to you."

"They wanted the money for themselves," Gil replied. "During the night, I took it and left."

"What did you tell Burton?" Gifford asked, not believing what Gil had just said.

"I didn't tell him nothing."

"What did he want to know?"

"He wanted to know who killed his pa," Gil said. "I told him I didn't know nothing except what I heard in town."

"What about you shooting Ashley? Did he ask if I ordered you to do it?"

"Yeah, he asked that, but I told him you had given orders not to sell supplies to them. He said that if Ashley dies, he was coming after you."

"Why did you shoot him?" Gifford asked.

"I was with Duke when Burton stood him down, and I wasn't going to let Ashley do it to me," Gil explained.

"Couldn't you see he wasn't wearing a gun?"

"He had a coat on. I thought he had a gun under it," Gil lied. "You gotta get me out of here."

"I'll see what I can do," Gifford replied as he turned to leave.

"You've got to do it. I ain't gonna hang alone," Gil called out.

When Gifford heard that, he knew he had to do something. He went back to his office, where Duke and Lew were still waiting.

"What did you find out from Gil?" Duke asked.

"He said he heard you two planning to kill him. He got nervous when I asked him if he had told Burton anything. I think he talked."

"He was afraid that the money we gave him was our pay to kill him and not let him out of the area," Duke said.

"You got any idea what he told Burton?" Lew asked.

"I'm not sure," Gifford said. "But I know that if he's going to hang, he's going to do a lot more talking, and we can't have that. He told me that he was not going to hang alone."

"What do you want us to do?" Duke asked.

"We need to wait and see if Ashley lives. If he does, Gil won't hang, and we may not have to do anything. If Ashley dies, we'll have to get rid of Gil before he can talk."

⚬⚬⚬

Jake and Lance were met by Logan as they rode into the ranch. "Did you find Gil?"

"We caught him," Lance said. "He's at the marshal's office."

"How's Howard doing?" Jake asked.

"Not good. Mrs. Ashley has been with him almost all the time since he got home. Doc was out here yesterday."

"Can you take care of my horse?" Jake asked, getting off and handing Logan the reins before heading to the house.

Elizabeth heard them ride in and was waiting when Jake walked in. "We've been worried about you."

"We're fine," Jake assured her.

"Did you find Gil?"

"He's in jail. How's Howard?"

"Sally is with him," Elizabeth said. "You can go in and see him. While you're in there, I'll get some food together for you and Lance."

Jake slowly opened the door to the bedroom. Sally was sitting by the bed, sleeping. Howard was still having a hard time breathing but looked to be asleep. Not wanting to wake either of them, he closed the door and went back to the kitchen.

Lance had returned to the house and was sitting at the table. He watched Elizabeth, who was busy at the stove putting food together. "How's Howard?" he asked.

"They were both sleeping," Jake said. "I didn't want to disturb them."

"Sit down," Elizabeth instructed. "Your food is almost ready."

When Jake sat down, Elizabeth handed him a cup of coffee before going back to finish preparing their food. While drinking it, he tried to plan what he would do next. Gil had told him that Gifford was stealing cattle from the ranchers, but how was he going to prove it? The marshal was one of Gifford's men, so he wouldn't do anything about it even if Gil told him. If anything was going to happen, Jake knew he was the one who would have to do it.

He suddenly snapped out of his thoughts when Elizabeth said, "Here, eat. It's probably been a few days since you had a good meal."

Lance laughed and said, "He ain't a bad cook, just not as good as you."

"Thanks. That sure does smell good," Jake said as he looked at Elizabeth.

Logan came in while they were eating and sat down. Jake asked, "Was there any trouble while we were gone?"

"It's been quiet since you left. I had some of the boys watch the herd, and they haven't seen anyone around. You think more cattle will come up missing?"

"Gil told us that Gifford is the one taking cattle from the ranches a little at a time," Lance said.

"What else did he tell you?" Logan asked.

"He said he didn't know anything about who killed Pa," Jake said. "I think he was lying. Somehow I get the feeling that Gifford's behind that as well."

"Elizabeth, come quickly," Sally suddenly called out. "We need the doctor."

Jake, Logan, Lance, and Elizabeth went rushing into the bedroom. Sally was panicking at the way Howard was breathing and looking paler than before.

Jake turned to Logan and said, "Hurry to town and get the doctor. Tell him Howard doesn't look good."

Logan ran out to the corral, got his horse, and rode to town.

Elizabeth took one look at Howard and shook her head. Going to him, she tried to see what she could do to ease his breathing. She raised him some, which seemed to help. Then she opened his shirt and saw that the wound was infected. There was a bad smell from it, and pus was oozing out. She looked at Jake and said, "It's not good."

Sally heard her and broke down crying. Jake went to his sister and wrapped his arms around her to try to comfort her.

It was an hour later when the doctor showed up. He took one look at Howard and knew that he did not have long to live. "What have you done for him?" he asked Elizabeth.

"I've just been trying to make it easier for him to breathe. I tried to keep the wound clean, but it keeps seeping. What more can we do?"

"I'm afraid there's nothing we can do but wait," Doc said. "If you've got coffee, we might all need some."

When Elizabeth went to the kitchen, Lance left the family with the doctor. She returned with Doc's coffee, but the others didn't want any. "What else can I do?" she asked.

Sally looked at her and said, "You're doing a lot by taking care of the men for me."

Jake, Sally, and Doc stayed by the bed as Howard lost his fight and died. Seeing her husband take his last breath, Sally broke down crying and almost fainted.

Seeing her reaction, Doc gave her some medicine to help her relax. Once Sally had calmed down to where the doctor felt she would be all right, Jake walked him to the front door and said, "Thanks for your help.

When you get back to town, tell the marshal that Howard died. He needs to get Gil's trial going. Remind him I'll be in town to look for Gifford as well."

Once the doctor was gone and Sally had recovered, Elizabeth helped her prepare Howard's body for burial.

When Logan heard that Howard had died, he started to build a coffin with some of the other men. Once Howard was prepared and the coffin ready, they helped Jake place the body in it. One of the hands rode over to the neighbors to let them know about Howard's death and tell them that he would be buried the next day.

The next morning, Howard's grave was dug near Mr. and Mrs. Burton's. Lance rode to town to get the preacher to perform the service. By the time they returned, several of the neighbors and some of the townsfolk had shown up.

After Howard was laid to rest, the family and ranch hands covered the grave. Elizabeth was busy preparing food for the guests with some of the other women. After everyone had eaten and given their condolences to Sally, they started to leave. A couple of the neighbors stayed to help clean up.

By the time everyone left, Sally was exhausted. Going into the room where Howard had died, she lay down but couldn't sleep. Thinking about him, she started crying uncontrollably until she was drained of all emotion and fell asleep.

After Sally had left, Jake sat with Logan and Lance. "We need to make sure that Gil hangs for what he did. I got the feeling Gifford will try to get him out of jail. When Gil hears Howard died, he knows he'll be hung for killing him and will do a lot of talking. I believe he'll try to spread the blame for what he did."

"What do you want us to do?" Logan asked.

"I think we need to lend the marshal some help until this is over," Jake said. "When Gil goes to trial, Gifford will try to keep him quiet. He may try to break him out or kill him. When we caught Gil, he said Duke was going to kill him then, so now they'll have to keep him quiet."

"What are you going to do about Gifford?" Lance asked.

"I ain't sure," Jake said. "Depends on what Gil says before he hangs. We know that Gifford is having his men steal cattle, and if we can prove it, we could get him hung as well."

"He's a smart one," Logan said. "It ain't going to be easy to prove that he is stealing the cattle."

"I know he's behind Pa's killing as well. We still haven't been able to find that Sharps rifle to prove it. If one of his men has it, it would tie him to the killings. First thing in the morning, I want one of you to go to town and watch the marshal's office. I'll be in later."

Lance and Logan went to the bunkhouse, leaving Jake to sit by himself. He heard a noise coming from the kitchen and got up to see who was there. Elizabeth turned around as Jake came in. "How come you're still up?" he asked.

"I wanted to finish cleaning up. Would you like some coffee and pie before you go to bed? The coffee is still hot."

"Thanks," Jake said. "I'll have some if you'll join me."

Elizabeth got them each a piece of pie before she poured two cups of coffee. She sat down and asked, "What's going to happen now?"

"I don't know. It all depends on what Gil has to say."

"My heart breaks for Sally. What do you think she'll do?"

"Half this ranch is hers," Jake said. "She'll stay here."

"Are you going to stay and help her?"

"I will. Are you thinking of leaving?"

"No," Elizabeth said. "I would only leave if Sally wanted me to go."

"I'm sure she'll need your help more now than before," Jake said. Looking straight at her, he added, "I wouldn't want to see you go either."

Hearing that, Elizabeth couldn't meet his eyes. She liked him, along with the rest of the family. They had all made her feel welcome. She had been doing some thinking about him too, but it was still too soon after losing her husband.

They chatted a while longer about the ranch and how best to help Sally during this difficult time. When they finished their coffee, they both got up, said goodnight, and went to their rooms.

◌

The next morning, Logan rode to town, and everywhere he looked it was quiet. As he rode by Gifford's office, it appeared that no one was there. He noticed that the street was empty like the town had been deserted.

He stopped at the marshal's office, where Shafer was sitting behind his desk, not looking too good. "Something wrong?" Logan asked.

"What do you want?" Marshal Shafer grunted.

"Jake figured that you could use some help keeping Gil in jail now that Howard died. He is still in jail, isn't he?"

"Yeah, he's in his cell. Doc came by and told me that Mr. Ashley died. Now what's Jake going to do?"

"He wants to make sure that Gil is tried and hung," Logan said.

"He told me he'd be going after Mr. Clemens too," the marshal said. "If he kills Clemens, he'll be hung for murder."

"Not if it's self-defense," Logan countered.

"Well, you can go back and tell Jake that I don't need his help," Marshal Shafer said.

"That ain't the way Jake sees it," Logan argued. "I think I'll stick around."

"Well, you ain't welcome to stay in my office. I suggest you get on out of here."

Outside, Logan went across the street to the mercantile. Finding a chair in front of the store, he sat down. Mr. Hanson saw Logan and came outside. "Sorry to hear about Mr. Ashley. Do you think Gil will hang?"

"Thanks. He is going to hang. Jake sent me to make sure that nothing happens to Gil. He thinks Clemens will try to get him out of jail."

While they were talking, they saw Marshal Shafer come out of his office and go to Gifford's law office. There, he found the door locked, so he went to the saloon and found Lew. "Go tell Mr. Clemens that Jake Burton has sent one of his men to make sure nothing happens to Gil before he hangs."

Logan continued to watch as Marshal Shafer left the saloon and went back to his office. Shortly after, he saw Lew come out and ride out of town. He looked up at Mr. Hanson and said, "Well, it won't be long now before Clemens knows that the marshal has help in keeping an eye on Gil."

"What do you mean?" Hanson asked.

"One of Gifford's men just rode out of town. The marshal must have told him that I was here to make sure Gil remains in jail."

"With Howard dead, when do you think they'll have the trial?"

"I don't know when the judge will be coming through," Logan said. "When he does, I hope he'll be able to get enough men for the jury who will go against Clemens and convict Gil."

"A lot of townspeople want to see Gil hang for killing Howard. He will as long as Clemens doesn't threaten those who are picked for the jury," Hanson said.

"Jake thinks Clemens was behind his pa's killing. Knowing what he does, he'll go after Clemens too."

"We're willing to help him any way we can," Mr. Hanson said as he turned to go back into his store.

Marshal Shafer sat at his desk and watched Logan. He saw him talking to Mr. Hanson and wondered what he told him. Clemens strongly suggested that Gil should escape. However, with Logan watching, Shafer wouldn't be able to let him escape without Jake Burton finding out. The only thing he could think of was to shoot Gil as he was trying to escape. He had told Lew to inform Clemens that Logan was watching the jail. With that being the case, trying to set up an escape where he could shoot Gil would be hard. He knew that Clemens was not going to be happy about the jail being watched, but he wasn't sure who would be worse to face: him or Burton.

For the first time since Clemens had given him the marshal's job, he wished that he had not taken it. When he started as marshal, it sounded simple. All he had to do was follow what Mr. Clemens wanted, and his men would do all the dirty work. Now knowing some of the things that Clemens's men had done, he could be in as much trouble as Gil just by association with them. How could he get out of this?

Lew rode into the Clemens ranch and was met by Duke. "I thought I told you to stay in town and make sure that the marshal let Gil escape."

"Burton sent one of his men in to watch the jail and make sure that Gil didn't get out," Lew told him.

"Who did he send?"

"Shafer said it was Logan, their foreman."

Going to the house, they found Gifford in the study. He looked up as they walked in and asked, "What are you doing here? Did Gil get away?"

"He ain't going anywhere," Lew said. "Burton sent his foreman in to watch the jail. He may be sending others to help him. Shafer looked scared. I don't think he's going to stand up to Burton and his men."

Gifford sat thinking, not saying a word. He finally said, "We need to find out when the judge is going to be here. Maybe we can get Gil released by the court. Do you know if the marshal has sent for him yet?"

"I don't think he has since he was going to let Gil escape," Duke said.

"Lew, I want you to go back to town and tell Marshal Shafer to send for the judge," Gifford ordered.

"Won't Gil hang for sure if he goes to trial?" Lew asked.

"Not if he doesn't make it to trial."

14

THE MARSHAL

WHEN LEW RODE INTO TOWN, he went directly to the jail. "What do you want?" Marshal Shafer asked when he entered his office.

"Mr. Clemens wants you to send for the judge."

"I thought he didn't want Gil going to trial."

"He changed his mind," Lew said.

"Why?" Marshal Shafer asked.

"He didn't say. All you need to know is he wants you to get the judge here for a trial."

"All right. I'll send for him."

Logan watched as Herman, who Marshal Shafer hired to take a letter to the Judge, went to the livery stable, got a horse, and went back into the marshal's office. He wondered if they were going to set up Gil's escape. When Herman came out, he was carrying a letter that he put in the saddlebag.

Logan crossed the street and stopped Herman before he could ride out. "Where does the marshal want you to take that letter?"

"I don't know if it's any of your concern," Herman said.

"If it concerns his prisoner, it concerns me."

"Well, I suppose it ain't gonna hurt nothing. He wants the letter to be delivered to the district judge in Durango."

"What's he asking the judge for?" Logan asked.

"He didn't say."

"Why didn't he send it on the stage?"

"I guess he's in a hurry," Herman replied.

Logan let him go and wondered why the marshal was in a hurry to get the letter to the judge. He was about to go back across the street when Marshal Shafer, who had been watching, came out of the office. "Logan, you got no right to bother Herman. He's on official business."

"Just making sure you don't do something to get yourself in trouble and that Gil remains in jail," Logan said.

"It ain't none of your business what I do as marshal. You and Jake Burton need to stay out of my way," Shafer growled.

"Seems strange that you're just notifying the judge about your prisoner seeing how he's been in your jail for a few days."

"I've been busy. What are you still doing in town? I think I told you that I don't need any of the Double B's help."

"Just following the boss's orders to make sure nothing happens to Gil before he hangs." Logan left the marshal and went back across the street.

It was the middle of the afternoon when Jake and Lance rode into town. They found Logan sitting in front of the mercantile.

"How are things going?" Jake asked.

"Things have been quiet," Logan said. "The marshal sent a letter to the judge in Durango this morning."

"Has Gifford Clemens been in town?" Lance asked.

"Nah, but he has been told that we're watching the jail. The marshal sent Lew out to tell him right after I stopped by his office."

"How did the marshal take the idea that we're watching him?" Lance asked.

"He got nervous and has been staying in his office."

"Anyone else been to see the marshal?" Jake asked.

"Lew returned and talked to him," Logan said. "I don't know what he was told, but right after Lew left, the marshal got Herman to go to Durango with a letter for the judge."

"Maybe they weren't going to ask the judge to come before we decided to make sure that Gil stayed put for his trial," Jake commented.

"Think Gifford had plans to let him escape?" Lance asked.

"That could have been their plan," Jake answered. "If so, we'll have to wait to see what they plan next."

"How long do you think it will take for the judge to get here?" Logan asked.

"At least a week," Jake replied.

"We ain't going to be able to watch the jail for a week sitting out here," Lance said.

"I'll go talk with Marshal Shafer." Jake walked over to the marshal's office. Shafer had just poured himself a cup of coffee and had his back to the door when it opened. When he saw Jake, he asked, "Now what the hell do you want?"

"Heard you sent for the judge."

"Yeah, I did. That ain't none of your concern."

"How come it took you this long to send for him?" Jake asked.

"What difference does it make?"

"Seems to me that you weren't in a hurry to have Gil's trial since it has been four days since I turned him over to you. If you had sent for the judge the following day, he would have been here soon. Now it will be at least another week before he can get here."

"Still ain't no concern of yours," Marshal Shafer said.

"What changed your mind about asking for the judge? Is Gifford Clemens planning on Gil escaping so there won't be a trial?"

The marshal's face turned red with anger. "Gil ain't going nowhere. So what difference does it make if I delayed asking for the judge?"

"I aim to see that Gil doesn't escape," Jake said. "My boys and I will ensure he stays here until the judge arrives with or without your permission."

"You ain't no deputy. You don't have any jurisdiction or authority here. If you or your men interfere, I will put you all in jail with Gil."

Jake said, "If something happens to Gil before he can go to trial, I will come after you and see you hang in his place."

"You can't threaten me. I am the law here."

"That is not a threat, Marshal. That is a promise."

Jake left the office and rejoined his men. "What did the marshal say?" Logan asked.

"He said we don't have any right to be here."

"What do you want us to do?" Lance asked.

"We're gonna keep watching the jail to make sure Gil doesn't escape," Jake said.

"We ain't gonna be able to stay here on the street," Lance restated.

"I'll talk to Mr. Hanson and see if we can use the room above the mercantile."

"What if the marshal lets him out the back door? We can't see the back of the jail from here," Logan said.

"I warned the marshal that if anything happens to Gil, I will come after him and make sure he hangs in Gil's place," Jake explained.

"What if Gifford gets Gil out? The marshal won't be able to stop him," Logan said.

"I don't think Marshal Shafer will hang around if something happens to Gil."

Jake went into the mercantile to look for Mr. Hanson and found him standing behind the counter. "Hi, Jake. What can I do for you?"

"I was wondering if you might let us use your room upstairs where we can keep an eye on the jail."

"How many men are you going to leave here?" Mr. Hanson asked.

"Logan and Lance. They can take turns watching the jail. I want to make sure nothing happens to Gil before the judge gets here."

"That would be fine with us. Tell them to come in."

After Jake had left his office, Marshal Shafer started pacing. He was worried about what Jake had said about him hanging in Gil's place if something happened. He tried to figure things out and just couldn't come up with any answers. So far, Gifford Clemens had been the only one to talk to Gil, but he had overheard Clemens telling Duke that he did not want Gil talking to a judge. What did he have planned for Gil? Was he going to have Duke kill him so he couldn't talk? If they killed Gil, Shafer knew that Jake Burton would hold him responsible. He needed to talk to Clemens and tell him that. Maybe he could take care of Burton as well.

Gil had heard Jake when he talked to the marshal. He could hear the marshal pacing nervously about the office now, and it got him thinking. When he saw how worried the marshal was, he thought that maybe he could put pressure on him to let him go. "Marshal," he called out.

"What do you want?"

"I heard what Jake Burton said to you," Gil told him.

"Yeah? What concern of it is yours?"

"If I go to trial, I'll tell the judge what I know."

"What do you know?" the marshal asked.

"I know that you've been helping Gifford steal cattle and run the ranchers out."

"That's a lie. I ain't had anything to do with rustling cattle."

"That isn't what I understand," Gil said. "You were along on some of those raids to keep the ranchers busy while their cattle were rustled."

"How do you know that?" Shafer asked.

"I'll tell Gifford that you were the one who told me. He'll want to keep you quiet as well."

"I didn't tell you anything."

"Gifford doesn't know that," Gil said with a smile.

"You ain't gonna be able to tell it to the judge. Clemens will stop you before you go to trial."

Gil thought about what the marshal said. "It may be too late."

"What do you mean?"

"You'll see what Burton does," Gil said, trying to bluff the marshal into believing that he had talked to Jake when they had caught him.

"What did you tell Burton?"

"If something happens to me, you'll find out."

The marshal went back to his desk, sat down, and began to worry about what Gil told Burton. If he told him about the cattle rustling, maybe what Burton said about him making sure he'd hang was true. Now he became very nervous. There had to be a way that he could get out of there without Clemens or Burton coming after him.

Jake rode into the Double B and put up his horse. Greg caught up with him on the way to the house. "Mr. Burton?"

"Hi, Greg. What can I do for you?"

"Mr. Burton, now that Mr. Ashley is gone, will Ma and I be allowed to stay here?" Greg asked.

"You're welcome to stay here as long as you like. My sister can use your mother's help, and Logan tells me you are becoming quite a cowboy."

"Thank you, Mr. Burton. I was afraid that we would have to leave." Relieved, Greg turned to go back to the barn.

Sally met Jake as he entered the house. "How are you doing?" he asked her.

"I miss Howard. The medicine the doctor left helps me get through the day. But every time I go by the room where Howard died, I start to cry."

"I'm glad to see the medicine is helping you some. We all miss Howard, and we'll miss him for a long time to come."

"Didn't you just return from town?"

"I went in to check on Lance and Logan," Jake replied. "They're watching the jail from the room above the mercantile."

"What's going on with Gil?"

"He's in jail, and Logan said that the marshal sent for the judge," he responded as they walked into the parlor. "He should be here in a week."

"Gil needs to hang for what he did. I hope the judge gets here soon and gets the trial over with so he can be hung," Sally said, sitting down.

"I hope you're right, but I think Clemens is up to something. He may try to get Gil out of jail."

"How long are you going to leave Logan and Lance watching the jail?" Sally asked.

"If I have to, I'll send some men in to replace them, but I want someone watching the jail until Gil is hung. The marshal isn't happy with me about them being there either. He wanted me to bring them back to the ranch. He seemed rather nervous when I talked to him."

"But you left them in town. What do the Hansons think about the men staying at the mercantile?"

"Mr. Hanson does not have a problem with the boys staying. I think he likes the idea of having the two of them there."

"Does the marshal know they're watching the jail?" Elizabeth asked as she walked into the room. "Sorry, I couldn't help but overhear."

"He knows. I told him that if anything happened to Gil before the trial, I would see to it that he is hung in his place," Jake said. "He now has me as well as Gifford to worry about."

Jake went to the den. With Howard gone, he would have to take over the books along with running the ranch. Logan could take care of the men, but Jake had to make the decisions about what to do to keep the ranch running and make sure there was money to pay the hands. While he sat and looked at the books, he wasn't sure if he was going to be able to figure them out. His pa took care of the books when he was alive, and then Howard took over. Maybe Sally would be able to help. He would have to talk to her.

He was still puzzling over the books when Elizabeth came in. "Supper's ready." When she saw the look on Jake's face, she said, "You look like you're having some trouble with those books."

"Thanks," Jake replied. "I don't think I understand them."

"Maybe I can help," she said. "I helped my pa before I got married."

"When you get a chance, maybe you can sit down with me and we can look at them," Jake suggested.

Lew rode back to the Clemens ranch and informed Gifford that Marshal Shafer had sent a letter to the judge. Gifford immediately started making plans about what he would do to keep Gil from talking. He sent for Duke and asked, "How much does Gil know about what happened to Randolph Burton and Marshal Owens?"

"I don't think he knows anything. I haven't talked to any of the men about it, and they don't know what my involvement was in their death."

"Are you sure they don't suspect something? Because the day you went after Marshal Owens, I overheard one of the men say he thought someone followed you," Gifford said.

"I hadn't heard that from the men. Did they say who?" Duke asked.

"They thought it was Gil but didn't know for sure. If he followed you, he might know that you killed Marshal Owens."

"Well, you just make sure that you haven't been doing any talking," Duke said. "If I get arrested for killing Marshal Owens and Randolph Burton, you're going to hang with me."

"Maybe if Gil followed you, he might've said something to the marshal, and that's why the marshal thinks he might have also talked to Burton."

"You need to find out what Gil told Burton. If he has men watching the jail, how are we going to get to Gil before the judge gets here?"

"I'm going into town in the morning. I'll talk to Gil again," Gifford said. "Maybe I can find out if he did follow you and what Burton knows."

The next morning, Gifford rode into town and went to his office before going to the jail. From his office window, he was unable to spot anyone watching the jail. *Maybe Burton doesn't have anyone watching.* Going to the jailhouse, he opened the door and found Marshal Shafer sitting at his desk eating. When Shafer saw him, he almost choked on his food.

"I want to see Gil," Gifford stated.

"He's in his cell."

"I need to talk to him alone."

The marshal didn't like Gifford's attitude but got up and left his food, knowing it was going to be cold when he got back. He led Gifford to Gil's cell and headed out the front door. He wanted to know what they talked about, so he went around the corner of the building, where he would be able to hear what was being said. If Gifford had a plan to get Gil out, he wanted to know what it was since he might be able to use it to get away as well.

Gil was still eating his breakfast when Gifford appeared. "Are you going to get me out of here?" he asked.

"I'll take care of you," Gifford said.

"How? You gotta get me out of here first."

"I have some questions I want you to answer," Gifford stated.

"What kind of questions?"

"I want to know where you were the day that Marshal Owen was killed."

"What difference does it make where I was?"

"If you want me to help you," Gifford said evenly, "you'll tell me what I want to know."

"If you don't get me out of here, I will tell Burton and the judge that you had Marshal Owen killed by Duke," Gil threatened.

"What makes you think that Duke killed Marshal Owen?"

"I followed him. I know where he hid the rifle he used."

"What did you tell Burton before you were brought in?" Gifford asked.

"I didn't tell him that you and Duke were involved in the killing, but if something happens to me, he'll be able to find out where that rifle is and who it belongs to."

"How?"

"I moved it to where he'll find it one of these days unless I get out of here and can move it again," Gil warned him.

"Tell me what you told Burton."

"Not until I'm out of here," Gil stated. "If he finds out that you were involved in killing his pa, he ain't gonna wait for a trial. He will kill you himself."

"How do I know that you'll do what you say if I get you out?" Gifford asked.

"You're just going to have to trust me. If I don't get out of here or get killed, Burton will be coming for you."

Disgusted with Gil, Gifford left the jail and returned to his office. Gil was not as dumb as he thought. If he gave Burton information about where to find Duke's rifle, it could tie the murder back to him and Duke, and he could be in danger of being hung as well. Gifford sat at his desk and stared out the window while several thoughts crossed his mind. *Where did Gil put the rifle that Burton could find it? Has Burton found it? Naw . . . if he had, he would have gone after Duke already. Maybe Gil is lying. But he does know that Duke owns a hidden rifle. How would he know that if he hadn't followed him?* He felt confused and didn't know what he would do.

Marshal Shafer had heard that Duke killed Marshal Owen. He knew if Gifford found out that he had listened to them talking, he would be killed as well. When he realized Gifford was getting ready to leave, he had hurried to the front of the jail and waited for him to come out. Gifford walked past him without saying a word.

With Gifford gone, Shafer went back into the office and sat down. While he finished his breakfast, he kept thinking about what Gil had told Gifford. The doctor's reports he had read said it looked like both Randolph Burton and Marshal Owen had been killed by the same gun. If Gil saw Duke kill the marshal, then he had to have killed Randolph Burton as well. Shafer thought that maybe he could get Gil to tell him where to find the rifle. If he could get his hands on the gun, it might be what he needed to save himself.

Believing that he found his salvation, Shafer finished eating and went back to Gil's cell. "What did Gifford want?" he asked.

"He's going to get me out of here, or he'll be hanging with me," Gil said smugly.

"How is he going to get you out?"

"He didn't say."

The marshal picked up the breakfast dishes and took them back to the café. When he returned to his office, he was relaxed, knowing that he now had a plan. He would be happy to wait for the judge to arrive. If Burton found the rifle, he wouldn't care if Gil escaped or got killed, and Burton could get Duke and Gifford as well.

Later, the marshal went to the saloon and found Kelly Peters, one of the local men who did work only long enough to buy whiskey. Shafer walked over to where he was sitting at a table, drinking. "I need you to ride out to the Double B Ranch. Can you do it?"

"What do you want me to go out there for?" Kelly asked.

"I want you to tell Jake Burton to come in and talk to me. Do you understand?"

"Yeah. I can go there for a dollar."

The marshal handed him a dollar and watched Kelly leave to make sure he didn't sit and drink it up before going. Kelly got his horse and rode out.

While the Marshal walked back to his office, he noticed Gifford was watching him through his front window. *So what?* he thought. *At least I have a plan to save myself.*

Clemens had seen Shafer go to the saloon. He didn't think anything about it until he saw him come out with Kelly. Watching Kelly ride out of town, Gifford wondered what the marshal was up to and where he sent Kelly.

Puzzled, Gifford went back to thinking about what he could do to Gil to keep him from talking. If he talked to the judge and the information got out that Gifford had something to do with killing Marshal Owen, they would know that he also had something to do with Randolph Burton's death. That could lead to him being hung with Gil. Now he would have to have Duke get Gil to tell him where his rifle was before he killed him. If he didn't find out where it was located, he might have to run and leave everything he had built behind like he had to when he left Denver.

Not coming up with any answers, he decided to leave town and rode back to his ranch. Duke saw him riding in and knew from the look on Gifford's face that something was on his mind. Gifford motioned for Duke to come to the house.

"What do you need?" Duke asked.

"Gil knows that you killed Marshal Owen."

"How does he know that?"

"The men were right; he followed you the day you killed the marshal. He saw where you hid the rifle you used and moved it. Have you checked lately to see if it's where you hid it?" Gifford asked.

"I ain't been out there since I killed Marshal Owen. I'll go see if the rifle is still there."

"Gil told me that Jake Burton would be able to find it and would know who it belongs to if we didn't get him out soon," Gifford said.

"I'll go check on it now. If it's not there, we need to get Gil out of jail and find out where he put it."

Duke left to get his horse. Riding about a mile from the ranch, he came to a small cave where he had hidden the rifle. Going inside, he started looking around and found it empty. He knew Gil had to be telling the truth.

He returned to the ranch and found Gifford still in the den. "Did you find it?"

"It's gone," Duke said. "Gil must have moved it."

"Tomorrow we'll go into town and get Gil out of jail. Once you get the rifle back, kill him."

"Do you think he talked to anyone else?" Duke asked.

"He only said that he talked to Burton. I thought he was lying, trying to force me to get him out of jail, but with the rifle missing, we have to believe that he talked to him. He also said that when Jake finds the rifle, he'll know who it belongs to."

❦

Following up on the marshal's message, Jake rode into town and tied his horse in front of the jail, which he entered and found empty. When he heard the front door open, he turned around as the marshal came in. "What do you want to talk to me about?"

"Gil has been doing a lot of talking lately," Marshal Shafer said. "I need to know what he has told you."

"Why don't you ask him? Why do you need to know what he told me?"

"If you are withholding evidence from me, I will arrest you."

"What he told me ain't got nothing to do with killing Howard," Jake said.

"If it ain't got nothing to do with killing Howard, then you can tell me."

"What he told me ain't gonna help you. When I get something that will, I'll let you know. Until then, just know this: you could be in as much trouble as Gil."

Jake got up and left the marshal without any of the information he had been looking for.

15

THE ESCAPE

THE NEXT MORNING, THE CLOUDS covering the sky made the dawn as dark as the mood Gifford was in, knowing that he could be in trouble. The only light he had was in the hope that it would rain, which would help his plan to get rid of Gil as soon as they found out where the rifle was hidden.

The temperature continued to drop as the wind picked up. Gifford and Duke rode to town, glad to see the streets deserted. There wouldn't be any witnesses around while they got Gil out of jail. Not seeing any of the men from the Double B Ranch Duke said, "It looks like the men watching the jail have left."

"You might be right," Gifford said. "They had been sitting out front of the mercantile, letting the marshal know they were still here. With them gone, that will make what we have to do easier."

The clouds opened, and the rain started just as they reached Gifford's office. "I'm glad it held off until we got inside," Duke said. "The rain will keep everyone indoors today. How do you plan to get Gil's horse from the livery?"

"Have him take mine," Gifford said. "After you kill Gil, let the horse loose, and it will go back to the ranch."

"Don't you think Burton will know you had something to do with the escape?"

"When you go to the jail, I'll make sure that I'm seen so Burton can't accuse me. They'll think Shafer let him go and that Gil just took the nearest horse to escape."

Standing by the window, Duke looked out. "It looks quiet at the marshal's office."

"When the marshal leaves, you go get Gil," Gifford said. "Just make sure you don't kill him until you get your rifle back."

Marshal Shafer looked out the window and saw the heavy gray clouds. He figured it would be a good day to stay inside.

While he stood watching, he had seen Gifford and Duke ride into town and figured they might have a plan to get Gil out. He put that thought aside and went to the stove, where he put on a pot of coffee. While he waited, he heard rain start pelting the roof. Cussing to himself that he hadn't gone to the café earlier, he knew he would have to go out in the rain now to get Gil's food. *Too bad it didn't hold off until I got back*, he thought.

Upstairs at the mercantile, Logan continued to watch the street while Lance slept. Lance woke up when he heard him move around and asked, "Anything going on?"

"Duke and Gifford just rode in," Logan reported.

Having to relieve himself, Lance went downstairs and out the back door. It had just started to rain when he left the building. When he returned, he said, "It's getting cold, and the wind is blowing. We could get some hail with this rain."

"Glad we don't have to be out in it. This kind of weather will keep people from moving about. Why don't you go get something to eat? I'll go when you get back," Logan suggested.

When Lance got to the café, he sat in the back. Two other men were sitting near the window, talking in low voices so Lance couldn't hear their conversation. When he finished eating, he returned to the mercantile to allow Logan to get something to eat.

The marshal was thinking about getting something to eat but didn't want to venture out in the rain. "Hey, how about some breakfast?" Gil hollered from the back.

"You'll get something to eat when I get good and ready to go get it," Marshal Shafer said.

"How about some coffee? I can smell it brewing."

The marshal poured him a cup and took it to the cell. Gil grumbled, "Thanks."

Shafer put on his slicker and said, "I'm going over to the café and will bring your breakfast back."

The rain beat against his face as he made his way to the café. He sat down and ordered his breakfast along with one for the prisoner.

The waitress brought Gil's meal when the marshal had finished eating. He opened the door, and the wind blew it out of his hand, almost knocking the tray of food to the floor. When he recovered, he walked out. The wind and rain beat on him as he made his way back to the jail, adding to the marshal's discomfort.

Duke stood by the window in Gifford's office, watching the jail and hoping to see the marshal leave so he could get Gil out. He couldn't see what was going on inside, so he didn't know what the marshal was doing. He could make out a shadow of someone as he moved around and figured that had to be Shafer. He became bored and looked around; finding a newspaper, he picked it up and started to read. The main article was about an Indian attack that had happened a few months back. Engrossed, he missed seeing the marshal head to the café. After Duke finished the article, he put the paper down and moved his chair closer to the window.

He looked up and down the street and found it still empty. "Do you think the marshal will go out?" he called.

"He's got to feed Gil," Gifford said. "He'll be going out soon."

It was almost an hour before the café door banged loudly enough to get Duke's attention. "Damn," he said.

"What's up?" Gifford asked.

"The marshal made it to the café without me seeing him. He's on his way back."

Gifford mumbled under his breath, upset that Duke had missed his chance.

"Why don't you just tell Shafer to let Gil go?" Duke asked.

"We need to make sure we're not connected with his escape. Gil has to be killed before he can tell the judge what he knows. If you don't get that rifle back before Burton finds it, we will both be hung."

Gil heard the door open and hoped it was the marshal returning with his food.

The marshal kept going over in his mind what he overheard Gil telling Gifford. If Gil knew who killed Randolph Burton and Marshal Owen, he might be able to get Gil to tell him. With that information, he could blackmail Gifford and get enough money to get out of the territory. Going back to Gil's cell, he said, "I overheard what you told Gifford."

"Huh?" Gil said.

"I said I overheard what you told Gifford about who killed Marshal Owen."

"What did you hear?"

"I heard you tell Gifford that you know where the rifle is that killed Marshal Owen. You also said if anything happens to you, Jake Burton would find it."

"What do you want?" Gil asked.

"If you tell me where to find the rifle, I can help you get out of here."

"What good is the rifle to you?"

"It could help me get out of here alive," Marshal Shafer replied.

"How do I know I can trust you?"

"You don't have a lot of choices; you're just gonna have to trust me."

"If I agree, you've got to get me out of here first. Then I'll take you to where I hid the rifle," Gil said with a scowl as he started to eat. He was afraid that the marshal was working with Gifford just to get the rifle and that he could be killed.

"If I let you out, how do I know that you'll lead me to it?" Shafer asked.

"I ain't gonna tell you where to find it while I'm still in here. You get us a couple of horses and let me out of here, and I'll take you to where I hid it."

The marshal went back to his desk and sat down. He would have to figure out how he was going to get their horses saddled and ready. If he went to the livery now, Bret, who ran it, would wonder what he wanted the horses for with the raining like it was. He couldn't tell him it was to let Gil out. Maybe he would wait until tonight. He could then go to the livery and get the horses after Bret had closed for the night.

At the same time, Gil kept thinking about what the marshal said. Several thoughts kept going through his mind. Is the marshal working with Gifford? Maybe he wasn't, and it would be Gil's best chance to get away. The rifle wasn't tied to the marshal, so why was he so interested in it? He would wait and see what Shafer would do.

Meanwhile, Gifford was worried about the weather. The marshal might stay in his office and not leave. Duke may have to kill him as well as Gil. Gifford couldn't risk the town finding out about what he had done.

After sitting there for three hours, he decided to go over to the jail. He got up and told Duke, "I'm going over to talk to Gil. If he knows that we're going to break him out, maybe he can get the marshal to leave long enough for us to do it."

He put on his hat and slicker to walk to the jail. Inside, he was surprised to find the marshal had fallen asleep at his desk. Shafer jerked awake at the sound of the door opening and saw Gifford. "What can I do for you?" he asked.

"I want to talk to Gil," Gifford said.

"I suppose you want me to leave again," the marshal said, knowing he would have to go out in the rain.

"I need to talk to him alone."

The marshal stood up and put on his slicker. Outside, he made his way around the building to listen to want they were saying.

Gifford waited until the marshal was gone before talking to Gil. "Have you come to get me out?" Gil asked when he saw who it was.

"I came to tell you what I need you to do."

"What can I do here in jail?"

"I need you to get the marshal to leave so I can have Duke let you out," Gifford said. "Once you're out, I need you to take Duke to his rifle."

"So you do believe that I have the rifle."

"Duke said it wasn't where he put it. If he couldn't find it, then you must have moved it, and we don't want Burton to find it."

"If I take Duke to his rifle, I'll need some money to get out of here," Gil said.

"What happened to the money I gave Duke to give to you?"

"I don't know. Maybe you need to ask Burton. He's the one who brought me in."

"All right. I'll make sure you get the money you need," Gifford said.

"How do I know that Duke won't kill me after he gets his rifle? When we were in Mesa Verde, I heard him tell Lew that he planned on killing me."

"I'll make sure Duke follows my orders not to kill you—that is unless you don't take him to the rifle."

"What do you suggest I do to get the marshal to leave?" Gil asked, not believing what Gifford said about not killing him.

"Act sick so he needs to get the doctor."

When Gifford turned to leave, Gil asked, "How will you know when the marshal leaves?"

"Duke is watching the jail from my office. We'll know when he leaves."

Gifford walked back to his office, and Duke said, "When the marshal came out, he went around the jail and hasn't come back yet."

"Keep watching and see where he comes from," Gifford said.

Overhearing what Gifford told Gil about Duke watching the jail, Shafer knew that Duke had to have seen him go behind the building. He had to make sure that they didn't know he was listening to what Gifford said. Keeping the jail between him and Gifford's office, he made his way to the stable. Inside, he found it was empty except for horses, so he saddled his and Gil's. Now when he let Gil out, all they had to do was make it to the livery without being seen.

The marshal walked up the main street, where Duke could see him, and then returned to his desk in the jailhouse. Duke saw him and told Gifford, "It looks like he went to the livery. He's coming up the street now."

Gil was sitting in his cell, waiting for the marshal to return. He knew that Shafer had probably listened to what Gifford said. Not being able to hear him move around, he called out, "Marshal, are you here?"

"What do you want?" Shafer asked.

"We need to talk."

The marshal got up and went to the cell. "Did you hear what Gifford said?" Gil asked.

"I heard."

"What are you going to do?"

"I have two horses saddled at the livery," the marshal told him.

"How are we going to get to them?"

"We can go out the back door and get to the livery without Duke seeing us."

"Are you sure we won't be seen?" Gil asked.

"I went there when Gifford left. I'm sure Duke couldn't see me until I came back."

"When are we going to leave?"

"Soon," the marshal said, turning to leave Gil. He knew that getting that rifle would put him on Duke and Gifford's good side.

Opening the safe, he took out the money Burton had given him when Gil was brought in. He picked up Gil's gun and the keys, opened the cell door, and let Gil out. He then opened the back door and looked out before exiting. Not seeing anyone, they made their way to the livery, where they took their horses out of the stalls, went out the back through a corral, and rode out of town.

Not only had Duke been watching, but Lance had been as well. He had seen Gifford go to the jail and the marshal go behind the building. From the mercantile, the jailhouse did not block the view of the livery, so when Gifford left, Lance had also seen the marshal make his way there. He woke Logan and said, "I think something is going on over at the jail."

"What do you mean?"

"Gifford went in, and when he left, the marshal went to the livery. Watch the jail while I go check it out."

Lance made his way to the livery and found that Bret wasn't around.

When he looked in the stalls, he found two saddled horses. One looked like the horse Gil was riding when they caught him. *Why are these horses saddled? Are they planning Gil's escape? But why would the marshal be going with him, or is the second horse for someone else?*

When Lance got back to the mercantile, Logan asked, "What did you find?"

"There are two saddled horses in the livery. One of them is Gil's, and I think the other belongs to the marshal."

"Do you think they're going to let Gil escape?"

"I can't think of any other reason for having those horses saddled," Lance said.

"Maybe one of us should stay here and watch the jail and the other go to the livery to watch the horses," Logan suggested.

"I'll go back to the livery. If you see the marshal leave with Gil, you know that's where they'll be heading."

"If I see them leave, I'll meet you there," Logan said.

A short while later, Logan saw the marshal and Gil make their way to the livery. He left the mercantile and arrived at the livery just as they were riding out of town. Inside, he found Lance busy saddling his horse. "They just rode east out of town," Logan said.

"We need to hurry so we don't lose them."

Gil rode in front of the marshal, knowing that he was going to have to take him to the rifle if he wanted to get away. As soon as Shafer had the gun, Gil was going to head to Santa Fe.

An hour after they left town, Gil turned south. Three miles later, he came to the cave where the rifle was hidden. When they entered, Gil found a torch and lit it. In the back of the cave lay the rifle wrapped in a blanket. Gil picked it up and handed it to the marshal.

Lance and Logan followed their trail. As the rain kept wiping out the tracks, they had to follow closer than they wanted to so they could spot them occasionally through the rain. Keeping just out of sight, they almost missed where the two turned south. If Lance hadn't been watching their tracks, they would have ridden right past it.

When the two were back in sight, Lance said, "I wonder where they're going."

"They must have a plan," Logan replied. "If the marshal was just going to let Gil escape, he would have stayed in town. Maybe Shafer decided to leave with him after Jake threatened that he would hang if Gil escaped."

The rain caused them to lose sight of the two again, so they were surprised when they came upon Gil and the marshal's horses tied near an opening of a cave. They tied their horses out of sight and waited. It wasn't long before they saw a light coming toward the entrance of the cave. Seeing the marshal coming out of the cave and carrying a rifle, Logan said, "I wonder if that's the rifle used to kill Randolph and Owen."

"Do you think Shafer and Gil were the ones who killed them?" Lance asked.

"We need to find out."

Stepping into the open with their guns drawn, Logan said, "Hold it, Marshal, and drop the rifle. Gil, you stay where we can see you."

Before they could be stopped, the marshal and Gil ducked back into the cave without dropping the rifle. Drawing their Colts while they moved, they fired. Lance and Logan fired back as the two men disappeared into the cave, taking cover. Logan knew it was going to be hard to get them out. He looked around and couldn't see anything that would offer him and Lance protection from the rain and still allow them to see the entrance of the cave. He pulled his slicker closer around him and waited.

"I thought you said we could get to the livery without being seen," Gil said inside the cave.

"I didn't know Burton still had men watching the jail," the marshal said. "I ain't seen them since yesterday."

"What are we going to do?"

"They're sitting in the rain. I don't think they'll sit there all day."

"Well, we ain't going anywhere with them out there," Gil said. "Maybe we can make a deal with them. Burton wants to know who killed his pa and Owen. We can tell him who owns this rifle."

"You killed Burton's brother-in-law," the marshal snapped. "He ain't gonna forget that."

"I ain't gonna stay in here. I ain't gonna hang."

Gil moved to the entrance of the cave and looked out. The rain was coming down hard, which made it difficult to see more than a few feet. Taking a chance, he made a break for his horse. Just as he reached it he heard, "Hold it, Gil."

Gil froze. Then he turned and fired in the direction the voice had come from. Lance had moved, and Gil's bullet went wild. Returning fire, Lance hit Gil in the chest.

Gil dropped his Colt and fell to the ground. Lance went over and found him still alive. "Did you and the marshal kill Randolph and Marshal Owen?"

Gil looked up at Lance. "No. It was Duke."

"Is that Duke's rifle the marshal has?"

Gil just nodded and then died.

Lance jumped as Logan came up behind him. Seeing Gil lying on the ground, Logan asked, "Did the marshal come out with him?"

"No," Lance said. "He's still in the cave. But Gil talked before he died."

"What did he say?"

"He said the rifle the marshal has belongs to Duke, who was the one who killed Randolph and Marshal Owen."

"We need to get that rifle," Logan said.

Marshal Shafer had heard the shots fired. He moved to the entrance of the cave and looked out to see what had happened, calling out, "Gil!" Not hearing a response, he wondered if he should try to make it to his horse. He hadn't heard Gil's horse leave, only the two gunshots.

Logan heard Shafer call Gil's name. "Marshal, come on out. Gil is dead."

Marshal Shafer came out of the cave, carrying the rifle. Lance was standing by Gil's horse, pointing his Colt at the marshal as he walked toward them. "Hand that rifle and those shells to Logan," he said.

"I'm keeping the rifle."

"I said to hand them over to Logan, or you can join Gil here."

Handing the gun and shells to Logan, Shafer asked, "Did Gil say anything before he died?"

"He said plenty," Logan replied.

"What are you going to do with the rifle?" Marshal Shafer asked.

"We're taking it to Jake Burton," Logan said. "He'll want to know who it belongs to."

"Why did you let Gil out of jail?" Lance asked.

"I needed that rifle as protection from Duke and Gifford. Gil said he would take me to where it was hidden, and if he didn't get it, Jake Burton would. Then he would find out who it belonged to," Marshal Shafer explained.

"What else do you know about the deaths of Randolph Burton and Marshal Owen?" Logan asked.

"I overheard Gil and Clemens talking about the rifle belonging to Duke and that he was the one who killed them."

"Well, he was right about Jake Burton wanting to find out who it belongs to," Lance said.

"What are you going to do to me?" Shafer asked.

"We ain't gonna do anything to you," Logan told him. "If I was you, I would leave the territory as fast as you can."

The marshal got on his horse, deciding to take that advice while he could. If he went back to town and Gifford found out Burton had the rifle, he would be killed. With the money he had, he would be able to start over somewhere else.

Lance and Logan watched Shafer ride away. "Do you think he'll go back to town?" Lance asked.

"Don't look like he's headed that way," Logan said. "We need to take this rifle back to the ranch."

Duke had continued to watch the jail. After two hours, he still hadn't seen the marshal leave. "Why hasn't Shafer gone for the doctor?"

"He should have by now," Gifford said. "Let's go check."

Getting up, they put their slickers on and went to the jail, where they found the office empty. In the back, they found the cell door open. Gifford was surprised that both Gil and the marshal were gone. "How the hell did they get out of here without you seeing them?"

"They must have gone out the back door," Duke said.

"Go check the livery and see if their horses are gone."

Duke went while Gifford returned to his office. At the livery, Duke found both Gil and the marshal's horses gone. He looked out back, but the rain had washed away any tracks. When he got back to Gifford's office, he told him what he found and asked, "What do you want to do?"

"We need to wait and talk to the marshal when he gets back," Gifford said.

"Do you think he will come back?"

"If he took Gil to get the rifle, he'll be back."

While he sat there, Gifford began to worry. He got up and started walking back and forth across the room, only stopping to look out the window, hoping to see the marshal. While he was pacing, he kept asking himself, *Why didn't Shafer tell me he was going to get Gil out? Does he know about the rifle? Did Gil tell him about it, or did he overhear me talking to Gil?* If Shafer had the rifle, Gifford reckoned he would have Duke kill him, and they could frame Jake Burton for it. By the time the marshal returned, he would know just what he was going to do.

16

THE RIFLE

LANCE AND LOGAN RODE INTO the Double B Ranch and went right to the barn to get out of the rain, which had not let up. They were soaked to the bone. Wanting to get into some dry clothes before going to the house, they put their horses up and went to the bunkhouse, which was empty.

"Where is everyone?" Lance asked.

"They might be up at the main house. I don't think Jake would have them out checking cattle today."

After changing their clothes, they went to the house and found everyone eating in the kitchen. Jake saw Logan carrying a rifle and asked, "What happened?"

"Marshal Shafer let Gil out of jail," Logan said.

"Did Gil get away?"

"No, he's dead," Lance stated.

"Who killed him?"

"I did," Lance said. "He tried to shoot me."

"What about Marshal Shafer?" Jake asked.

"We think he left the territory," Logan replied. "They had this rifle with them."

"What rifle is that?"

"This is the one that killed your pa and Marshal Owen," Lance said. "Gil told me about it before he died."

"Is it Gil's?" Sally asked.

"No, it belongs to Duke," Logan explained. "We believe the marshal didn't have anything to do with their deaths, so we let him go."

"Does Gifford know you got the rifle?" Jake asked.

"Not unless the marshal went back to town," Logan said. "What do you want to do now?"

"We need to see what Gifford does. If we can prove that this is the rifle that killed Pa and Marshal Owen, we can get Duke hung for the killings. We may even get Gifford arrested."

"Who do you think would arrest them?" Sally asked.

"We may have to go to Durango," Jake said. "If they won't do anything there, we'll have to take care of it ourselves."

By the end of the day, Gifford and Duke still didn't know what had happened to the marshal and Gil. Duke finally asked, "Do you think they both cleared out?"

"I don't know what the marshal would gain by letting Gil go. If Gil was able to get the drop on him, the marshal would have left him in the cell or dead. If they both left the territory and Burton finds the rifle, we might be able to say that the rifle belonged to Gil. There wouldn't be anyone in town or at the ranch who could say that it didn't."

They decided there was nothing more they could do, so they rode back to the Clemens ranch.

Jake was getting ready to go into town the next morning, when Sally asked, "Can I ride along with you? I need to get out of the house for a while."

"Yeah."

When they arrived, Jake stopped in front of the mercantile. Inside, he saw Mr. Hanson, who asked, "What happened to Lance and Logan? I saw they were gone yesterday."

"They followed the marshal out of town. Have you seen Shafer today?"

"Can't say that I have," Hanson said. "Did something happen to him?"

"That's what I came in to find out," Jake said. "Sally, while you're getting what you need, I'm going to the jail."

Jake left and found the door to the jailhouse open. Going in, he could tell that no one had been there that morning. The stove was cold, and there were food trays from the day before sitting on the marshal's desk. In the back, he found the cell door open and the cell empty. Satisfied that the marshal had not returned, he went back to the mercantile.

"Was the marshal there?" Sally asked.

"No. It looks like no one has been there since yesterday."

"I wonder what happened to him," Mr. Hanson added.

"Logan thinks he left the territory."

"Why would he do that?" Mrs. Hanson asked as she entered from the back.

"He let Gil out of jail yesterday, and they both rode out of town together."

"Unless someone goes after them, Gil will get away," Mrs. Hanson said.

"He won't get away," Sally stated. "Gil is dead."

"Have you seen Gifford?" Jake asked.

"He was in town all day yesterday," Mr. Hanson said. "I haven't seen him today."

Jake paid for their supplies and loaded them into the wagon. Before leaving the mercantile, he said to the Hansons, "You need to watch for Gifford. I don't know if he had anything to do with Gil escaping or not. There's no telling what he'll do when he learns that both the marshal and Gil are gone."

"We'll keep an eye on him," Mrs. Hanson promised.

As they were riding back to the ranch, Sally said, "I noticed that you didn't say anything about the rifle."

"I don't want them to know we have it," Jake said. "If Gifford finds out, he may not stay around long enough for us to prove he was involved with the killings. First, we have to prove it was the rifle that shot Pa and Marshal Owen."

"How are you going to do that?"

"I have to prove that the casing I found came from that rifle," Jake said. "If that is correct and I can prove that the rifle belongs to Duke, we'll have our killer."

"How are you going to prove that the casing came from the rifle?"

"I'm going to take it to the sheriff in Durango."

Gifford sat in his den and wondered what had happened to Marshal Shafer and Gil. A bigger concern was what had happened to Duke's rifle. *Did Gil get the rifle and leave with it, or did he give it to the marshal? Shafer should have returned last night.* He needed to know what was going on, so he called for Lew.

Lew arrived, and Gifford said, "I want you to go to town and find out if Marshal Shafer returned last night."

"What for?"

"He and Gil rode out of town yesterday, and I need to know if either or both of them came back."

Lew got his horse and rode to town. He stopped by the jail and found it empty. Looking inside, he determined that the marshal had not returned. Confused about what was happening, he went to the saloon. While he sat at a table and drank a beer, he overheard two men talking at the table near him. The first man said, "I heard that the marshal has one of Gifford's men in jail for killing Howard Ashley."

The second man said, "I was in the mercantile this morning, and Jake Burton and his sister were there. After they left, I overheard the Hansons talking about Gil being dead and the marshal leaving the territory."

"How did the Hansons know Gil was dead?"

"When I asked, they said that Sally Ashley said one of their men had shot him."

When Lew heard this, he decided to go to the mercantile and talk to the Hansons. He finished his beer and left. Once there, he found Mr. Hanson putting merchandise on the shelves and walked over to him.

Hanson turned around and asked, "Can I get something for you?"

"I heard that Jake Burton was in here this morning."

"Yes, he was. Did Gifford send you here to find out why he was here?"

"No," Lew said. "I heard some talk in the saloon that Burton said Gil had been killed and told you about it."

"He said that Gil had been shot," Hanson confirmed.

"Who shot him?"

"One of Jake's men."

"Does he know what happened to the marshal?" Lew asked.

"No, but he thinks he left the territory."

Lew thanked Mr. Hanson and left. He rode back to the ranch, where he found Gifford in the den at his desk. Duke was in a chair off to one side. When Lew entered, Gifford asked, "What did you find out?"

"Burton was in town this morning and told Mr. Hanson that Gil had been shot and the marshal left the territory."

"Did he say who shot Gil?" Duke asked.

"One of Burton's men."

"Did he say anything else?" Gifford prodded.

"No, just what I told you. I went by the jail and could see no one had been there during the night."

"I want you to go to Durango tomorrow and see if Jake sent someone to report to the sheriff what happened to Shafer or Gil," Gifford ordered. When Lew left, he said, "I wonder if Burton's men got the rifle before Gil was shot."

"Could be that the marshal has it," Duke replied.

"We need to find out where that rifle is."

"If Burton has it, I'm sure he'll be coming after us."

Jake needed to find out if the rifle was the one that killed his dad. Putting the shell casing he had found in his pocket, he wrapped the rifle in a blanket and headed for Durango.

Jake returned later that night. Stabling his horse and finding the house dark, he made his way to his room and went to bed. During breakfast the next morning, Sally asked, "What did you find out in Durango?"

"The sheriff said the casing came from the rifle."

"Is he going after Duke?" Logan asked.

"Mancos is out of his jurisdiction, and he can't do anything to help. He said to have the local marshal take care of it. I told him we didn't have a marshal, that he had disappeared."

"What are you going to do?" Lance asked.

"He said I should send a telegram to the army and request that they send someone," Jake explained. "I sent the telegram, and while we're waiting for word that the army is coming, I'm going to make sure Duke doesn't leave the country before they get here. Gil told Lance before he died that the rifle belonged to Duke, and I want to see him hung for it."

"Are you going to let Clemens know you have the rifle?" Elizabeth asked.

"Not yet," Jake said. "I want to get Duke alone to tell me who ordered him to kill Pa and Marshal Owen."

Lew rode into Durango and stopped at the saloon before going to see the sheriff. He had just stepped down from his horse when he saw Jake ride into town. Hidden behind his horse, he waited to see where Jake went. When he stopped in front of the jail, Lew moved to where he could watch him. He saw Jake take something wrapped in a blanket with him.

Jake entered the jail, and Lew moved to the side of the building, where he could see and hear what was going on. Jake unwrapped the bundle and took out the Sharps rifle. He explained to the sheriff that it belonged to Duke Sanders. Hearing that, Lew wondered why he had come to Durango. He saw Jake take something from his pocket and hand it to the sheriff. He watched as the sheriff took a look at the casing. Jake took a cartridge from his pocket and gave that to the sheriff, who put it in the rifle and then took it out. The sheriff then took the spent casing and compared them. When he finished looking at the two, he said, "The casing you found looks like it could have been fired from this rifle. There are similar marks on the side of the spent casing that match the one I just took out."

Lew heard Jake say that he believed the rifle was used to kill Randolph Burton and Marshal Owen. Lew knew that if Gifford had ordered Duke to kill the two men, he would be interested in knowing that Jake had Duke's rifle and that the sheriff told him there was nothing he could do because it was out of his jurisdiction.

It was late in the afternoon when Lew arrived at Clemens's ranch. Gifford was in the house, eating dinner. He saw Lew ride in and got up from the table to take him to the den. "What did you find out?"

"Jake Burton was there," Lew said.

"What was he doing there?"

"He had a rifle with him that he took to the sheriff."

"What kind of a rifle?" Gifford asked.

"I overheard him telling the sheriff that it was a Sharps Linen .52-caliber. Jake said it belonged to Duke."

"That's interesting," Gifford said. "Why did he take it to the sheriff in Durango?"

"He had a shell casing that he said he found where Randolph Burton and Marshal Owen were killed. The sheriff said that was the only Sharps he had seen since the war and the casing Jake found had been fired from that rifle."

"How did he figure the rifle belongs to Duke? Did he say how he got it?"

"No."

"What did he want the sheriff to do?"

"Arrest Duke," Lew said. "But the sheriff said it was out of his jurisdiction and couldn't do it."

"Did Jake say what he was going to do next?"

"No. It sounded like they were done, so I got out of there before he saw me."

"When you go to the bunkhouse, don't say anything about the rifle to anyone . . . including Duke," Gifford instructed. "If he asks, just tell him that the sheriff didn't know anything."

Lew left, confused why Gifford had said not to say anything about the rifle. If it was Duke's rifle, Gifford had to know that he shot Burton and Owen.

Back in the bunkhouse, Duke asked, "What did you find out in Durango?"

"Not much. The sheriff didn't know anything," Lew said as he went to get something to eat.

⚭

After Lew had left, Gifford thought to himself, *So Jake Burton has Duke's rifle. Now we know where it is.* He knew it wouldn't take long for people to figure out it was Duke who killed Randolph Burton and Marshal Owen. *Jake will think I'm involved with their deaths. I need to get rid of him.*

He went back to his meal and continued to think about what actions he was going to take. He would wait until morning and talk to Duke.

The next morning, Gifford called Duke to the house. When he walked in, Gifford said, "I know where your rifle is."

"Who has it?" Duke asked.

"Jake Burton."

"How did you find that out?"

"Lew overheard Burton talking to the sheriff in Durango."

"He told me that the sheriff didn't know anything," Duke said.

"I told him to say that so the rest of the men wouldn't know about the Sharps," Gifford explained. "We need to figure out how we're going to get it from Burton. If we kill him and don't get the rifle, we still have a problem."

"What about Marshal Shafer?" Duke asked.

"We don't have to worry about him. He won't be coming back."

"What will the sheriff from Durango do?"

"He won't get involved," Gifford said. "It's out of his jurisdiction. We need to find where Burton has the rifle and get rid of him."

"Why don't we take our men and raid their ranch?"

"He has too many men there. We need to get him when he's away from the ranch. Lew said he would come looking for you. You need to keep out of sight until we figure out where he has the rifle and how we can get it. I want you to ride up to the summer cabin and stay there until I find out what's going on."

17

HUNT FOR DUKE

AFTER BREAKFAST, JAKE SAT WITH Logan to work out a plan to capture Duke. "We need to find out if he is at Clemens's ranch. You and I will ride out there to watch the ranch, and I'll send Lance into town to see if Duke shows up at Gifford's office. We have to be careful that Gifford doesn't find out I sent word for the army, or he may try to get Duke out of town before they arrive."

"How are we going to get him if he's at the ranch?" Logan asked. "They will have most of their hands there to help him."

"I figure that he'll leave the ranch at some time, and we can grab him then."

"What are you going to do with him after you capture him?"

"We'll have to bring him here and hold him until the army arrives," Jake said.

Logan went to the barn to get their horses, while Jake went looking for Lance. He found Lance in the corral and called him over. "I want you to go into town and watch Gifford's office to see if Duke shows up. Don't tell anyone we have his rifle. Logan and I are going over to Clemens's ranch to see if he's there."

Lance left the horses he was working with and went to saddle his. By the time he finished, all three men were ready to leave. Lance left for town, while Jake and Logan rode to the Clemens ranch.

It took about two hours for Jake and Logan to get to the ranch and find a spot where they could watch the property without being seen. They had left the main trail and stayed out of sight until they found a place where they could see both the ranch and the main road. With field glasses, Jake settled down and scanned the buildings. Several men were working around the ranch, but none of them was Duke.

Early that morning, Duke had left for the summer cabin, while Gifford rode to town. He had wanted to go after Jake, but Gifford had told him to remain out of sight until they figured out what Jake was up to. It didn't take very long for Duke to reach the cabin, put his supplies inside, and take care of the horses. He walked around the area to make sure no one had been there recently. He decided that he would go out and check the surroundings every morning and evening. Back at the cabin, he settled down and waited.

Gifford wanted to remain near his office to give the impression that everything was all right. Although Jake didn't know that Gifford had found out about the Sharps rifle, he thought that Jake might get careless, and he would have his chance to get rid of him. He hoped that Jake would come into town to look for Duke. He had not mentioned to anyone that he had sent Duke to the cabin. Even the men at the ranch didn't know he left and wouldn't until Gifford returned from town without him.

Lance saw Gifford's horse tied at the hitching post in front of his office. He didn't find Duke's horse anywhere. He thought that if Duke had come to town with Gifford, his horse should be there too. *Maybe he'll show up later.* He decided to go to the jail to see if the marshal had come back. If the jail was still empty, he would watch Gifford's office from there.

Later that afternoon, Gifford left his office and rode out of town. Lance saw him leave and knew for sure that Duke was not going to show up. He mounted his horse and rode back to the ranch. When he stopped at the house, he found that Jake and Logan had not returned, so he asked at the bunkhouse if anyone had seen them. No one had seen them since they rode out that morning. Concerned they might have run into trouble, Lance called Pete and said, "Get a horse. We're going to look for Jake and Logan."

"Where?" Pete asked.

"They rode over to the Clemens ranch this morning to look for Duke. If they ran into trouble, they might need help."

While they were saddling their horses, they saw two men riding in. "That looks like them now," Pete said.

As the two rode up to them, Lance asked, "Did you see Duke?"

Jake said, "No. He wasn't at the ranch. I take it he didn't show up in town?"

"Gifford spent the day in his office, and no one else showed up," Lance said. "The jail was empty, so I decided to watch Gifford's office from there. I looked around the jail and found that the marshal hasn't returned either."

"If Duke wasn't at the ranch and didn't show up in town, I wonder where he is," Jake questioned. "Maybe Gifford sent him to find the marshal. If they think Gil told the marshal where to find the rifle, Duke would want to get it back."

Logan said, "While we watched their ranch, some of their men drove cattle in. We didn't get a chance to check their brands, and we don't think they belong to Gifford."

"Has anyone been out checking our stock?" Jake asked.

"One of the men is with the cattle," Logan replied. "I don't think they're taking any of ours."

Over the next week, Jake continued to send one of the men to town and one to the Clemens ranch to watch for Duke. By the end of the week, Duke had not shown up at either place. That evening while all the men were eating supper, he said, "Pete, I want you to go to town and stop by the saloon. Have a few drinks and then let it slip that I have Duke's rifle at the ranch. Maybe we can get Duke to come here."

The next morning, Sally called Pete to the house before he left. "Would you pick up some supplies while you're in town?" She handed him a list. "You're going to need to take the buckboard."

"Yes, Miss Sally."

When Pete got to town, he stopped at the mercantile and gave Mrs. Hanson the list. "I'm going over to the saloon and will come back for the supplies later."

In the saloon, he found men from the Clemens ranch. He ordered a whiskey and a beer at the bar. One of the men asked, "Don't you work for Jake Burton?"

"Yeah, I work for him. Why do you want to know?"

"Word is that one of Burton's men killed Gil and run the marshal off. Was that you?"

"No," Pete said. "I ain't been off the ranch for a month."

"Who done it then?" the ranch hand asked.

"Lance did, I guess. Word is that Gil tried to shoot him, but Lance shot him first. Mr. Burton wasn't too happy about it."

"Why wasn't Burton happy about Gil being killed?"

"He wanted to see Gil hang. He wanted to find out who killed his pa and thought that Gil knew."

"I guess he won't know now," the ranch hand said.

"Oh, he knows. He's got the rifle that belongs to Duke at the ranch. The sheriff in Durango said it was the same one that killed his pa."

"He has it at the ranch?" the ranch hand asked, surprised. "What's he going to do with it?"

"He wired the army and got word that they're coming. He wants to give it to them when they get here."

Pete finished his drink and went back to the mercantile. He watched the saloon from inside the store and saw the man he talked to leave and go to Gifford's office. It wasn't long before he saw Gifford and the other men ride out.

After he loaded the supplies, Pete drove back to the ranch. Jake saw him unloading the buckboard and asked, "Did you let it slip that I have the Sharps?"

"Yeah. Some of Gifford's men were in the saloon and asked me about Gil and the marshal. They became very interested when I said you had the rifle. I also let it slip that the army was coming. While I picked up the supplies, Gifford and his men rode out. What do you think they'll do now?"

"I'm not sure," Jake said. "But I'm sure they will do something."

"Do you think they'll come here and try to recover the rifle?"

"Knowing the army is coming, they'll want to get the rifle before they get here. Gifford may try to raid the ranch. We need to make sure there are plenty of men here to protect the women at all times."

Gifford rode back to his ranch. When he heard that the army was coming, he knew they had to get the rifle before they arrived. It was time to act. He sent Lew to the cabin to instruct Duke to return.

Duke met Lew and asked, "What brings you out here?"

"The boss wants you back at the ranch."

"What's going on?"

"He said that Burton sent for the army."

"Did Gifford say what he wanted me to do?"

"No, he just said I should come get you."

By the time Duke and Lew returned to the ranch, Gifford had called the men together. When the two walked into the house, he was laying out his plan. "We are going to raid the Double B Ranch."

"Why?" one of the men asked.

"We need to get a special Sharps rifle from them," Gifford replied.

"They have too many men there for us to just ride in and take it," another man said.

"Not all of you are going to the ranch. Most of you will be going after their cattle. Duke and I, along with six men, will go to the ranch to recover the rifle."

"If they're all at the ranch, how will they know we're after their cattle?" the first man asked.

"We'll make sure they know their cattle are being rustled. When they come to stop you from taking them, you'll scatter the herd and leave," Gifford explained. "After that, the rest of you scatter as well and ride back here. I don't want their cattle. I want their men away from the ranch while Duke and the rest of us go after the rifle."

"What's so important about that rifle?"

"It could cause all of us a lot of trouble with the army coming here."

"What does the army have to do with us?" the second man asked.

"They're coming to investigate the deaths of Randolph Burton and

Marshal Owens," Duke said. "If they get the rifle, it will end what we have here, and some of us could be hung for rustling."

"Tomorrow we go after Burton's cattle and that rifle," Gifford instructed.

The men got up to leave, talking among themselves. Duke and Lew remained with Gifford.

"When the men go after the cattle, eight of us will go after Burton. If he leaves with his men, we'll take his sister as well as the rifle. We'll make sure he comes after her alone," Gifford told them. "When he does, we'll kill him and his sister and take over the ranch."

"What about the army?" Duke asked.

"By the time they get here, there won't be any Burtons or Ashleys to have a reason for them to investigate. Without them and the rifle, they won't have any proof."

The next morning, Pete rode from the upper pasture to the Double B. "Our herd is being rustled," he shouted.

The men jumped up, leaving their food, and headed for their horses. Jake called to Logan and Lance. "Logan, I want you to go with the men and see what's going on. Lance, I want you to stay here with me. I don't like it that the herd is being rustled, but I think it might be Gifford's men trying to get us away from the ranch."

Logan rode with the men and left Jake and Lance at the ranch with the women. Gunfire erupted when they caught up with the rustlers who were moving the herd. As instructed, Gifford's men rode through the middle of the herd, scattered the cattle, and rode away. Logan saw what was going on and called the men. "Half of you round up the cattle and drive them back. The rest of you come with me; we're going back to the ranch."

Gifford and his men sat on their horses, overlooking the Double B Ranch, and waited. They watched as the ranch hands got their horses and quickly rode out. Once the men were far enough away, they took their rifles out and rode down to the house.

Jake was in the front room looking out the window in time to see them ride into the yard and recognized Gifford in the lead. He told the women to go upstairs and stay away from the windows. Lance went to the front door and waited. As the riders approached the front of the house with their rifles across their saddles, they spread out. Jake came out with his rifle in hand.

Gifford sent three of the men to the back of the house when he saw Jake come out. Lance saw the men ride around the house, so he went to the back as well. When they rode up, Lance saw that they already had their guns out, so he started shooting and knocked one of the men from his horse. The other two found cover in the trees behind the house before Lance could get a shot at them.

Jake heard the shot and took a quick shot at Gifford but missed as he ducked back inside. Gifford, Duke, and the rest of the men left their horses and spread out behind the corral and barn before they opened fire on the house.

As Jake worried that he and Lance may not be able to hold them off, he heard shots coming from the upstairs window. He remembered that Elizabeth had helped when they were attacked by the Indians, and he knew that his sister knew how to handle a rifle. Maybe the four of them could hold them off until the ranch hands returned.

Jake saw one of Gifford's men go down from a shot he knew had to be fired by one of the women. He saw where Gifford took cover and knew that Duke had to be near him. Trying to locate Duke, he almost got hit as glass shattered near his face. As the man who fired the shot stood up to get a better line of fire, Jake shot and hit him in the shoulder. Unable to hold his rifle, the man drew his Colt and returned fired.

Jake went back inside and moved to a different room in the house, where he tried to locate Duke to get a shot at him or Gifford. He was moving past a window when Duke took a shot at him and missed. As Jake opened a window, his Henry was knocked from his hands when Duke took a second shot. Jake saw the movement; taking out his Colt, he shot. He saw the man drop as another bullet hit the window near his head. Locating Duke, he took a shot at him. He thought he hit him but wasn't sure.

Sally had taken a rifle upstairs, and Elizabeth had her husband's rifle with her. Elizabeth was shooting from the front while Sally went to the other side to help Lance at the back of the house. Elizabeth spotted Duke and saw that he was wounded, but he was still able to hold his rifle. She fired and hit him in the leg, causing him to fall behind a water trough and out of sight. Thinking she had killed him, she started to shoot at some of the other men.

Lance had shot two of the men, and Sally shot at the third, causing him to duck. Hearing the increase in gunfire coming from the front of the house, Lance went to help Jake. Not knowing that Lance left, Sally went to help Elizabeth.

The man at the back of the house noticed he was not drawing fire and made his way to the back door. Before going in, he drew his Remington. He quietly opened the door and made his way through the kitchen. Though the doorway, he spotted Jake standing by a window with his back to him, aiming at Gifford. He fired and hit Jake in the back, driving him forward against the wall and onto the floor. At first, Jake didn't know what had hit him, and then he felt the pain. Lying there, he wanted to move but couldn't.

Lance heard the shot behind him. Turning, he saw a man in the doorway with his gun still smoking. He fired, killing him. When he saw Jake lying on the floor, he went to check how badly he was hurt. He found him alive, so he moved him against the wall.

Elizabeth saw some of the men rushing the house. Not waiting, she aimed and started firing. Sally saw what was happening and joined her. With the two of them putting up a resistance, they drove them back.

Logan and the men had gotten close enough that they could hear the gunshots coming from the ranch. As the house came into sight, they saw that it was under attack. Logan told the men to spread out as they moved in and opened fire on Gifford and his men.

Seeing the ranch hands returning, Gifford ran to his horse and rode out, leaving Duke and the rest of his men to fend for themselves. It wasn't long after he had deserted his men that they surrendered.

Lance came out of the house to help Logan, who asked, "Where's Jake?"

"In the house. He has been hit. Sally and Elizabeth are taking care of him."

Duke, who had been lying behind the water trough, started to crawl to his horse, when Richard, one of the Double B men, spotted him. Duke shot at Richard and hit him. Logan heard the gunfire and turned in time to see Richard fall as Duke made his way to his horse. Logan was not about to let Duke get away and went after him.

Duke pointed his gun at Logan and pulled the trigger, but the hammer fell on an empty chamber. He threw his gun at Logan and missed.

Logan grabbed him by the shirt and hit him in the face, causing Duke to fall to the ground. Lance held his Winchester on him while Logan dragged him to his feet. Some of the other men went to help Richard.

Logan said, "Carl, go to town and get the doctor. Lance, tie Duke up."

Shaking his head to clear it, Duke asked, "What about my leg?"

"If you're lucky, you'll bleed to death before you can be hung," Lance said, tying Duke's hands behind his back.

"Lance, take him to the house," Logan said. Pointing to a couple of the ranch hands, he added, "Take the rest of Clemens's men and tie them to a post in the barn."

Lance removed the neckerchief from Duke's neck and tied it around his leg to stop the bleeding. Half pushing and half dragging him, he took him to the house.

Inside, Sally and Elizabeth had put Jake on a bed, where they were tending to his wound. When they heard someone come in, Sally went to see who it was. Finding Logan and Lance with Duke, she went back to help Elizabeth.

"This bullet has to come out," Elizabeth said as Sally came back into the room. "Who came in?"

"Logan and Lance have Duke with them."

While they were talking, Logan came into the bedroom. "How's Jake?" he asked.

"We're going to need a doctor," Elizabeth said.

"I sent Carl to town to get him."

"Why did you bring Duke in the house?" Sally asked. "I want to see him dead."

"Jake has the army coming to take care of Duke. He wants to try to get Duke to tell him who gave the order to shoot your pa and Marshal Owen. If he tells us it was Gifford, he will hang as well."

❧

Gifford rode back to his ranch. Lew saw him and went over, asking, "Where are Duke and the rest of the men?"

"I believe they're dead," Gifford said.

"What happened?"

"Burton's men got back before we could get in the house. They had us pinned down. I was lucky to get out of there."

"You're sure the rest of the men are dead?" Lew asked.

"I saw Duke go down, and the rest were out in the open when Logan and his men rode in. When I rode out, I saw that two of the men who had gone to the back of the house were dead. I think Jake is dead as well. I saw him go down when someone shot him from inside the house. That was right before Logan showed up."

"What about the rifle?" Lew asked.

"If Duke and Jake are dead, we won't have to worry about the rifle. If the army comes and asks what happened, I'll just tell them Duke must have taken some of the men to go after Jake."

"I'll let the rest of the men know," Lew said and left to go to the bunk-house.

Sally was outside on the porch when the doctor arrived. She led him to the bedroom, where he took a look at Jake. "That bullet has to come out. Can you help me?" he asked, looking at Elizabeth and Sally.

"I can," Elizabeth said.

"Sally, can you get us some hot water?" he asked.

Sally went to the kitchen and put water on the stove, while the doctor and Elizabeth got Jake ready for the surgery to remove the bullet.

Jake was awake when the doctor started probing for the bullet. Biting on a piece of rawhide, he passed out from the pain. Elizabeth watched to make sure that he kept breathing. Sally saw what the doctor was doing, felt faint, and had to leave the room.

When the doctor finished, he told Sally that the bullet had not hit any vital organs and that Jake should recover quickly.

Two hours after the doctor removed the bullet, Jake woke up. Elizabeth was sitting by the side of the bed, watching him, when he opened his eyes. He tried to smile, but his face paled as pain shot through his back.

"What did the doctor say?" Jake whispered.

"He said you're going to be okay. Lance wants to see you. Can he come in?"

"Yes." When Lance came in and sat down, Jake asked, "What happened after I got shot?"

"Logan rode in with some of the men and captured those we hadn't killed. Two of them are tied up in the barn. Duke was shot in the leg and is being looked at by the doctor. Doc thinks he may lose his leg, but Duke doesn't want him to take it off."

"What about Gifford?" Jake asked.

"Gifford got away. Do you want us to go after him?"

"No, the army should be here soon. They can take care of him."

Elizabeth looked at Lance and said, "You need to let him rest. Now, out you go. You can talk to him later."

Leaving some of the ranch hands with Lance to guard Gifford's men and to bury the dead, Logan took the others to help round up the scattered cattle. By the time they got back to the herd, most of the cattle had been gathered. They drove them back to the pasture and returned to the ranch.

Sally was in the kitchen, preparing supper, when they returned. When she heard them ride in, she went to get Elizabeth to help her.

As the men got closer, they saw the damage to the house. When they sat down to eat, Pete was the first to ask where Jake was. Lance told him that Jake had been shot and was resting in the other room.

"Will he be all right?" Pete asked.

"The doc said he'll recover." By the time they finished eating, Lance had told them the full story about what happened.

Three days later, Logan went to town to find out if Gifford was still around. Jake had told him not to say anything about them holding Duke and the men as prisoners.

Logan entered the saloon and ordered a beer. While he was standing at the bar, the barkeep asked, "Don't you work at the Double B Ranch?"

"Yeah, I work there. Why are you asking?"

"Word around here is that Jake Burton was killed in a raid a few days ago. It's been said that Duke was killed during the raid as well. He had taken some of Mr. Clemens's men with him, and they were all killed. Clemens claims he didn't know anything about the raid or why Duke wanted to attack the Double B. He was sorry to hear that Jake was killed and wondered if Mrs. Ashley would consider selling the ranch."

"I don't know if she would sell or not," Logan said.

"Mr. Clemens said he'd buy it if she wanted to sell it."

Logan finished his beer and rode back to the ranch. He found Jake sitting on the front porch as he rode up to the house. Dismounting, he joined Jake and said, "You look good for a dead man."

"What are you talking about?" Jake asked.

"Gifford has been spreading the word around town that you were killed by Duke. He believes Duke is dead as well and wants to know if Mrs. Ashley wants to sell the ranch."

"He's going to be surprised when he finds out that Duke and I are still alive," Jake said.

"When do you want him to find out?" Logan asked.

"Not until the army arrives."

18

THE HANGING

THE ARMY ARRIVED IN TOWN two days later. When they rode in, they stopped in front of the empty jail and noticed that it had not been used for some time. When Captain Ward looked across the street, he saw the law office of Gifford Clemens. Hoping to get some information, he entered the office and found Gifford at his desk. "Sir, do you know where I might find a Mr. Jake Burton?"

"I heard he was killed," Gifford said.

"When did this happen?" Captain Ward asked.

"A few days ago. His ranch was raided by outlaws, and he was killed. His sister, Mrs. Ashley, is still at the ranch if you want to ride out there."

"Where is the ranch?"

"It's about four miles northeast of town," Gifford said. "Head east to the first road that goes north; it will take you right there. It's called the Double B. Tell Mrs. Ashley that I'll be coming out to see her soon."

Captain Ward thanked Gifford and left.

Logan saw the captain and his troops as they approached the ranch. At the house, he found Jake talking to Sally and told them that the army was riding in. When the soldiers rode into the yard, Jake, Sally, and Logan were standing on the porch, waiting for them.

"My name is Captain Ward, ma'am. Are you Mrs. Ashley?"

"Yes, I am," Sally said. "But I think you're here to see my brother, Jake. This is him."

"Mr. Burton?" Captain Ward said, surprised to find Jake alive. "I just heard in town that you were dead."

"Yes, sir," Jake said. "I heard that was what was being said, and I didn't want the truth known until you got here."

"I'm glad you're alive," Captain Ward said. "You are the one we were told to see."

"Step down, Captain, and tell the men to do the same. They can relax while we talk. Would you join me in the house?"

"Sergeant O'Hare, have the men take care of their mounts, and then you join us in the house as well," the captain said.

Jake took them into the den and offered them a seat, introducing the captain and sergeant to Logan. Then he began telling the captain why he had sent for the army. "After Gifford Clemens came to the Mancos Valley, several of the ranchers were run out. Their cattle had been rustled to the point where they were forced to sell their ranches. We found out that Clemens had taken cattle from us and sold them to the miners in Animas Forks."

"If he's stealing cattle, why doesn't the local law take care of him?" Captain Ward asked.

"Marshal Owen was investigating it, along with the killing of my father, when he was killed. Clemens appointed Marshal Shafer, who also worked for him."

"When we stopped in town, we didn't find the marshal," Ward said. "Do you know where he is?"

"Word is he left the territory." Jake took out the casing he had and handed it to Captain Ward. "I found this casing where my pa and Marshal Owen were killed."

Captain Ward looked at it and handed it to Sergeant O'Hare, who said, "I ain't seen one of these since the war. You said you found it where your father and the marshal were killed?"

"Yes," Jake said.

"Do you know who owns the Sharps that fired it?" the sergeant asked.

"Yes. Duke Sanders. I have the rifle." Jake got up, went to the other room, and returned with the Sharps. He handed it to Captain Ward. "It was confirmed by the sheriff in Durango that this is the rifle that the bullet was fired from."

"How did you get it?" Captain Ward asked.

"Our man Lance took it from one of Clemens's men."

"Can we talk to Lance?" Sergeant O'Hare asked.

Jake turned to Logan and asked him to go find Lance. While Logan was gone, Jake said, "I found this Concho where Marshal Owen was killed. I don't know if it belonged to the marshal or whoever shot him."

The captain took it and looked it over. "I haven't seen one like this before. Let me keep it for now."

When Logan returned to the den with Lance, Captain Ward asked, "Do you know who the Sharps belongs to?"

"Gil, a man who worked for Mr. Clemens, told me it belongs to Duke Sanders," Lance said.

"Can you tell us how you got this rifle?"

"Gil was in jail for killing Mrs. Ashley's husband. Jake had me and Logan watch the jail from the mercantile when we saw Marshal Shafer leave with Gil. We followed them to a cave, where they recovered the rifle. When we tried to stop them, Gil tried to get away. He shot at me, and I shot back, hitting him. Before he died, he told me that the Sharps belonged to Duke."

"You said that Gil was in jail for killing Mrs. Ashley's husband?" Captain Ward repeated.

"Yes, he killed my brother-in-law, Howard Ashley, and was in jail waiting to be tried," Jake said. "He said that he was going to talk, and we believe he was going to name Gifford Clemens and tell us what he was involved in. When we caught him, he told me some of the things he wanted to tell the judge."

"If what you say is true, Duke Sanders will be arrested, and if Mr. Clemens is involved, he'll be arrested as well. Do you know where we can find this Duke Sanders?" the captain asked.

"I have Duke and two of the men who raided our ranch. We captured them when they were trying to steal the rifle back," Jake said.

"Where are they now?" Sergeant O'Hare asked.

"Tied up in the barn."

"We'll take them to town, where there's a jail," Captain Ward ordered. "Will you and your men be willing to testify at a trial?"

"We'll be there," Jake said.

The men got up and walked over to the barn.

Duke had heard the horses when the army rode in and some of the men talking, and he thought it was Gifford. But when the barn door opened and the soldiers entered, he knew the army had arrived.

Captain Ward looked around and saw the three men sitting on the floor, tied to posts. Walking over, he asked, "Are you Duke Sanders?"

"Yes," Duke replied.

"You are under arrest for the murders of Randolph Burton and Marshal Owen."

Duke sat there, not saying a word. He knew he was going to go to jail but hoped that Gifford would be able to get him out.

"Sergeant O'Hare, put these men on their horses so we can take them to town," Captain Ward ordered.

"Captain, if you wouldn't mind, I'd like to ride along with you," Jake said. "I understand that Clemens thinks Duke and I are dead. I'm not sure what he'll do when he finds out we're still alive."

"Are you going to be able to ride?" the captain asked. "I noticed your back is hurt."

"I should be able to make it. I was shot, but there's no infection, and it has been healing."

"All right, you can ride along."

Lance and Logan thought they should ride with Jake since he hadn't fully recovered from his wound. "What do you think Gifford is going to do when he finds out that you and Duke are still alive?" Logan asked.

"He may try to leave town," Jake answered.

Gifford was at his desk when the soldiers rode into town. He couldn't see who they had with them, but he did notice that some of the men were not soldiers. *Maybe some of the men from the ranch rode in with them,* he thought. When they stopped in front of the jail, the first one he recognized was his man Larry. When he spotted Joe, he was surprised that they were still alive. He figured that they had been killed when Logan arrived with some of the ranch hands.

At the window, he saw that Duke was also with them. *If the army arrested Duke, they must have the Sharps rifle as well. But maybe they won't be able to connect me to the killings unless Duke talks.* Clemens thought if Duke didn't talk and Jake Burton was dead, he could still get the Double B Ranch. When they stopped in front of the jail, Captain Ward said, "Sergeant, take these three men in and lock them up."

The captain wanted to talk to Clemens. He did not have enough proof to arrest him, but he hoped to find out more by talking to him. He went across the street to Gifford's office, only to find it locked. He would have to go out to the Clemens ranch to talk to him, but since it was late in the afternoon, he decided to wait until morning.

When Gifford had seen the captain headed toward his office, he hurried out the back door and made his way to the livery, where he got a horse and rode back to his ranch. Now that he knew Duke was still alive, he needed to find out what he had told the army. He figured Captain Ward must know he was involved in the raid, or he wouldn't be coming to his office. Joe and Larry were involved with the rustling and had also been at the raid, and they knew Gifford had been there as well. Had they said anything to the captain? With the three of them in jail and the army guarding them, Gifford knew he was not going to be able to get to them. In the morning, he would find out how much the army knew.

The next morning, Gifford rode into town and entered his office from the back. He opened the shade, looked out the window, and saw very little movement around the jail. He unlocked the front door and sat at his desk, waiting.

One of the soldiers saw Gifford in his office and told the captain that he was in town. Captain Ward walked over and said, "Mr. Clemens, I would like to have a word with you."

"Captain," Gifford greeted him. "What can I do for you?"

"I have some of your men in jail for raiding the Double B Ranch. I would like to know what you know about it."

"I'm afraid I don't know anything about it," Gifford said. "But as their lawyer, I would like to talk to them."

"When you get a chance, come over to the jail, and you can talk to them." Captain Ward got up to leave.

⊱⊰

Jake had gotten up that morning with a fever. When he went to the kitchen, Elizabeth saw that he looked flushed and asked, "Are you feeling all right?"

"My back feels a little warm."

"Let me take a look at it. You should have stayed home and not rode into town yesterday. You may have irritated it."

Lifting his shirt, she found that his wound looked red and felt warm. "I think it's infected. I'll get some medicine to help draw the infection out." She left and soon returned to the kitchen, where she applied medicine and put a clean bandage on it.

"That should help," Elizabeth said with a forced smile. She was worried because it had been long enough for the wound to heal and there shouldn't have been any infection. She would check it again later.

That afternoon, Private Anderson rode out to the ranch. Sally led him to the den, where Jake was resting. "What can I do for you?" Jake asked.

"Captain Ward said he'll be holding the trial in the morning and requests that you and your men be there."

"Where is he holding it?" Jake asked.

"In the saloon," Private Anderson replied.

"You can tell the captain we'll be there."

After Private Anderson left, Jake went to the barn to inform Logan and Lance. Elizabeth saw him coming back to the house and said, "I want to look at your back."

"It's all right," Jake assured her.

"I still want to look at it," she insisted. "I don't want the infection to get worse or anything else to happen to you."

Her last statement took Jake by surprise. As he looked at her, he could see the warmth and concern in her eyes, and that affected him. He looked at her in a new light, thinking, *She is a fine-looking woman.* Perhaps someday she would be that someone special who he could spend the rest of his life with. Maybe he would talk to Sally, who had gotten close to her, and she would tell him how Elizabeth felt.

The next morning, Elizabeth checked the wound and saw that the redness seemed to be clearing up. She put more medicine and a fresh bandage on it before he went into town.

Sally told Jake she wanted to go to town as well. She was curious about what would happen at the trial. She also said that Elizabeth was going to come because they had been involved when the ranch was raided.

After hitching the horses to the buckboard, they drove to town with Logan and Lance following. Several horses were already tied in front of the saloon. When Jake stopped, he helped the ladies down and told them to wait while he took the buckboard to the livery. When they entered the saloon, Jake saw that the tables had been moved and chairs set up to allow people to face a table located near the back of the room. That table was where the captain would oversee the trial, and there were three chairs behind it.

Several people were already waiting when they entered. Men were standing at the bar and drinking, so Jake led the ladies to the far side of the room and found chairs where the five of them could sit and wait for the trial to start.

At the jail, Captain Ward went to check on the prisoners. Duke was standing in his cell with a nervous look on his face. The captain saw that he had something in his hand that he kept rubbing. "What do you have there?" he asked.

Duke looked at him and opened his hand. The captain saw the Concho he was holding and recognized it as being like the one Jake had found. Taking it from Duke, he laid it beside the one he had received from Jake and found them to be the same. He figured that Duke had to have been at the location where the two men had been killed.

"Get the prisoners ready to go to trial," Captain Ward ordered his men.

The captain entered the saloon, escorted by Sergeant O'Hare and Private Anderson, and they went to the back of the room. Sergeant O'Hare was carrying the Sharps and laid it on the table in front of them. The three men sat down. Behind them, the three prisoners were escorted in by two privates, who made them sit to the right of the table, where they could be guarded.

Captain Ward took out his army Colt and used the butt to bang on the table. When he had everybody's attention, he said, "The bar is closed. I want to see all glasses off the bar, and there will be no more drinking while this trial is going on."

He waited until the bar was cleared and the glasses removed. "Ladies and gentlemen, with no law enforcement present here, the US Army is now in charge. This trial is being conducted under martial law. That means I'm the governing factor in this trial. It is made up of the board you see in front of you, and our decision is the law."

He waited until everyone absorbed what he had just said. Looking toward the prisoners, he stated, "I need the three of you to stand." Once they were on their feet, he continued. "You are being charged with the murders of Mr. Randolph Burton and Marshal Owen."

Larry quickly said, "We don't know anything about no murders. We were ordered to help Duke get a rifle from the Double B Ranch."

"You work for Gifford Clemens, don't you?" Captain Ward asked.

"Yeah, we work for Clemens," Joe said.

"Did he order you to go after the rifle?"

The three men did not say anything.

"Is Gifford Clemens in the room?" Captain Ward asked.

Gifford had entered the saloon from the back door without being seen and made his way to a dark corner in the back of the room. He wanted to be out of sight, where he could watch and hear what was said; if need be, he was close enough to the back door so he could leave. He heard Larry tell the captain that he had been ordered to go to the Burton ranch to get the rifle. When he heard Captain Ward ask if he was in the saloon, he didn't wait around.

One of the men standing near the back of the saloon pointed toward the back door. "He was just here. I saw him standing over there." Everyone looked to where he pointed.

Hurrying back to his office, Clemens made sure that no one was watching him. The streets were empty as everyone was in the saloon watching the trial. After opening his safe, he cleaned out the money he had in there, knowing he was going to have to get out of the territory. Then he got his horse and rode back to his ranch, where he took more money out of the safe there. After grabbing his clothes, he rode out.

Not seeing Clemens after having his men take a look around the saloon, Captain Ward went on. "Was Mr. Clemens with you on the raid of the Double B Ranch?"

Joe said, "He was there."

"How come he wasn't caught with you?" Sergeant O'Hare asked.

"We saw him ride out when Logan and his men rode in."

"Did Mr. Clemens tell you why he wanted Duke to recover this Sharps rifle?" Captain Ward asked, pointing to it on the table in front of him.

"He just told us to come with them," Joe said.

Larry added, "I overheard talk in the bunkhouse about a Sharps Linen .52 rifle that belonged to Duke. I ain't never seen one till you brung it."

"Did you hear that the two men mentioned in this trial had been killed?" Captain Ward asked.

"I heard talk that Marshal Owen had been killed," Larry said. "I don't know who did the killing."

"If you had nothing to do with the killings, why did you go on the raid?" Captain Ward persisted.

"We worked for Mr. Clemens, and he ordered us to go," Larry simply said.

"You two can sit down." Turning to Duke, the captain said, "Duke Sanders, you are charged with the murders of Randolph Burton and Marshal Owen."

"I don't know what you're talking about," Duke protested.

Captain Ward picked up the evidence. "Is this your Sharps rifle?"

"No. I ain't seen it before."

"There are two men here who are willing to testify that you are the owner of this Sharps rifle," Captain Ward stated. "If you look under the wrap on the butt of the rifle, you will find the initials DS."

Duke said, "Lots of men have Sharps rifles."

"Not like this one that was used during the war by snipers. We also have evidence that it was used in the killings of Randolph Burton and Marshal Owen. Did you kill them?"

"I ain't killed no one," Duke said.

"Do you work for Mr. Gifford Clemens?"

"I don't know a Gifford Clemens."

"How come these two said they work for Mr. Clemens and were ordered to go with you to recover this rifle? Do you deny that Mr. Clemens was with you when you raided the Double B Ranch?" Captain Ward asked.

Duke stood looking nervous, not saying a word.

"I have four people who saw Mr. Clemens with you when you raided the ranch. Did he order you to kill Randolph Burton and Marshal Owen?"

"I didn't kill nobody," Duke repeated.

"We already know that this is the rifle that killed the two men and you are the owner," Captain Ward asserted.

"I didn't kill nobody," Duke said again.

"Are you telling us that someone else used your rifle to kill them?"

Again, Duke stood there not saying a word.

"Mr. Sanders, is this your Concho?" Captain Ward held up the Concho Jake had given him.

"Yes," Duke said. "You took it from me this morning."

"How about this one?" The captain held up the one he had taken from Duke.

Duke stood with a nervous look on his face, not answering.

"Sit down, Mr. Sanders," Captain Ward said. "Jake Burton, are you in the room?"

Jake stood up. "I am."

"Would you tell us what you know?"

Jake walked up to the table and stood looking at the panel.

"Do you know who the rifle belongs to?" Captain Ward asked.

"It belongs to Duke Sanders."

"How do you know this?"

"One of my men recovered the rifle from Gil after he escaped from jail," Jake said.

"Why was Gil in jail?" Captain Ward asked.

"He was awaiting trial for killing my brother-in-law, Howard Ashley. When Lance and I captured Gil in Mesa Verde, he told us that Gifford Clemens had been driving ranchers out of the area. Knowing that he was going to be hung for killing Howard, he said he wasn't going to hang by himself."

"Did Gil shoot Randolph Burton and Marshal Owen?" Private Anderson asked.

"I don't think so," Jake said. "I'm sure if he had been the one to shoot my pa, Duke and the others would not have tried to get the Sharps from my ranch."

"Did you see who rode into the ranch that day? Is there anyone else at your ranch who saw who rode in with these men?" Captain Ward asked.

"I saw Gifford Clemens ride in with these men. Lance, my sister, and Elizabeth saw them as well," Jake said, pointing at the three prisoners. "There were five others killed during the raid."

"Thank you, Mr. Burton. You can sit down," Captain Ward said. "Is Lance here?"

"I am, sir," Lance said, standing up.

"I understand you are the one who spoke to this Gil and took the Sharps from him. Tell us what happened that day and why you were following Gil and the marshal."

"Mr. Burton wanted us to watch the jail to make sure that Gil did not get away and would stand trial. When I saw the marshal and Gil leave the jail, Logan and I followed them to see where they were headed. We followed them quite a while before they stopped. They went into a cave, and we waited. They came out carrying that rifle. When we called them, that is when they started shooting. It was raining heavy, making it hard to see when Gil tried to get away. I caught him trying to get on his horse. When I called him, he shot at me, and that's when I shot him. Before he died, he told me the Sharps belonged to Duke and that he saw Duke shoot Owen."

"What happened to the marshal?" Captain Ward asked.

"Shafer had done nothing except let Gil out of jail, so we let him go," Lance explained. "Before he left, he said that he had overheard Mr. Clemens and Gil talking in the jail about the Sharps rifle and the shooting. He heard Gil say that he had followed Duke the day Marshal Owen was shot. He saw Duke hide the rifle, so he took it and hid it where Duke couldn't find it."

"Thank you, Lance," Captain Ward said. "That will be all."

Lance sat back down while the three men at the table talked together. When they finished conferring, Captain Ward pointed to Joe and Larry. "You two are guilty of raiding the Double B Ranch and will go to jail for five years. Duke Sanders, we find you guilty of the murders of Randolph Burton and Marshal Owen. In three days, you will be hung by the neck until dead. Men, take the prisoners back to jail. When we capture Gifford Clemens, he will be tried and hung as well for ordering the murders of Burton and Owen. This court is adjourned."

Elizabeth, Sally, Jake, Lance, and Logan felt some relief as the trial came to an end. However, even knowing that justice was served would not lessen the sorrow these men had caused from the loss of their loved ones. As they left the saloon and rode back to the ranch, they had an empty feeling in their hears.

That night at supper, Jake recapped for the men what had happened and told them of the upcoming hanging. Later that evening, he walked outside, wanting to clear his head and get some fresh air. Walking past the corral, he saw Elizabeth standing by a tree. He walked over to her and said, "I see you needed to get some fresh air as well."

She looked at him and smiled. "I have been thinking how nice you and your sister have been to Greg and me even with all the troubles your family has been going through. I know Adam had dreams of someday having a place of our own. I do miss him, and sometimes at night, I feel so lonely that I cry. I'm sure Sally must feel the same way and you, too, from the loss of your father."

Elizabeth bent her head, and Jake could hear soft sobs coming from her. He put his arms around her and held her against his chest. Elizabeth continued to sob. They stood like this for some time. When Elizabeth finally stopped crying, she looked up into Jake's face. Jake leaned down and he kissed her on the lips. She didn't know how to react at first, but then she started kissing him back.

After they separated, Jake said, "I'm sorry. I shouldn't have done that."

"I'm not sorry you did that," Elizabeth said. "I know Adam hasn't been gone long, but I have been thinking of you, especially when you were wounded. You have been so kind to me that my heart felt heavy at the thought I was going to lose you as well."

"I have been thinking about you too," Jake said. "You are a fine-looking woman and one that would make any man proud to have for his wife. I know you only lost your husband a while ago, but in time, if you would, I'd like to take you for my wife."

Elizabeth didn't know what to say. She looked up at him, and a smile formed on her face. Reaching on her toes, she kissed him again. This time, her kiss had more passion.

Jake asked, "How do you think Greg might feel about us getting together?"

"I'll talk to him. I know he has come to think of being here with you and the men in the bunkhouse as a home again. I'm sure he would want to see me happy. I'm just not sure how he would feel since I know he misses his father. We have talked at times, and he does not want to leave."

Arm in arm, they walked back to the house. Hearing a noise in the kitchen, Elizabeth went to find out what was going on, while Jake headed to his bedroom. In the kitchen, Sally was busy getting things ready for the morning. When she looked at Elizabeth and saw a glow on her face, she asked, "What are you so happy about?"

"I am so happy. Jake asked if I would be his wife," she said.

"What? That is great," Sally said. "That means you'll be my sister. When will you get married?"

"I have to talk to Greg before we make any plans. Please don't say anything to Jake until we're ready to tell everyone, if it comes about."

The two women laughed and talked as they finished getting ready for the morning.

Three days later, Jake rode to town with Logan and Lance. They wanted to see the hanging of Duke Sanders and find out if the army had caught Clemens.

There were a lot of people in town who were interested in seeing the hanging. The gallows had been built next to the jail, and at five minutes to twelve, Duke Sanders was escorted there from his cell. Jake watched as they took Duke up the gallows stairs. Duke's face was showing no emotions even as he knew he would not walk back down those steps. He refused to say any last words, and the rope was put around his neck. Jake had hoped that he would confess to what he had done.

When the trap door opened, Duke dropped through the hole. His neck was broken, and he died instantly. It all seemed to go in slow motion as Jake watched. In the end, it still did not bring comfort for the loss of his father.

After the body was brought to the undertaker, Jake went to see Captain Ward in the jail office. "Mr. Burton, what can I do for you?"

"I was wondering if you had any word about Gifford Clemens."

"No. When we checked his office after the trial, we found he had cleaned out his safe. We went to his ranch, and he wasn't there. We don't know where he went."

"Did he leave any cattle there?" Jake asked.

"There was a herd in the pasture."

"I would like permission to look at the brands, and if I find any that have been altered, I would like to return them to their owners."

"You have my permission," Captain Ward said. "When we checked his office, we found some papers still in the safe. Some of them were loan papers that we gave back to the people who had borrowed from him."

"How long will you be remaining here?" Jake inquired.

"As soon as we can appoint a new marshal, we'll be leaving. Do you know of anyone who would be good at the job?"

"I don't," Jake said. "But you might want to talk to Mr. Hanson at the mercantile."

"Thanks. I will."

19

THE WEDDING

Two weeks after Elizabeth and Jake had talked, Jake remained busy sorting the cattle at the Clemens ranch and returning them to their owners. He found fifty head of their own that he had the men drive back to the ranch.

Sally came down to talk to him one night while he was putting up his horse. "How is the separating of the cattle going?"

"We are about done. Since Gifford left the territory, his ranch hands seemed to have gone as well. I guess they followed him."

"What are your plans?" she asked.

"What do you mean? We have the ranch to run."

"I mean about Elizabeth."

"She can stay here," Jake said.

"That's not what I meant. When are you going to ask her to marry you?"

Jake stood there for a while, looking at the ground before he answered. "We talked some. I ain't sure if Greg wants her to get married."

"She wants to marry you," Sally said. "We have talked, and she said she would if Greg would accept it."

"What do you think if I ask her?" Jake asked.

"I think it would be great. She would make a wonderful sister."

"But I don't know how Greg is going to feel."

"You need to think about what you want to do." Turning away, she walked back to the house and left Jake with his thoughts.

Two nights later, Jake was standing on the front porch when Elizabeth came out. "Would you like to go for a walk?" he asked.

"Yes."

The sky was clear, and there was a full moon that lit up the night almost like day. They stepped off the porch, and neither said a word as they walked side by side toward the tree where they had first talked.

They stopped under the tree, and Jake turned to her. "I have wanted to talk to you."

Elizabeth stopped him by grabbing his head and pulling it down to hers, kissing him. "I have wanted to do that since the last time we kissed."

Surprised, he was at a loss for words. Seeing the look on his face, she kissed him again.

Once Jake was able to get his breath back, he asked, "Have you spoken to Greg about us?"

"I talked to him. He got excited when I told him."

"I haven't heard any of the men saying anything," Jake said.

"I told him not to mention it to them. I wanted to wait and make sure you still wanted to get married."

"Yes, I do," Jake said. "That is if you do."

"You can't tell by the way I kissed you?"

"You must have been talking to Sally. She asked me when I was going to ask you."

"The night when we first talked about it, she was in the kitchen," Elizabeth explained. "She guessed something had changed in me, and I told her. I told her not to say anything, but I was too excited to keep it to myself."

"When do you want to get married?" Jake asked.

"I'll need to get a dress made, and we need to make arrangements for a minster. Oh, there is so much to do that I don't know how long it will take. Maybe Sally can help me."

Jake laughed. "Sally will be happy to help you. She has been bugging me about asking you. I'm sure the sooner the better for her.

"We need to go tell her and Greg." Elizabeth grabbed Jake's hand and dragged him toward the house.

They saw Greg coming out of the barn, and Jake said, "He is becoming quite a ranch hand."

"He told me the men seem to like him," Elizabeth commented.

"Greg," Jake called out. "Come here. We need you in the house."

Greg came over to them and asked, "Did he ask you, Ma?"

Elizabeth wrapped her arms around Greg. "Yes, he did."

"Does that mean I'll be able to tell the men now?"

"We're going to talk to Mrs. Ashley first," Elizabeth said. "Then you can say anything you want to the men."

"Some of them have been wondering if you had a hankering for my ma," Greg told Jake with a smile on his face.

In the house, they found Sally sitting in the parlor. She looked up as the three of them came in. "Well, did you finally ask her?"

"He sure did, Mrs. Ashley," Greg said. "Does that mean you will be my aunt?"

"It sure does. Now when are we going to have this wedding?"

"I'm going to need your help," Elizabeth said. "I need a dress, and I would like to have the wedding here if that's all right with you."

"I still have my wedding dress," Sally told her. "I think it will fit you if you'd like to see it."

"That would be nice," Elizabeth replied. "I don't know where else I would find one unless I made it."

"Jake, you and Greg go away and let us ladies do the planning," Sally instructed. "When we need you, we'll call you."

Jake and Greg walked outside and stood on the porch. Greg asked, "What do you want me to call you when you marry my ma?"

"I ain't thought about that," Jake said. "What would you feel comfortable calling me?"

"I ain't sure. I look at you as my boss. When you marry my ma, I guess you will be my pa. I still miss my pa a lot though and don't know if I would feel right calling you Pa."

"You could call me Jake. You're becoming a young man. From what I have seen of the work you're doing around here, you're quite a cowhand too."

"Thanks. Logan showed me a lot," Greg said, still excited about the news. "I think I'll go to the bunkhouse and let the men know about you and Ma."

After Greg left, Jake walked down to the corral. He stood there looking at the horses, when he heard shouts coming from the bunkhouse. Smiling to himself, he knew that he would be getting teased in the morning.

Back at the house, he found that the women were not in the parlor and went upstairs. As he went past Sally's room, he heard the two women talking. Smiling, he went to his room and got in bed.

Sally and Elizabeth had waited until Jake and Greg left before Sally said, "Let's go upstairs and look at the dress. We may have to make some changes to it. Once we get it done, we can come up with a date for the wedding."

Elizabeth was excited as they went upstairs. Going to her closet in the bedroom, Sally pulled out her dress, which was wrapped in yards of muslin. Once Sally took the muslin off, Elizabeth became breathless and said, "That is the most beautiful dress I have ever seen. Are you sure you want me to wear it?"

"Yes, of course," Sally told her. "Now get out of that dress and get into this one so we can see how it fits."

Once Elizabeth had the garment on, they saw that it wouldn't take much to make it fit. Sally got her sewing basket and began to pin it. When she was finished, Elizabeth slipped out of the dress and handed it to her. Sally quickly began to sew the new seams.

"Let me do that," Elizabeth said.

"You are too excited," Sally replied, laughing. "I wouldn't want you to stick yourself and get blood on it."

It didn't take Sally long to make the changes, and Elizabeth put it back on. "It fits perfectly," she said. "Now we can make the other arrangements tomorrow."

It was late by the time they finished the dress, and the women were tired. They knew they had to get up early. Elizabeth went to her room. Lying in bed, she couldn't sleep.

When morning came, she was tired and had a hard time getting up to go to the kitchen to help Sally. When she entered the kitchen, she saw that Sally had already started breakfast.

Sally looked at Elizabeth with a smile on her face. "Did you have a hard time sleeping last night?"

"Yes, I did."

By the time breakfast was prepared, Jake arrived. "I heard you two up late last night. What were you doing?"

"We made a wedding dress for Elizabeth," Sally said.

The men came in just as she had finished speaking. Seeing Elizabeth, Logan said, "Good morning, Mrs. Burton."

Elizabeth's face turned red. "Now, Logan, you behave yourself, or I will make sure your breakfast is burnt. All of you sit down and behave yourselves."

Sally smiled while she watched Elizabeth, knowing that she was enjoying what Logan and the others were saying. During breakfast, the men asked when the wedding was going to be.

Jake said, "We have not set a date."

After breakfast, the men left before Sally and Elizabeth sat down with Jake. Sally said, "Jake, you need to go to town and talk to the minister."

"When do you two think we can be ready for this wedding?" he asked.

Elizabeth said, "Sally and I were thinking that we could have everything ready a week from Saturday."

"I'll go to town and see if the minister is available," Jake said.

"I would like to go with you," Elizabeth told him. "I have some things to get from the mercantile."

"Let me get the buggy, and we'll head to town."

Elizabeth waited as Jake drove up with the buggy. He got down and helped her into the seat. As they drove into town, Elizabeth kept talking about how happy she was. "Once we are married, we'll have to decide where we want to live."

"What do you mean? We'll stay in the house."

"Do you think Sally will mind if we stay there?" she asked.

"She said she'd move into the room I'm in. She wants us to have the room that she and Howard had."

"What if Sally gets married someday?"

"I've been thinking about that. Maybe we can take over the Clemens ranch. I don't think he'll be coming back," Jake said.

"Who would run the ranch for Sally?" Elizabeth asked.

"Logan will run it until Sally remarries."

"There's so much we'll have to work out."

Reaching town, their first stop was the minister's home. They knocked on the door and waited for him to answer. "Jake Burton, what a nice surprise. Mrs. Hamman, won't you come in?" he invited.

Taking them to his den, he asked, "What can I do for you?"

"We have come to ask you to marry us," Jake said.

"I would love to. When would you like this ceremony to take place?"

"A week from tomorrow," Elizabeth told him. "We want it held at the ranch. That is, if you are available."

"Yes, I believe that I'm available. Is there anything special you want in the ceremony?"

Elizabeth said, "As you know, I lost my husband during an Indian attack. I would like your reassurance that I'm not doing this too soon."

"Mrs. Hamman, there is no certain time that one must mourn the loss of a loved one," the minister said. "You have to follow your heart and feelings to guide you on that."

"I would also like that you call me by my name, Elizabeth Hamman, and not Mrs. Hamman at the ceremony."

"I see no problem with that."

When they finished going over the details, Elizabeth and Jake left. At the mercantile, they found Mrs. Hanson arranging one of the shelves. As they entered, she turned around and said, "Hello, Mrs. Hamman, Jake. What can I do for you?"

"Jake and I are getting married," Elizabeth said excitedly. "We would like for you and Mr. Hanson to come and help us celebrate."

"When are you getting married?" Mrs. Hanson was getting excited at the thought of a wedding.

"A week from tomorrow," Elizabeth told her. "We were wondering if you would be kind enough to spread the word that everyone is welcome."

"We would be happy to. I believe after what has been going on around here, there will be a lot of people there to help you celebrate. Will you have a dress by then?"

"Sally is letting me wear hers. There are some other things I would like to get, if you know what I mean."

"Just leave a list with me, and I'll take care of it," Mrs. Hanson said.

Things were busy at the ranch over the next week. Besides the normal activities, the men helped get ready for the wedding. Lance and a couple of the ranch hands built an arch to be used by the bride and groom.

The morning of the wedding, neighbors and folks from town started arriving early. Mrs. Hanson and Mrs. Dobbs were two of the first ladies to arrive. Going into the kitchen, they helped Sally prepare the food. Logan and some of the men had dug a pit the day before and started roasting a steer to feed everyone.

Jake had gotten up that morning wanting to see Elizabeth, but Sally wouldn't let him. "You will get a chance to see her when she comes out for the ceremony. Now you get out of the house and go to the bunkhouse with the men."

As the guests arrived, Jake greeted them. When the men were alone, they told him stories about how nervous they were when they got married. They also thought that he was a lucky man to find a woman like Elizabeth. "After what she has been through," Mr. Dobbs said, "you know she is a strong woman. She will make a great wife."

A short time later, Captain Ward and his men arrived. "Captain, it's good to see you," Jake said. "Have your men relax and enjoy themselves today."

"Thank you. The men have been looking forward to this since the word got around town that there was going to be a wedding. Some of them brought their instruments to help with the music."

Everyone mingled, waiting for the minister to arrive. By the time he got there at one o'clock, everything was ready, and everyone was ready for the wedding to begin.

Jake stood by the minister with Greg at his side as they waited for Elizabeth. When the music started, Sally was the first one to come down the aisle. After she stopped in front, everyone stood up as Logan escorted Elizabeth down the aisle. Some of the women made comments about how nice her dress looked. When Jake saw her, it took his breath away.

Greg leaned over to Jake and said, "Ma sure looks nice."

Jake replied, "She sure does."

Once Elizabeth made her way to the minister and Jake took her hand, it was hard to tell who was the most nervous. Jake could feel her hand shaking in his as he looked at her and smiled.

By the time the minister pronounced them husband and wife, they had both settled down. When he kissed the bride, Jake started to blush as he had never kissed a woman in front of anyone before. Elizabeth saw him blush and smiled. "Get used to it, fella, because we will be doing it a lot more."

All the ladies got up and helped put the food on the tables set up in the yard. Once everyone had eaten, the music started. Elizabeth and Jake were the first ones to dance. Soon, others were dancing with them. When the dance ended, Elizabeth mixed with the women, and Jake joined the men.

The women wanted to know where Elizabeth had gotten her dress. They were surprised to find that it was the one Sally wore when she got married.

When it started getting dark, the guests prepared to leave. The bride and groom stood side by side as people stopped to congratulate them before departing. Exhausted, Elizabeth and Jake sat down after everyone had gone. "We need to thank Sally," she said. "She has done most of the work today."

They found Sally in the house, and Elizabeth went over and hugged her. "I don't know how I can thank you for what you have done for us."

Smiling, Sally said, "Now I can call you my sister." She hugged her. "I know the two of you are tired, so I'm going to leave you alone."

After Sally left, Jake blew out the lamps, and they went to their room.

Elizabeth asked him to wait outside until she was ready. She opened the package that Mrs. Hanson had brought for her. Inside, she found everything she asked for. Holding up the pink transparent negligee with red trim and low-cut front, she wondered what Jake would think. Smiling, she removed her clothes and put it on. Looking in the mirror, she was happy with what she saw. She took the bottle of perfume and dabbed some on her neck and between her breasts. Satisfied that she was ready, she called for Jake.

As Jake entered the room, his mouth dropped open when he saw her in the negligee. Her beauty made him blush. When he recovered, he said, "So this is who I married."

Elizabeth asked, "Is something wrong?"

"Ah, no. You are so beautiful." He picked her up and carried her to the bed.

In the morning, they were up early, knowing that work had to be done and the men needed to be fed. By the time they reached the kitchen, Sally had put the coffee on. Seeing them, she smiled and said, "It looks like you didn't get much rest last night. Just because you are married now doesn't mean you can shuck your job. Jake, go take care of your chores while we get breakfast ready."

"Maybe I shouldn't have gotten married," he said. "Now I've got two women telling me what to do."

Elizabeth grabbed the dishcloth and threw it at him as he left the room.

As the men filed in, they all said, "Good morning, Mrs. Burton." Elizabeth greeted each man as she served the food.

Two weeks after the wedding, Captain Ward sent word that he wanted to talk to Jake. Not knowing what the captain wanted, Jake had Logan ride into town with him. Captain Ward had set up his headquarters in the marshal's office. There, they found him sitting at the desk. "Captain, you sent word that you wanted to talk to me?" Jake said.

"Yes, please have a seat. I received a dispatch yesterday from Denver that you might be interested in. As you know, Gifford Clemens left town before we could arrest him, and I sent the word out to be on the lookout for him. The dispatch stated that Clemens had gone back to Denver, where he killed a man. He was convicted and hung the day you got married."

"I'll tell Sally that the man responsible for killing Howard is now dead," Jake said. "What's going to happen to his ranch?"

"As far as the army knows, he did not have any family, leaving the land up for grabs. If the bank owns any of it, then it will belong to them. You might want to check with Mr. Dobbs and see what he knows."

"Thanks." Jake got up, and he and Logan went to the bank.

Mr. Dobbs was in his office when Jake walked in. Shaking Jake's hand, he said, "I wanted to talk to you. What you did for us here has made Mancos a safe place to live again. What can I do for you?"

"Mr. Dobbs, I want to know if the bank has any interest in Gifford Clemens's ranch."

"Let me look," Mr. Dobbs said, "but I don't think we do. You remember he had taken control of the bank and was trying to get your ranch."

After going through the books, he said, "No, the bank has no interest in the Clemens ranch. If you want it, you need to find the title."

"Do you know where I might find it?" Jake asked.

"I don't know if anyone has been in his office since he left. You might look there or even at the ranch. I understand nobody has been out there since the men he had working for him left. If you can find the title, you should be able to get the ranch, or you'll have to find Mr. Clemens."

"I was just talking to Captain Ward, who told me that Clemens was hung in Denver the day I got married," Jake said.

"If you can find the title then, you can claim the land. The captain said that they found loan papers in Gifford's safe and returned them to the people whose names were on them. The title was not there, so it could be at the ranch."

After thanking Mr. Dobbs, Jake and Logan went to Clemens's law office and found the back door unlocked. Jake found the safe unlocked and looked inside. He didn't find anything that looked like a title or deed.

On the way back to the ranch, Logan asked, "Are you going to check Clemens's ranch?"

"We can ride over there tomorrow and see if Gifford had a safe there. If I could get his place, that would make a nice wedding present for Elizabeth, and Sally would still have our ranch. Don't say anything about this to anyone."

The next morning, Logan and Jake rode over to the Clemens ranch. They looked around, and it didn't look like anyone had been there since they separated the cattle. Those who had gotten their cattle back were happy and were trying to work their ranches again. There were still about two hundred head that bore the Clemens brand roaming the pastures.

Going into the house, they looked for a safe. Jake found it in the den. Luckily, the door to the safe was hanging open.

Logan had been going through the rest of the house and found it to be in good shape. Going to the den, he saw Jake looking in the safe. "I see you found it."

"Yes."

"Did you find the title?"

Still looking inside, Jake finally found what he was searching for. Along with the ranch title, several deeds had been signed by the original landowners releasing their land to Clemens. None had been processed through the land office in Durango. "We need to return these deeds to the people who are still around," Jake said.

"What are you going to do with those who are not here?" Logan asked.

"I don't know. It doesn't seem right to just take it."

"You've got more right to it than most. You lost your pa and Howard to Clemens, and these folks were given money for their land."

"What would you do?" Jake asked.

"I don't know. I don't want the land. I'm happy working for you and Mrs. Sally."

Taking the papers, they rode back to the Double B. That night, Jake sat in the den and started looking at the deeds. He separated those for which he knew the owners were still in the area and set them aside to be returned as soon as he could. The remaining ones amounted to a lot of land. Some of it backed up to the Double B.

It became clear to Jake that Clemens had worked hard to try to take over the whole valley. Most of the deeds butted up to Clemens's ranch. If Jake was to take the ranch and the surrounding land, Sally would have their original ranch and the land that backed up to it. He and Elizabeth would have their ranch nearby, and he could help Sally until she remarried.

The next day, Jake started returning the deeds that he could and kept the land and the house that Clemens had lived on. When the titles were transferred, he and Elizabeth moved into the house. She was happy that they had their own home. Living with Sally at the Double B was good, but to Elizabeth, it didn't feel like it was her home. They were still neighbors and would see each other often.

Greg and some of the men moved to the ranch with them. Logan stayed with Sally, and Lance became Jake's foreman. The cattle that were still on the land, along with some that Sally insisted Jake have, gave them a good herd to build on. When it came time to sell cattle to the miners, the two ranches worked together, driving them to Animas Forks and Rico.

A year after they started their ranch, Elizabeth gave birth to a little girl named Helen, after her mother. Sally and Logan were married two years later, and she gave birth to a boy named Howard, after her late husband.

With peace restored in the valley, both families continued to grow as their ranches prospered.

ABOUT THE AUTHOR

LOWELL F. VOLK IS A retired software engineering manager with a BS in computer science and a master's degree in business. He has been living in Pleasant View, Colorado, since 2014, after retiring from General Dynamics. He became a member of the Montezuma County Sheriff's Posse and worked part time in court security as a deputy for the Montezuma Sheriff's Office. He also serves on the board of directors for the Pleasant View Fire Protection District. Lowell and his wife, Mary Lou, have five children: Terri, Scott, Paula, Lowell Jr., and Kathy. Besides writing, Lowell enjoys horseback riding, deer and elk hunting, and early American history. In his spare time, he is restoring a 1953 Chevy three-quarter-ton pickup.

CPSIA information can be obtained
at www.ICGtesting.com
Printed in the USA
FSHW011131060720

9 781627 878098